CROWN OF FLAMES

THE FIRE QUEEN – BOOK TWO

CROWN OF FLAMES

SAYANTANI DASGUPTA

Illustrations by

VIVIENNE TO

SCHOLASTIC PRESS

New York

Library of Congress Cataloging-in-Publication Data available

ISBN 978-1-338-76681-3

1 2022

Printed in the U.S.A.   23
First edition, October 2022

Book design by Abby Dening

To all the elders we have lost.

We will not forget your stories.

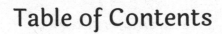

Table of Contents

CHAPTER 1

Burning Crowns and Other Serious Bummers

It all began with me being forced to wear a crown of flames. Which, as you can imagine, was a bummer. A serious bummer.

Since I'd officially/unofficially joined the rebellion against the Serpentine Empire, I'd been having trouble sleeping. It was probably because of the bounty that Sesha, that two-faced slimeball son of the Serpentine Governor-General, had on my head. But being hunted down by a boy I used to kind of–sort of like would stress anyone out, amirite?

So I'd done what I always did when I couldn't sleep. I'd snuck out a bunch of dusty old books from the school library and started reading. That's when it happened. I was lying in bed, in the middle of looking through a crumbling, silver-covered volume called *Thakurmar Jhuli*. Like I had since I was a lonely kid, I was reading the words aloud to myself, only softly, so as not to wake my water-clan roommate, Kumi. That was when I felt the strange, sucking sensation of being pulled out of my own reality. One second, I was Pinki the fire rakkhoshi, reading in my dorm in the middle of the night, and the next moment, I whirled, as if through a wormhole, right out of my own body, my own place, and most bizarrely, my own time.

Now, if you've never traveled unexpectedly through a time vortex magically created by an old book you stole from your school library, I don't recommend it. At least without a helmet and some anti-nausea medication.

When my vision cleared and stomach sort of settled, I found myself in a royal court lined with high columns and majestic silk banners. Snoring Kumi wasn't there, or anything else from my familiar room. I was still queasy, but had to stifle the urge to yuke, because before me, upon the high throne, was a fierce rakkhoshi queen. Her long, matted black hair flowed over her sharp horns and broad shoulders like a mighty river from a mountain. Her dark, all-seeing eyes swirled like two galaxies on her face, and the longest, sharpest tusklike fangs I'd ever seen curved like small daggers over her unsmiling lips. In other words, she was all that with an extra helping of awesome-sauce.

I was seriously impressed. Especially since I recognized her.

"Hidimbi!" I breathed, trying not to burp. I was pretty sure burping was inappropriate behavior when meeting a legendary queen of old.

The Queen looked unsurprised. "I've been waiting for you, young fire rakkhoshi."

"But how? I mean, you're dead!" I couldn't help but point out.

I agree, this wasn't my finest conversational moment. But ask yourself if you would do any better in the same situation. Hidimbi was not only the mother of Ghatatkach, my school's namesake and founder, but the last Demon Queen who had ruled over an independent Demon Land, before the Serpent Empire had come and colonized all the different peoples of the Kingdom Beyond Seven Oceans and Thirteen Rivers. Hidimbi wasn't just a little dead, she was seriously dead. Like, starring-in-history-books-level dead.

At my words, however, the ancient queen seemed unbothered. To put a finer point on it, her exact response to me was "Pffft."

My emotions went quickly from awe to irritation. "What do you mean, 'pffft'?"

The Queen waved her hands as if my question was an annoying pest flying by her ear. "What is death? What is life? What is time?"

"Things whose rules we have to follow?" I suggested.

"Pffft!" Hidimbi said, yet again. "Which part of the time-line are you from? I mean, which Pinki are you?"

"I beg your pardon?" What did she mean which Pinki was I? I was me!

The Queen squinted as if sizing me up. "So the name Neel means nothing to you?"

"I don't think so?" I was starting to suspect the many

millennia she'd been dead had somehow messed with Hidimbi's head.

"Hmm, I thought not." I heard a distinct buzzing, which stopped as Hidimbi caught something out of the air. She opened her fist, revealing a fat bee sitting in her hand. "When you get back, ask about the consorts, will you?"

"Consorts?" I repeated as Hidimbi let the insect go and it zipped by my face. Was I imagining things, or did the little stinker blow a raspberry at me as it flew by?

The Queen's eyes followed the path of the flying bee. Then she directed her attention at me again. "Do we rakkhosh still store our souls in bees in the future?"

"Yes, we do," I said impatiently, adding, as an afterthought, "Your Highness."

Hidimbi eyed me, pursing her full lips. "Maybe we should reconsider that. Not as safe as it seems."

I wanted to stomp my foot. If there was one thing I hated, it was feeling out of control. If there was a second thing I hated, it was being confused. I tried to get a handle on the situation. "Your Highness, what were you saying about consorts?"

"That you should *ask* about them?" Hidimbi snorted, rolling her huge eyes.

Wow, for a legendary queen of old, she really had an attitude. I was realizing that Queen Hidimbi reminded me of my own headmistress, Surpanakha, who didn't exactly adore me. I mean, yes, that probably was a little bit because of how much I interrupted her in class, and the fact that I wasn't great at following instructions. Also it could be because of that little incident when I'd almost burned down her outdoor banyan grove classroom. But I never said I was perfect.

"Now, onto the real business of the hour!" The ancient queen pointed a long-taloned finger at me. "Tell me, young rakkhoshi, what will you do with my crown? Will you use it to free your people, or serve yourself? Will you burn powerful with its magic, or let its powerful magic burn you?"

"Your crown?" I looked at the heavy golden mukut upon her head. "I don't want your crown! You're getting me confused with my friends Aakash and Kumi! I mean, I'm not even competing in the demonic royalty competition!"

Since the Serpent Empire began ruling the Kingdom Beyond centuries ago, they hadn't allowed anyone to be Demon Queen or King. The fact that they were permitting a demonic royalty competition to happen at Ghatatkach now was probably just a ploy to keep us rakkhosh in check. A little meaningless carrot to make us ignore the sting of the imperialist stick on our backs. But symbolic title or not, I also knew that whoever won Demon Queen or King this year would be the first person to wear Hidimbi's crown since Hidimbi herself. I just hadn't planned on it being me.

"Whether you want my crown or not, it is coming to you," Hidimbi intoned.

As she slowly took it off, her bulging arm muscles and pained expression told me how much the mighty mukut must weigh. I recognized the crown's central jewels—the legendary Chintamoni and Poroshmoni Stones—glowing white and gold, humming with intergalactic power like the stars they were. But if the history books were right, these magical jewels had been stolen from the rakkhosh many years ago. In fact, legend had it that only the true Demon King or Queen could summon the lost stones, which were actually living stars, back to the crown. And any imposter who presumed to put Hidimbi's crown on their head without the precious jewels back in place? Oh, no biggie. They'd just be burned to death by its power.

"I don't want your mukut," I repeated. "Believe me, I've never wanted to be Demon Queen. If you knew me, you'd know I'm way not into stuff like that! Leadership, sacrifice, honor—I mean, yuck!" I gave a shudder. "I swear, I'm really not about school spirit or royalty competitions. I'm much more of an independent operator, if you know what I mean."

"Time has a way of catching up to us all," said the Queen, her voice echoing strangely in my head. "As do our destinies. And, of course, bees."

I was starting to wonder if this was all just a dream. Everything—the throne room, the air, the words out of Hidimbi's mouth—was taking on that weird, otherworldly, wibbly-wobbly quality. But what if it wasn't a dream, and this was just the way time travel worked? What if Hidimbi put that crown on my head and it revealed me for what I really was—an imposter? If that happened, and the legends were true, then wearing that crown would spell my doom.

"I don't want your crown," I tried to repeat firmly. But my words floated out of my mouth in slow motion. I felt strange and stuck, like an insect caught in amber.

"Sometimes you choose the crown," said Hidimbi, moving from her high throne and down the marble steps toward me, "and sometimes the crown chooses you."

Her expression was beginning to seriously freak me out. "Wait, don't put that thing on my head!" I yelled. "I told you, I don't want your crown!"

And then, just as I had feared, the moment Hidimbi placed her weighty mukut upon my head, it began to burn.

Not slow, but sudden and fierce, like a raging inferno. My vision erupted in flames of orange, yellow, red. Soon, not just the golden crown but my head itself burst into flames that engulfed all of me in moments. And unlike when I created my own magical fire, these flames burned with a horrible, unspeakable pain. That's when I remembered that this had happened before. And I knew, in my bones, that it would happen again.

"Stop!" I screamed. "Stop, please! I don't want the crown! It burns, it burns!"

Everything got very loud, then very quiet. And all went dark.

CHAPTER 2

In Which I Totally Unfairly Get Blamed for Trying to Kill My Professor

Fire rakkhoshi, desist this caterwauling!"

I blinked my eyes through the smoke, only to realize that I was no longer in Hidimbi's court. I was no longer on fire either. I was in Surpanakha's outdoor classroom in the banyan grove in Ghatatkach Academy. Which meant I was back in my own time, my own place. Yet my neck ached from the weight of the mukut, and my nose burned with the smell of singed hair. Tentatively, I touched my hand to my head. There was no crown there anymore, and certainly no flames. So this whole visit to Hidimbi must have been a dream—or a nightmare, more like. It had to have been.

Surpanakha was staring at me over her spectacles. "Were you napping in my class again?"

"I'm sorry, Headmistress," I muttered, my head still spinning. "I didn't get a lot of sleep last night."

The fire-clan kids next to me were snickering. "I don't want your crown!" someone mocked. "It burns, it burns!"

"Was she dreaming about being crowned Demon Queen?" I heard someone else say. "As *if*!"

I whirled this way and that but couldn't find the two-faced finks who'd been talking. Even though I'd rescued all those human and rakkhosh kids from an undersea retraining center a few weeks before, a lot of my fellow students at Ghatatkach Academy of Murder and Mayhem doubted that the undersea raid ever happened.

"Fake news," they'd mutter when my friends Aakash the air rakkhosh, Kumi the water rakkhoshi, or I walked by. Even though we were the ones being oppressed by the snakes, most of these short-sighted rakkhosh ding-dongs believed the serpents' disinformation campaign, that we revolutionaries were just fame-hungry liars. They'd scoff at the idea that we'd risked life and fang to get those kids—including two of my own baby cousins—out of that horrible "school," where the snakes were literally stealing the voices out of their little throats! No, most of our classmates seemed to think it was just a publicity stunt, something connected to the upcoming contest for Demon Queen or King. I mean, it was enough to make a girl spit flames! And as much as I didn't like to admit it, being betrayed by my own people—the very community I'd put aside my selfish ways for and tried to help, thank you very much—well, it hurt. It hurt a lot.

I caught Aakash and Kumi looking at me from their own clan benches, worried expressions on their faces. "You okay?" Aakash mouthed at me, and I gave him a faint, hopefully reassuring smile.

"May I get back to our lesson, fire rakkhoshi?" Surpanakha was asking, her voice dripping with irritation. "Or do you have something else you'd rather be discussing?"

"No, no, I'm good," I said before suddenly realizing there *was* something I wanted to discuss. "Actually, there is something I wanted to talk about, Headmistress."

Surpanakha's eyebrows shot up straight to her hairline. If she'd had a nose, I'm sure her nostrils would have flared. "Oh?" she managed. The twin jackals sleeping at her feet gave a low growl.

"What's the legend about Hidimbi's crown again?" I tried to ignore the snarling jackals, who were seriously unnerving. "I mean, I know it's just a story, but the whole thing about the jewels that are missing on her crown?"

A number of my fellow rakkhosh students snickered at my words. Not just the air, land, and water clans, who naturally resented my superiority, but even some of my own fire clan too. Traitors. Had they forgotten I'd come into my full powers lately? I glared at them, and they shut right up. Clearly, they were smarter than they looked. No one felt like being incinerated before lunch.

"What do you care, fire rakkhoshi? Unlike your friends Aakash and Kumi, you're not even in the royalty contest." Surpanakha rolled her eyes. "But yes, the legends say that only the true inheritor of Hidimbi's power will be able to restore the Chintamoni and Poroshmoni Stones to the crown."

My roommate, Kumi, asked sharply, "And what happens otherwise, Headmistress?"

"Oh, blah, blah, blah." Surpanakha waved her hands in the air vaguely. "An imposter will be burned by the crown, which, upon touching their head, will immediately burst into flames."

I gulped, remembering exactly how this had happened to me. Kumi and Aakash, for their parts, looked unnerved.

"Then maybe we shouldn't use that crown, if it's, like, cursed or whatever?" Aakash suggested.

"Or dangerous?" I added. "Why put any of us at risk?"

"Don't be ridiculous!" scoffed the headmistress. "When a new King or Queen is elected, Hidimbi's crown will be brought up from the Academy's inner sanctum, next to our soul-bees, where it has been kept safe all these years. And jewels or no jewels, it will be placed upon the head of our next ruler!"

I saw Kumi and Aakash exchanging alarmed looks.

"One more question, Headmistress," I barreled on, remembering Hidimbi's words. "What's this about the consorts?"

"Where did you hear about the consorts, Pinki?" It was Professor Ravan, the legendary professor who taught Honors Thievery and was Surpanakha's brother— incomprehensibly, since they were totally opposite in personality. He looked like he'd been wandering by the banyan grove and overheard my question.

"Oh, nowhere," I said vaguely. My brain whirred, trying desperately to come up with a plausible excuse that didn't involve a long-ago dead queen. "Maybe something I read?"

"Something you read?" repeated Surpanakha, narrowing her eyes. "Or something you *heard* from that two-faced lily-livered snake in the grass Sesha, son of the Serpentine Governor-General?"

Before I could protest, Professor Ravan jumped in. "Come, sister, we know that our dear Pinki only pretended to befriend Sesha back then. She fought him bravely, almost killed him during the recent rebellion."

Surpanakha grunted, but looked unconvinced.

"So what about consorts?" I asked, unable to loosen the grip of the dream upon my brain.

"Well, it's not common knowledge yet, but I suppose it won't hurt to tell you all!" Professor Ravan's dark brows flew up his forehead from enthusiasm. "The Serpentine Empire has only recently declared that whoever is chosen the next Demon Queen or King will get to pick a consort from another community—a chance to unite rakkhosh-kind with another group! Imagine the possibilities of that!"

There arose kind of a shocked gasp from the students. Rakkhosh partnering with other demons like khokkosh, witches like daini, ghostly bhoot, fairy pari, or (shudder) humans? Unthinkable!

But Professor Ravan didn't seem to think so. "You students don't remember, but this once was our tradition, before the serpents came. The snakes don't see it either, but this is a remarkable opportunity for us to unite against the Serpentine Empire."

I tried my best not to steal a look at Surpanakha, who, as rumor had it, had gotten her nose cut off millennia ago after romantically pursuing some princely human brothers. She clearly didn't have a problem with rakkhosh-human dating. And of course legendary Hidimbi too had fallen in love with and married a great human warrior, with whom she had given birth to Ghatatkach himself.

"What're the exact details of this consort business?" asked Kumi.

"Yeah, can whoever wins choose anyone to be their consort?" added Aakash. His eyes were a little shiny, and I wondered if he was thinking about the beautiful moon maiden Chandni, on whom both he and Kumi had developed crushes during our rebel raid.

There were some giggles from the crowd of rakkhosh students, and the sound of someone making smooching sounds.

"Cut it out, gasbags!" Aakash said good-naturedly. But he threw a gust of wind so unnecessarily strong, several students fell off their tree trunk benches. One small air rakkhoshi was lifted so high by the gust, she got stuck in some banyan branches overhead and had to get rescued by her clan-mates.

As all this was going on, I couldn't help thinking about Arko, the sun-blessed human prince who had also helped us during the undersea raid. Arko was handsome, funny, noble, kind—all the things I used to think I hated. But if

I was being really honest, there was very little about Arko that I hated, and a lot about him that I liked very much. If I was given a choice to pick a consort, what would stop me from choosing him?

"Choosing a consort is not about romance; it's about picking a political partner," snapped Headmistress Surpanakha. "It's about uniting rakkhosh-kind with another group from the Kingdom Beyond for strategic—not kissy-face—purposes."

"It's what you three learned in your wonderfully successful raid," continued Professor Ravan even as a few fake-news students scoffed under their breaths. "There is power in numbers, and the only way to defeat the snakes is not to let them divide and conquer the different inhabitants of our land."

Yet my naturally suspicious nature told me this was a too-easy answer. "But, professors, isn't the timing strange?"

"What do you mean, Pinks?" Aakash asked.

"It's weird enough that the serpents would allow us to elect a new Demon King or Queen, after all these years," I began.

"It's a symbolic title only, remember?" Kumi interrupted. "Like with the humans' rajas. The snakes think it'll keep us quiet and satisfied, less likely to rebel against their rule."

"Okay, but what about this consort thing," I argued. "Isn't the timing suspicious? I mean, right after the resistance is reborn, right after we run a successful raid on that monstrous underwater school, suddenly this consort business happens?"

"Oh, the raid! The glorious raid!" someone said in a high, dramatic voice, adding, "More like the raid that never happened."

"Never fails to bring up that make-believe raid, our Pinki," a land-clan hulk named Gorgor said loudly. "You'd think she had no other claim to fame. Oh, right, wait, she doesn't!" he guffawed.

I shot him an evil look. What I wanted to do was shoot a smoke bomb straight up his nose, but Surpanakha always got hot under the horns at the unauthorized use of our powers in her classrooms.

Gorgor's comment seemed to irritate my roommate, Kumi, too. "Shut it, land dork!" she hissed, spitting seawater and flashing her pointed teeth. "If Pinki says there's something fishy with this consort stuff, there is!"

I felt a surge of gratitude at her support.

"Yeah, shut it, Gorgor," repeated Aakash, who had been busy arranging his windswept coiffure over his horns. "Professor Ravan says we're the spark that reignited the fires of the revolution against the Serpent Empire. Those snakes are hissing scared!"

I suppressed a grimace. What Aakash was saying wasn't exactly true. Professor Ravan had said that *I* was the spark that reignited the fires of the revolution, not *we*, just me. But maybe this wasn't the best time to correct my air-clan friend.

"Exactly!" I focused my attention back on my professors. "Think about it: The Empire won't take an embarrassment like that undersea raid lightly. They're publicly denying it, yes, but they know it happened, and who was involved. This consort business must be some kind of a trick, or a trap!"

I smiled in a satisfied way. Wow, my subconscious sure was smart. It had dreamed up that whole Hidimbi time-travel scene just to make sure I wouldn't ignore how suspicious this consort business was. Never mind how my subconscious had learned about the consort stuff in the first place. That was a detail I was choosing to ignore.

"Your concern, even if a bit misplaced, is commendable, Pinki! Even more reason for you to join the competition for Demon King or Queen!" Professor Ravan walked over to the headmistress and placed a giant hand on her shoulder. "Wouldn't you agree, sister?"

Surpanakha shrugged his hand off. Her eyes glittered

with malice, not for her brother, but for me. I knew she'd always resented how much Professor Ravan believed in me. "Oh, I don't think our Pinki cares that much about leading demon-kind," she murmured, her eyes turning into dangerous slits.

"That's not true!" I protested. "I do care! That's why I'm trying to tell you my suspicions!"

I looked to Kumi and Aakash for support, but my roommate just shrugged. Aakash, for his part, seemed to have lost the thread of the conversation and was busy flexing his biceps for a group of admiring air-clan rakkhosh who were oohing and aahing their approval. He grinned cheesily at them as he bounced his muscles like they were yo-yos.

Professor Ravan scratched at his considerable moustaches. He was old and getting gray around the temples, but yowza, was he still scary muscle-y. "If you're that worried, Pinki, you should absolutely run for Demon Queen, have an opportunity to make a real difference for our community—and for all the communities in the Kingdom Beyond."

"No, I'm sorry. I don't think so, Professor." I crossed my hands over my chest, shaking my head. Even though I knew it was a dream, I couldn't forget the feeling of that burning crown upon my head. "I just wanted to bring up my concerns, not throw my hat, or, er, mukut or whatever in the ring or anything."

Surpanakha's smile widened. "See, brother? Your little protégé isn't interested in real responsibility, or wielding her power for good. She just wants to be an alarmist, and do headline-grabbing exploits that bring easy fame and flashy glory."

At Surpanakha's words, I felt fire shoot from my gut straight to my brain. I mean, to hear this crap from my classmates was one thing, but it was quite something else to hear it from my own headmistress.

"Actually, Professor Ravan, I change my mind. I'll run for Demon Queen," I spat out before I could stop myself. "Of course I'll join the royalty contest. Why not?"

I shot the headmistress a triumphant look as her brows drew together with fury.

In the meantime, Professor Ravan's grin grew even wider. "Capital! Capital!" He clapped his hands together. "I am so delighted to hear you will enter this important race to determine our new leader! You will make your revolutionary parents so proud! Imagine, whoever of you wins will be the first rakkhosh to once again wear the great Hidimbi's crown!"

At the mention of my parents, as well as Hidimbi, my stomach dropped. Then I mentally kicked myself. I was Pinki the fire rakkhoshi! I wasn't intimidated by the inheritance of my family's rebellious history! Never mind my father had died in serpent prison and my mother had been under house arrest for years. And I certainly wasn't afraid of a nightmare queen, or a burning crown conjured by my underslept and overactive imagination, was I?

"So, Pinki, you're really going to join the royalty competition?" asked Aakash. I could tell from the looks on both his and Kumi's faces that neither of them was super keen to have me in the running.

"I guess." I shrugged, trying not to look too invested in something so mundane as a royal title. I remembered how Hidimbi had asked me whether I would burn with the crown's power or allow the crown's power to burn me. I shuddered, not wanting to imagine what would happen if the legend of the crown turned out to be true.

And then, just like it had in the dream, a noise distracted me. The familiar, deep, buzzing noise of a rakkhosh soul-bee.

I could tell that the other students in the grove heard it too. Students from each of the clan trees were looking around as they tried to locate the origin of the sound. Unlike regular honeybees, hornets, or wasps, rakkhosh soul-bees were magicked to be strong and fierce, and the sound they made was equally powerful.

"Where's that coming from?" a land-clan kid next to me growled, swatting at the air. There were students from all different clans standing up now, creating chaos in our grove classroom.

"Students, sit down! Stop swatting!" Surpanakha shouted. "I don't know how or why, but someone's soul-bee has escaped from the secret sanctuary under the Academy and into the open!" She was glaring at me, like it was my fault this had happened.

Then, suddenly, it was obvious to everyone whose soul-bee had escaped. Because Professor Ravan, looking quite pale and sweaty beneath his facial hair, fell to his knees with a groan.

"Brother!" The headmistress tried to catch him, but the reverberations of Professor Ravan's collapse shook the entire grove.

Our fierce firebrand of a professor, who had been so supportive of my revolutionary efforts, sagged like a crumpled bag on the ground. Ravan's eyes were rolling back in his head, and he was clutching at his chest, making a terrible sound.

The students rushed forward, all except me. I was riveted to my spot, watching Professor Ravan's agonies in a state of shocked horror.

"Wake up, brother! Wake up!" Surpanakha was trying to revive him, wielding some kind of complicated magic that swirled out in waves from her hands. But nothing she was doing was of any avail. "Find his soul-bee! Students, find that bee!"

"Pinks, snap out of it!" Kumi slapped me across the face with a wave of seawater. "We've got to find his escaped soul-bee!"

All us students ran this way and that in disarray, hunting the skies. But even though we could hear its buzzing, we couldn't seem to find the escaped soul-bee.

Then guards from the Academy honeycombs were on the scene, shouting, "It's Hidimbi's crown! Someone stole the crown from the Academy's sanctum! We gave the thieves chase, but they got away!"

"It must be the snakes!" I exclaimed. "They let the bee out of the sanctum when they were stealing the crown!"

"But why?" Kumi demanded. "I mean, they want us to have the royalty contest!"

"Plus, how?" Aakash asked. "The Academy's got, like, mad security around it."

I didn't know how to answer my friends, but knew I was somehow right. Sesha's slimy face floated as if before my eyes.

In the meantime, Professor Ravan was writhing around on the ground, moaning in agony. There was a pink froth at his mouth, and his dark eyes were unfocused and afraid. It was as if his very soul was being tortured by some invisible hand.

"Whoever did this better run!" the headmistress shrieked as she tried to hold her brother's convulsing form. "I'll curry up their liver and stew up their feet!"

And then, horribly, Ravan's eyes focused for a brief second on one object: me.

"Pinki!" he moaned, before descending into his half-conscious, writhing state again.

It was just a moment, but it was enough.

"*You!*" shrieked Surpanakha, her words laced with murderous fury. "You did this to my brother! I was right, you *are* still working with the snakes!"

"N-no!" I stammered. "Headmistress, I didn't! I'm not!"

But the headmistress was beyond all reason now. "You, with all your distracting talk of Hidimbi's crown, and finding out about the consorts! It was you who did this! I know it was! You let the snakes into the school!" Spittle was flying from her mouth, and her eyes looked red and crazed.

"Headmistress, please believe me!" I insisted. "I had nothing to do with this! You saw me . . . I was in your class!"

"Stop!" Surpanakha shrieked, a horrible sound that sent all the crows flying from the trees and the small animals scampering into the ground. "All I see is someone who teamed up with the snakes before, and is probably teaming up with them again!"

"But that's not fair. I didn't—" I began, but she cut me off.

"This is your fault, fire demoness!" seethed Surpanakha. Her eyes were glowing red coals, and her fangs and talons had sharpened with her emotions. "If my brother dies, it will be you who killed him!"

"Wait, that's not true!" I protested.

"Get out of my sight!" shrieked the nose-less teacher. "Get out of this school!"

In the meantime, someone had called for the medical team, and as they magicked Professor Ravan away to the school infirmary, the headmistress screamed one parting promise.

"If you don't find his runaway soul-bee and restore my brother to health, I'll hunt you down until the end of your days, Pinki, is that understood? In neither air, land, sea, nor even in the flames of fire will you be safe. I will hunt you down no matter where you run! I will make you pay for this!"

Farting fairy butts, this was really not my day.

CHAPTER 3

The Revolution Is Hiring: Wimps and Bullies Need Not Apply

To be a revolutionary, you really cannot be a wimp.

If you're one of those types who want to always keep safe and out of harm's way, then by all means, take up badminton or croquet. Alternately, join that needlepoint circle that meets at the local library every other Wednesday. But if you want to free yourself and your country of the yoke of imperialist tyranny, you can't expect not to break a talon or two, if you know what I mean.

So after I'd been accused of murdering my professor and effectively kicked out of school, I was ready to make war on whoever was responsible. And if that meant another, fiercer raid on the Serpent Empire, so be it. If Sesha was at the bottom of whatever was going on, I'd not just find out but make the jerk of a colonizer pay. Oh, I couldn't wait to make him pay. But first, I needed to find my rebel friends Arko and Chandni and have them help me find Ravan's soul-bee. Hidimbi's burning crown, on the other hand, could stay stolen for all I cared. I wasn't sure if the legends were true or not, but I'd rather not have to find out.

On my way to the new secret rebel headquarters, I really just wanted to daydream about all the different ways I'd torture Sesha when I caught him. Fireballs up the nostrils? Shooting flames into the armpits? Smoke bomb to the belly? But instead of indulging in such pleasant musings, I had to take care of my baby cousins Kawla, Mawla, and Deembo, who had, of course, insisted on tagging along with me.

"Can we see Miss Chandni, please?" Mawla gushed. "I think she's just the bee's knees."

"No bee metaphors, please, buddy," I groaned, rubbing at my temples. "Everybody thinks I'm responsible for releasing Professor Ravan's soul-bee. I'd rather not hear anything more about those dratted insects right now, if you please."

We were all flying on the back of one of the school's helicocrocs—part bird, part crocodile, all sharp teeth and mace-like tail. I still didn't love flying, but it was the fastest way to get to the new rebel headquarters and find my revolutionary friends.

"Headmisthtress was cwying tears," said Kawla worriedly. "I was afwaid she'd box my eaws!"

"That's why I'm taking you three with me to the rebel headquarters." I patted her hand. "I don't want Surpanakha to take out her anger on you guys. Hopefully by the time we get back, she'll have cooled off and realized that Professor Ravan's illness wasn't my fault. Plus that I had nothing to do with that missing crown!"

Deembo, who was seated in front of me, just nestled her head back into my chest. Even though she could speak now, she didn't do so without real need, as if she was the only one among us who knew the priceless value of words.

When we landed at the rebel headquarters, a series of underground tunnels along the River of Dreams, the first thing we saw was shockingly unexpected.

"Pinkoo shona! Darling beetle bum!" A giant, gray-haired, snaggletoothed, and rheumy-eyed rakkhoshi stood at the tunnel entrance. On her shoulder sat a yellow bird with an onion-like white pagri on his head.

"Ai-Ma!" I exclaimed. "Toto!"

"Why, hello, your demoness-ship!" squawked Toto, eyeing Kawla and Mawla warily. His pagri wobbled a little with agitation. "Deembo, dear, do tell your siblings Toto is a friend and not on the menu?"

Both Kawla and Mawla jumped for the bird, trying to catch him with their sharp talons. Toto squawked, shot out a few tail feathers from his bottom, and flew out of their reach.

I ignored the silly bird and turned my full attention to my mother. "Ai-Ma, how did you get here? You're under house arrest!"

"Didn't you hear, my dung droplet? Your friends Arko and Chandni organized a protest before my cave complex, and before the complexes of all the older prisoners of war. They made such a stink, arguing that we old folks couldn't be of harm to anyone, and that it was cruel and unusual punishment to keep us imprisoned, that the snakes actually freed me—well, with certain conditions!" Ai-Ma showed me the glowing green cuffs circling her wrists and ankles.

"What are those? Monitors?" I pointed to the evil-looking devices. "Then Arko and Chandni didn't free you at all, they just changed the nature of your imprisonment!"

"Oh, pffft! You're such a Gloomy Gus!" Ai-Ma scooped Kawla, Mawla, and Deembo into her fire-hose-like arms and squeezed the stuffing out of them, much to their giggling delight. "It only just happened, or I would have sent you word! One day the magical gate guarding my caves was there, and the next, it had disappeared! Cuffs or no cuffs, I call that a win!"

"Well, I certainly don't!" I snapped, eyeing the cuffs with disgust. Also, what was with her saying *pffft*? "Do those hurt?"

"Don't worry about me, slimy fungus puff," Ai-Ma said with a gentle smile that made me feel even more strange and guilty. I mean, I'd never even thought to demand her freedom before. Chandni and Arko had done that. Chandni, whom Ai-Ma had once doted on as her beloved human "pet." Chandni, who was all beautiful perfection in Ai-Ma's eyes, the daughter she probably always wanted. On the other hand, what power did the snakes now have over her and all the other newly freed revolutionary prisoners through those dratted cuffs?

"I never demanded your release before because, well, how could I have known that the snakes would agree to it?" I muttered, as if answering an unspoken question.

Ai-Ma didn't answer, because she was distracted by my squealing cousins, who were still jumping up and down, trying to catch Toto. Toto, out of an understandable amount of caution, flew around Ai-Ma's head as she embraced the little rakkhosh.

"A teacher's soul-bee got free!" Mawla explained even as he followed Toto's flight with alert, and possibly hungry, eyes. "Everyone thinks it's the fault of Didi!"

"Headmistwess was vewy down!" added Kawla as she wiggled happily in Ai-Ma's arms, planting kiss after kiss on my mother's hairy cheeks. "Her bwother's sick, and thewe's a missing cwown!"

Ai-Ma shot me a questioning look, and I filled her in on all that had happened.

Then my mother got distracted by my cousins again as Deembo took a boiled egg out of her dirty pocket and held it up for Ai-Ma to share with her. I let my messy relatives have their slobbery, snotty, eggy lovefest even as I worried about Ai-Ma's newfound freedom. Again, it was the timing that worried me. The announcement about the consorts, the missing crown, the release of political prisoners, was it all somehow connected? But it made no sense. The serpents must be playing some kind of dastardly game.

I eyed, once again, my mother's magical cuffs. The mere sight of them filled me with fury. I mean, what the protesters had said was right; she was of little danger to anyone, as goofily warmhearted as she was. Yet still, the serpents insisted on putting her in those green cuffs? Why?

But before I had a chance to ask Ai-Ma more about her release, my cousin Deembo said the exact wrong thing. The thing I hadn't planned on telling Ai-Ma. Still cuddling in my mother's arms, the little rakkhoshi looked up and cooed, "The headmistress wants to eat her spleen, but Didi's running for Demon Queen!"

At this, Ai-Ma's face utterly transformed into that expression I dreaded the most: pride. Yuck. Is there anything worse than having your parents be proud of you?

"Have you decided to run, my darling slug bottom?" Ai-Ma put down my little cousins, her eyes shining with tears. "Oh, Pinkoo! Your babu would have been so proud of you! As am I! You are destined to be queen, and when you are anointed, I know your power will call forth Hidimbi's lost crown! Oh, I knew you couldn't have been born so bossy for nothing!"

I let my mother hug me and tried to ignore all her endearments as well as her mention of that dratted crown of flames. She rambled on about all the changes I could bring to the Kingdom once I was queen, how I could challenge the snakes' rule, bring freedom to the land, blah, blah. Ugh. Now that Ai-Ma knew I was running for Rakkhoshi Queen, there was no way to get out of it without breaking her hearts. Double ugh! How had I gotten myself into this situation?

Finally, Ai-Ma let me go, still snuffling, and Toto came back to land on her shoulder. I took a hard look at my mother, avoiding her still teary and ever-so-proud face.

She was dressed in some kind of homespun white sari that looked plain one moment, and the next, strangely shimmery. I noticed the pagri on Toto's tiny head was made of the same material.

"Wait, what are you both wearing?" I demanded, trying to change the subject away from the royalty contest.

Toto puffed out his yellow chest proudly. "Say, why are pagri jokes so hard to understand?" he squawked.

"Because there's a rumor you have a bad sense of humor?" asked Mawla.

"To be understhood," guessed Kawla, "they can't be vewy good?"

Deembo, in the meantime, had dropped an obviously raw egg from her pocket onto the ground. She giggled uproariously at the sight. "Look, my egg's runny—that's very funny!"

"No!" Toto squawked in indignation. "Pagri jokes are so hard to understand because . . ." He made a little trumpet sound with his beak. ". . . puh-puh-puh-puh! They go over your head!"

My three little rakkhosh cousins rolled around on the ground laughing, but I just rolled my eyes. I turned to my mother. "Ai-Ma, seriously, what are you wearing?"

My mother looked down at her sari and smiled a secret

smile. Her normally straggly hair was pulled back in a bun, and she wore a round red teep in the middle of her wrinkled forehead.

"Ah, my smelly jackfruit rind of a future queen! I see you have not yet heard about the resistance's new philosophy!" Ai-Ma waggled her salt-and-pepper eyebrows at me. She had one disturbingly long eyebrow hair that seemed to move with a life of its own. "Let me take you to dear Chandni and Arko, and all will become clear!"

I followed Ai-Ma and Toto into the resistance headquarters, my baby cousins in tow. Ai-Ma walked with a kind of slow shuffle, probably because of the snaky cuffs around her ankles. We made our way down a long series of tunnels, some with secret passages and doors leading off left and right.

The tunnels were gloomy and dank, and I wondered how the resistance had found this new hideout, after the original rebel hideout had been compromised a few months ago. Despite the public denial by the snakes that the undersea school raid had ever happened, the empire knew exactly who was responsible. As rakkhosh, Kumi, Aakash, and I had the protection of demon-kind as long as we lived in the secure grounds of Ghatatkach Academy of Murder and Mayhem, but our rebel friends didn't have the same protections. I'd missed Chandni and Arko, since they'd been effectively in hiding since our raid. Except, I guess, when they were out protesting for my mother's freedom without telling me.

Finally, my mother led us to an open cavern through which rushed the underground River of Dreams. It was the same river that ran beneath Ai-Ma's home and Arko's father's palace, the same river that connected our dimension with others. The air smelled sharply of river water, and after the suffocating atmosphere of the entry tunnels, I was relieved to feel a fresh breeze coming from an overhead opening to the cave. But what I saw next totally stressed me out. Big-time.

There was a girl in a white sari like Ai-Ma's sitting on a rock, staring stoically straight in front of her. Two guys on either side—both dressed alike in white dhotis and chadors—were haranguing and harassing her. But she just sat there, her expression unchanging. When the one on the right pulled at her arm, she just let him. The one on the left flung an entire glass of water in her face, and she just let him. I couldn't believe what I was seeing. They were pulling her hair and yelling in her face as she stared ahead, impassive. Why didn't she try to defend herself? Why did she just sit there? Was she too afraid? The flames in my belly were starting to roil to a full inferno. If there was one thing I couldn't stand, it was bullies.

"Get off of her, you cowards!" I yelled, huffing out two plumes of flames like arms. At one snap of my wrists, the flame arms closed their fists and punched the two bullies almost at the same time. They fell to the floor, yelling bloody murder. And to my shock, the girl they'd been harassing sprang to her feet to help them up!

"Hey! Prince Arko! She used violence!" complained one of the guys I'd felled as his victim was helping him to his feet.

"Lady Chandni, I thought that wasn't allowed!" yelled the other. "No fair!"

"I'm sorry, I'm sorry, it's just a misunderstanding," I heard a familiar voice calling. "This is the brave rakkhoshi Pinki whom you've all heard so much about."

At the sound of that voice, I whipped around, confused and relieved to see a very welcome face.

CHAPTER 4

Do-Goodery Is Such a Downer

My dear sister-friend!" I felt myself gathered into Chandni's arms.

"Good to see you too, moon girl!" I pulled back from her embrace and pointed to the two bullies who had been harassing the girl on the rock. "But what the heck kind of operation are you running here? Why are thugs like that allowed to bully people?"

Instead of answering, Chandni only laughed that annoying, sparkly little laugh of hers, then turned to receive the hugs and squeals of my little cousins.

"Pinki—how are you?" My three hearts sped up at the voice of the prince Arko. His face was a little drawn after weeks of being in hiding, but his eyes were still as warm as ever. I felt something squeeze in my stomach, like a fist

knocking out my breath. "What brings you out of the protection of your school grounds?"

"Never mind that," I said impatiently, spreading my arms to indicate the two bullies and their victim. "What is going on here, prince man?"

Arko laughed. "You misunderstood what you saw, Pinki. These are some of our new resistance recruits, practicing nonviolence training."

"Practicing what now?" I asked, trying to ignore the butterflies still flying around inside me at the sight of Arko.

"I'll take the children to see the river," said Ai-Ma,

scooping up my little cousins in her arms as Toto flew by her head. "As you two explain the new resistance philosophy to Pinki."

"What does she mean?" I asked, searching my friends' faces. "And also, why did you fight for my mother's freedom without telling me?"

"You know how much I adore Ai-Ma, how much I owe her," said Chandni. "As for the protests—we weren't sure they would work ourselves, so we didn't want to risk your safety by having you come off your school grounds if they didn't."

"Well, I'm the one who's her daughter!" I said angrily. "And anyway, you don't think those green serpent cuffs are a bit suspicious? I mean, what are the snakes planning for these old folks?" And then, realizing what I must sound like, I mumbled, "But thanks. I mean, for freeing her. And everything." As Chandni gave me a giant, gooby hug in response, I leaned over her shoulder to look at Arko. "So what is this new philosophy Ai-Ma keeps talking about?"

"We have been following the philosophy of satyagraha." Arko indicated everyone in the cave behind him with a sweeping gesture. "After that terrible, violent undersea raid, Chandni and I have realized we can't participate in the same evil acts as those we are fighting. In order to win this revolution, and get the Kingdom Beyond free, we must wield the power of truth, not weapons."

"The power of truth," I repeated slowly, not understanding where all this was coming from. This must be some goofy, moony idea of Chandni's for sure. But why was Arko going along with it? "Is that why you're all dressed like a bunch of extras in a weird play?"

"Like what?" laughed Chandni in that tinkly, delicate way of hers.

"Why are you all wearing homespun clothes? Made of what looks like"—I reached out to touch the chador Arko had slung over his otherwise bare chest—"moon threads?"

"It's been a while since we've talked," Arko said with a hearts-melting grin. "A lot has changed, Pinki."

Clearly it had. And not all for the good. It hadn't escaped my notice there was a new, comfortable vibe between Arko and Chandni. That they kept smiling at each other like loons. I felt fires of irritation begin to burn, deep and low in my belly.

"So, what? The anti-imperialist resistance has a uniform now?" I pointed to the lines of spinning wheels and looms in the corner of the cavern, and the rebels busy making homespun clothes out of piles of shimmery moonbeams. "We've all got to look like we're from the moon?"

"Part of our nonviolent protest is to not wear anything snake manufactured," explained Chandni. "We're making all our clothes ourselves."

"For real?" I scoffed. "Do you seriously think wearing moonbeam clothes is going to convince the Serpentine Empire to leave the Kingdom Beyond?"

"Not alone, maybe," agreed Arko with a twinkle of his dark eyes. "But all these small steps are part of a new philosophy of nonviolent resistance. We're making step-by-step arguments and turning public opinion—like arguing for the freeing of our elders who are political prisoners. It's all a part of the larger plan to get the snakes to quit the Kingdom."

Chandni enthusiastically pointed to signs some rebels were painting that had the same phrase on them: "Quit the Kingdom." She looked so smug and proud it made me a little acid-y.

"Good slogan, right?" Arko smiled at Chandni, and the way she smiled back was really just too much for my digestive system to handle.

"Look, don't get me wrong. I like the new slogan. 'Quit the

Kingdom'—it's catchy. Nice, uh, alliteration of the sounds,"
I said, suppressing a jealous burp. "I like—no, love—that
you were able to free all the old rebels from house arrest.
Green cuffs notwithstanding. But are you joking with this
passive nonviolent nonsense?"

Neither Arko nor Chandni answered, because just then,
some of the rebels started up a song that seriously got under
my skin. The chorus was "agun jalo"—light the fire. The
verses were about how fire burned and destroyed the old,
but also purified and created the new. As I heard the words,
I felt the burning crown upon my head again. What I didn't
know was if it was destroying or purifying me.

As the stars bloom in the dark fabric of night,
lightning changes darkness to light. So listen for
destiny calling your name. Light your soul on fire
with freedom's flame!

Then another rebel in a homespun dhoti and chador like
Arko's came up to us. I realized it was Aadil, the prince's
next younger brother. I gave him a shocked smile.

"How are you not a champak flower right now?" I
demanded, referring to the curse on Arko's entire kingdom
that doomed everyone but his six brothers to an enchanted

sleep every day, while his princely brothers were trans-formed into magical champak flowers, only returning to human form at night. Arko had evaded the curse because he'd been blessed with sun powers at birth. Yet the seven princes were still called the Seven Brothers Champak.

"Isn't seeing me in human form in the daylight an amaz-ing thing? I'm still not used to it!" Laughing, Aadil bowed to me. "In this underground cavern, we are not touched by the light of the sun, so our bodies do not know that it is day. It's the only way my brothers and I are evading the terrible champak curse. At least, that's what we assume, since we haven't been turning into flowers for weeks now."

"Congratulations?" I said, not sure what the etiquette was for people who'd evaded a curse on a flukey technicality.

"Pinki, here's the thing . . ." Arko cleared his throat, changing the subject back to the one we'd been discussing. "Nonviolence, when done correctly, isn't passive, but a form of active resistance."

"How do you all figure that?" As I looked around, I realized that many more of Arko's brothers were there in the cavern. In fact, there were five of them—Aadil, Ishan, Uday, Umran, and Rishi—all except the youngest, Rontu. I wasn't too surprised. That weaselly Rontu had always been a snake lover.

"There are examples of great resistance leaders from many other dimensions using nonviolence as a successful strategy," Uday was saying. "Even over the distance of space and time, they have walked the path before us, showing us the way."

"And when the snakes come to throw all of you in jail?" I pushed, thinking of my parents.

"We fill up their jails," said Ishan.

"Easier said than done; you don't know what jail does to you." I looked pointedly at Ai-Ma's back.

"There are sacrifices that will need to be made, but isn't it worth leaving behind a history we can be proud of for those who come after us?" Arko asked. "We are not just freeing ourselves in the present, but freeing our future descendants from the chains of violence, and the old, oppressive ways of exercising power."

"I don't get it!" I insisted. "You can win, or you can lose. That's it."

"But that's actually a trick—the idea that there are only two options," Arko insisted. "Nonviolence isn't about violently winning or losing. It's about choosing a third way."

I squinted at him. He'd changed so much in such a short time. There was a new seriousness and gravity to him that hadn't been there before. Was this the same boy who had fought so bravely—and violently—alongside me only weeks ago? The one who had encouraged me to embrace, rather than fear, my own inner fire? This nonviolence nonsense was giving me reflux. I mean, I'd only just embraced the full potential of my power, and now Arko was telling me to abandon it?

"So are we just supposed to make peace fingers or meditate while the snakes shoot bullets at us? Or better yet, put us in those green cuffs too?" I demanded. "I hate people who say that instead of changing the structures that oppress us, we all just learn how to do yoga or make mood boards or something. That's blaming oppressed people for their own oppression!"

"We're not doing that. We want to change the structures; we want to overthrow the snakes! We just want to do it nonviolently," said Chandni.

"So we are training all of our resistance team in how not to respond to violence," Arko explained. "That's what you saw when you walked in."

"You mean, you're training them in how to get beaten up without fighting back?" I stomped my foot. "Did you all forget how awful that undersea battle with the snakes was? How close we all came to dying?"

"Of course not." Chandni shook her head, making

her long, dark braids shake too. "You saved us, Pinki. We know this."

"We saved each other." I couldn't help but feel confused and betrayed. "I mean, did you forget how hard it was for me to actually tap into my power, come into my fire? But I did it. I did it and now you're telling me it's all for nothing?"

"The way of the enemy cannot lead us to victory." Arko's voice was gentle and schoolteacher-like. "As a great 2-D philosopher once said, 'The master's tools will never dismantle the master's house.' We have to choose a new path. Nonviolence can be powerful when done right, purposefully."

I felt like I was losing my mind. And honestly, like a little violence wouldn't be bad just about now. Just enough to bash my two friends in the head and get them to see some sense.

"Would being nonviolent have saved those kids we rescued from the undersea serpent retraining school?" I demanded. "Would me being nonviolent have saved either of you when you were being tortured by Sesha?"

"In the words of another great 2-D philosopher, 'Darkness cannot drive out darkness, only light can do that. Hate cannot drive out hate, only love can do that,'" said Chandni primly.

I wanted to scream. All this do-goodery talk was giving me some serious heartburn!

"First of all, who are these 2-D philosophers and what do they know? Secondly, what's with always equating darkness to bad things, to hate?" I demanded, holding out my arm. "We're all brown-skinned; are you saying we're all bad?"

"That's not what the quote means . . ." Chandni began, looking all delicate and flustered.

"Also, why shouldn't I hate those who are violent to me? Why is it always up to us with the least amount of power to bend and forgive?" I was practically shouting now, little tendrils of smoke escaping from my ears and nostrils. "Why is everyone so afraid of our anger and strength? I'll tell you why—because it challenges the power structures in place!"

"Pinki, please try and listen to what I'm saying. Violence does something to the person using it." Arko's dark eyes were boring into mine, as if he was begging me to understand. He ran his fingers through his hair. "I can't participate in the same evil as those I'm fighting. I have decided to walk the way of the satyagrahi and wield the power of truth, not weapons."

There was a moment of silent tension. Arko and I stared at each other, the space between us crackling with unspoken energies. Chandni looked from one of us to the other, her face inscrutable.

Then Toto flew over to perch on Arko's shoulder, announcing, "Toto has a riddle!" I had no idea why the silly bird always referred to himself in the third person. Without allowing anyone to respond, the yellow parakeet went on, "The ocean's pearl, a grain of sand, more precious than all the gold in the land. Life would be flat, life would be bland, without this diamond in your hand!"

As he'd probably intended, the bird's riddle cut through the tension that had built up between Arko and me. We both laughed, a little embarrassed.

I thought about Toto's clues even as the little bird turned his head this way and that, his beady birdie eyes on me.

"It's an old riddle, bird," I answered finally. "The answer is salt—that ocean's jewel without which life and all our food would indeed be bland. Way to be a non sequitur."

"You're a non-squee-tor!" Toto protested huffily.

"Non sequitur!" I corrected him with a snort of laughter. "It means you bring up stuff out of context, you big weirdo!"

"Toto is mentioning salt because we're also planning a salt march—a weeklong walk to the Ruby Red Sea shores in order to make our own salt." Arko was smiling again, his voice warm and light.

"Why are you making your own *salt* of all things?" I scoffed.

"The serpents make us pay for their overpriced salt, and we want to show them that, just like with our clothes, we of the Kingdom Beyond are self-sufficient!" Chandni said, a glint of pride in her face.

"We're also planning on making our own honey," announced Prince Umran, who had suddenly arrived from who knows where in a beekeeper's suit.

That got my attention. "That's actually the reason I came to find you," I said, looking around at the princes and Chandni. All this talk of peace and light had distracted me from my actual goal. "Just this morning, Professor Ravan's soul-bee escaped and then he fell really ill—he's in a coma in the infirmary now. It happened during a raid on our sanctum—maybe by the snakes, I don't know. Anyway, the headmistress blames me—I'm supposed to find his escaped soul-bee but don't know how to do it."

I bit my lip, not wanting to tell my friends about Hidimbi's missing crown. Honestly, because I had no intention of finding it. I mean, wasn't it kind of a blessing that the burning nightmare was gone?

"So what happens if Professor Ravan's bee dies?" Arko asked.

"He dies too," I answered grimly.

"I wouldn't know the first place to look for a soul-bee," Chandni began, then paused. "Except . . ."

"Except what?" I reached over and shook Chandni's arm a little. She looked at me, but hesitated.

Arko caught Chandni's expression, and it made his own harden. "No, Chandni. That's not an option. You're not doing that."

"It may be our only option if we're to help Professor Ravan and Pinki," Chandni insisted. "If the snakes really are responsible for this raid on the Academy's sanctum . . ."

By now I'd gotten the drift of where Chandni's mind was drifting. "You want me to go talk to Sesha."

Chandni nodded, her luminous face firm with resolution. "I want us to go talk to Sesha."

CHAPTER 5

Snaky Slimeballs Are Gonna Snaky Slimeball

There's no way to overstate how much of a snaky slimeball I knew Sesha to be. First of all, he'd once tried to trick me into finding Chandni for him because he was so in love with her. Second of all, even though his dad, the Governor-General, was completely evil and seriously mean to Sesha, the kid was still loyal to him. Thirdly, he'd once kidnapped my little cousins in some kind of twisted attempt to save Chandni from his dad. His ridiculous plan had been to hold them hostage until I convinced the moon girl to go into hiding and abandon the revolution. Finally, in a pathetic and gross attempt to get on his dad's good side, the loser had caged hundreds of kids and magically stolen their voices. Not to mention that he'd tortured Aakash and Kumi, and practically killed Chandni, Arko, and me during the undersea battle.

He was, to put it mildly, the worst. Despite the fact that I'd found him kind of intriguing the first time I met him. Chalk that up to my jealousy at how many minions he had working for him, including a whole host of maggots who were carrying his cape that day. And so, yes, I had once made a deal with him—because I was so desperate for his help to control my fire. But I'd soon discovered his idea of helping me was just to rein me in, limit me, and make me afraid of my own strength. The only reason I'd been able to finally learn to control my powers was because I'd found friends who helped me learn to embrace my anger and fire, and recognize that power as a part of me.

Yet despite all this bad history between us, there I was, on the back of Raat, Arko's black-as-night flying horse, off to see Sesha. I'd left Kawla, Mawla, and Deembo at the resistance headquarters with Arko and Ai-Ma. I would have left Chandni too, but as Arko rightly pointed out, Sesha was more likely to kill *me* outright than he was *her.*

"We're almost to the place he agreed to meet me," called Chandni from the back of Snowy, Prince Rishi's white-as-a-snowy-mountainside pakkhiraj.

"I don't know how you got that message to and then

back from Sesha so quickly," I groused again. Flying made my stomach upset and so I was feeling even grumpier than usual. I let out a little burp. "He must still be in love with you."

"I don't think he knows how to love anything but himself. But he certainly thinks he's in love with me." Chandni shrugged. "It doesn't matter. That kind of love isn't something I care about—or want—right now in my life. I have the love that counts. The love of my friends."

As silly as it was, I felt a little spark of jealousy flare up in me, because I knew that Chandni was talking about Arko. And maybe Ai-Ma. And yet, what she was saying made sense—she was talking about the love of friendship. What was wrong with me that I had to bring jealousy into the equation? Maybe it was the fact that I'd kind of had some chemistry with Sesha way back when he was trying to fool me into helping him. Maybe it was the fact that I'd only recently stopped resenting that Chandni was so tiny and cute and luminous she always made me feel huge and muscular and unnecessarily hairy in comparison. Or maybe it was the fact that she had orchestrated Ai-Ma's release, like she was Ai-Ma's real daughter and not me.

"There!" My tiny, cute, and annoyingly luminous friend pointed down toward the ground. "That's the grove I said I'd meet him."

Of course the grove in the Thorny Woods Chandni had chosen for our secret meeting with Sesha was in fact the first place I'd met him myself. It was also the place I'd first met Arko, back before I knew he was a prince and thought he was just a village schoolteacher named Shurjo. I remembered how I'd felt a sense of connection to Arko right away, as if the sun powers he was blessed with at birth had somehow called out to my own fire. I remembered how encouraging and gentle he'd been with the village school-children. It made sense, I guess, for him to turn to the path of nonviolence. But oh! It made me so frustrated to think of all Arko's battle fire going to waste.

Sesha was waiting for us in the grove, popping out from behind a wide Ashoka tree the moment we landed the horses. He was overdressed as usual, in an elaborate green velvet suit with a matching short cape. And hey, as if that wasn't enough, he was even sporting a circlet crown thing that he wore tilted rakishly on his green-black hair. Was he heading out for a self-indulgent photo shoot after this or something?

"You didn't say you were bringing *her*," Sesha snarled, sending a green wave of power in my direction the moment I dismounted my horse. Okay, so he obviously hadn't

forgotten the fact that the last time he'd seen me this up close, I'd been dangling him over a balcony, threatening to drop him.

"Super awesome to see you too, Sesha," I yelled as I threw a wall of fire to meet and burn up his power. He was such a snivelly little two-faced scumbucket of a snake. I was seriously regretting the fact that I'd let Chandni convince me to come see him.

"Gotten more control of your fire, have you?" Sesha snarled, hurling another piece of green lightning in my direction that I barely had time to duck. "Where did that pathetic fire girl go who just wanted someone to help her control her naughty flames?"

"Same place that pathetic daddy's boy went, the one who only wants to get his evil father's attention!" I yelled, throwing a huge smoke bomb toward his head. "Oh, wait, my bad, you're right here!"

Sesha's eyes turned a glittering bright green, and he looked ready to send another bolt of magic my way, but Chandni intervened first.

"Stop it, both of you!" bellowed the moon girl. Lifting her hands, she put us each in a sort of dome of shining moonlight so we were unable to use our powers on each other.

"Let me out of here; the last time I saw that creature she tried to kill me!" Sesha bared his sharp teeth as he pounded on the curved walls of the moon dome.

"But I didn't kill you, did I? Though that was obviously a mistake." I was happy to see that there was a bunch of my fire-smoke that had gotten trapped in the dome with Sesha, making the snake boy choke and cough.

"Sesha, you agreed to meet me without fighting," said Chandni coolly. "I'm not going to let you go until I know you won't try to attack Pinki either."

I stuck out my tongue at Sesha, tossing my fabulously

curly hair as I did. Immature, I know, but sometimes immaturity can be very deeply satisfying.

"You cool it too, Pinki!" Chandni turned on me like the Goody Two-shoes she was. "We're calling a truce so we can talk."

"This is over! Your message said you wanted to see me alone, Chandni." Sesha stomped his booted foot inside the moon dome, looking like a toddler about to have a tantrum over losing a toy. "I should have known not to trust you, you rebel scum!"

"Relax, Sesha," Chandni soothed. "We just want to talk. And I knew if I said Pinki was coming, you wouldn't agree to meet with me."

"You were right!" Sesha's eyes were big and bloodshot, and he was shooting me furtive looks almost like he was afraid of me. "Get that fire-breathing dragon out of my sight!"

"If you're going to be like that, then we'll have to leave." Chandni twitched her sari end around her waist and tucked it in, like she was preparing to remount her flying horse.

"Wait! No, don't go!" Sesha blurted out, reaching out his hand toward Chandni as if he couldn't stand to let her go. Ugh, why did everyone fall for the moon maiden so hard? "A temporary truce, I promise."

Chandni turned to me, hands on hips. The trees around her seemed to also be looking down on me, waiting for my answer.

"Fine, me too." I grunted, puffing out two small plumes of frustrated smoke. "A temporary truce."

As Chandni released us both from our domes, Sesha and I eyed each other warily like caged animals just freed, each trying to size up the other's intentions.

"We'll go away as soon as you answer some questions." Even as I said this, though, I let a couple little show-offy sparks burst out from my nose and mouth. I was gratified to see Sesha take a few alarmed steps back from me.

"Someone broke into Ghatatkach Academy's inner sanctum," Chandni said. "Were you responsible?"

Sesha narrowed his eyes at this, a slow smile spreading over his face. "You're here to ask me where Professor Ravan's soul-bee went. And more importantly, that old-fashioned crown?"

"Crown?" Chandni shot me a look. "You didn't tell us about a missing crown!"

Sesha burst into laughter. "Of course she didn't! Pinki here probably doesn't want it found—I mean, what with the legends about it bursting into flames the moment any pretender tries to put it on!" Somewhere in the tree line, a bird jabbered and jabbered as if imitating his mockery of me.

"Is that true?" Chandni asked.

"Let's keep our eyes on the prize here!" I exclaimed, hoping that my reddening cheeks weren't too obvious. Trust that slimeball Sesha to guess why I didn't want to find Hidimbi's crown. I cleared my throat, determined to change the subject. "So, Sesha, you're admitting you snakes *were* responsible for the break-in?"

"I didn't say that! But we snakes have our eyes and ears everywhere. We know everything that goes on in the Kingdom." Sesha's hands were clasped behind his back and he was pacing around like some kind of a storybook version of an evil villain.

"We know you do, which is why we came to see you," Chandni said with a sigh.

"At least *you* have a realistic sense of the world, moon maiden." Sesha raised one dark eyebrow in my direction. "But your demoness friend here is a disappointment! All brawn and no brains, obviously, just like she looks!"

"Come closer and say that to me, you slimy punk!" I took a snarling leap toward him. Flames and smoke erupted from my mouth, ears, and nose. Yes, I know, perhaps not the smartest thing in the middle of a forest.

"Calm down, both of you!" Chandni sent a shower of cool moonbeams to extinguish the tiny bush and brush fires my emotions had caused.

"You should keep that she-beast chained up!" spat out Sesha. But I did notice he had managed to leap several more feet away from me.

"Let's just cut to the chase." Chandni rubbed her eyes tiredly. "Do you know where Professor Ravan's soul-bee is or not?"

Sesha studied both of our faces, his evil villain nonchalance back in place. He lifted a wicked eyebrow. "Why should I tell you?"

Oh, I really couldn't stand this guy. "What do you want in return for the information?" I demanded.

"What do you have on the menu?" He leered at Chandni as he said this, and I seriously wanted to bite him in the kneecap.

"You'll tell us because you know that the empire's coming to an end," said Chandni calmly. "It's getting too expensive to govern, and the snake population itself is getting disillusioned with the cost of continuing to rule the Kingdom Beyond."

Sesha waved a casual hand. "That's all just media propaganda. None of that is true. The sun will never set on the Serpent Empire, no matter what anyone says. The reporters have it out for us; they're all lying rebel scum."

Chandni narrowed her eyes, but I cut in before she could say anything. "I need to know where my professor's soul-bee is, Sesha. Tell me now before we decide we were just joking about the whole truce thing."

I opened my balled fists to show Sesha the two orange-red fire orbs I had burning in them. But somehow, Sesha didn't seem scared. Not, in fact, at all. Instead, he started to laugh.

"If you actually think that the moon girl will let you go back on your word, you don't know her as well as you think you do!" He ran his hands through his product-greasy hair, as if readying himself for that Young Tyrant of the Year photo shoot. He leered again in Chandni's direction, and I don't know what it was, but there was something in his look that just pushed me over the edge.

Unfortunately, what I did next was so not smart.

CHAPTER 6

In Which I Stupidly Set Up a Fake Romantic Situation with Someone I Totally Can't Stand

If you tell me, I'll make you my consort when I become Demon Queen!" I burst out.

Immediately, I regretted the words, which came from that same awful jealousy that had burbled up in me before. It wasn't so much that Sesha liked Chandni—but more about the fact that everyone, including Arko and Ai-Ma, seemed to like Chandni so much. My offer also came from that same impulsive place that had made me enter the demonic royalty competition in the first place. What can I say, at least I was consistently on-brand. Foolish, but on-brand.

At my words, Chandni and Sesha turned to me, their faces comical pictures of surprise.

"You'll make Sesha what?" Chandni blurted out, her

eyes wide. "But. I mean. You don't even care about the contest. You don't want to be Demon Queen, right?"

"I used to not care about being Demon Queen," I corrected huffily. It felt kind of good to have caught Chandni so off guard. "Everyone can change, okay? You've changed, I've changed, the climate is changing, everything changes, okay? I've entered the contest, for your information, and I'm sure I'll win too."

"Okay, fine, I believe you," Chandni pressed on, her face a mix of unclear emotions. "But what is this about a consort?"

I couldn't help but feel a spark of joy deep inside to see her looking so upset. She might not be interested in romantic love, but clearly she still enjoyed being at the center of everyone's attention. Served her right for being so darn adorkable.

"You hadn't heard, Chandni?" Sesha puffed up a little. Seemed like someone else didn't mind making the moon girl jealous either. "The next Demon Queen or King will choose a partner from one of the other communities of the Kingdom Beyond. I think the thought was to ally with, say, the humans or the fairies. But Pinki's idea about a snake consort is pretty perfect, actually. With me as her consort, it will make it impossible for the rakkhosh to rise up against the Serpent Empire's rule."

Chandni shot an accusing look at me. "Is that true? Then you can't offer him that!"

My stomach flipped. I obviously hadn't thought this entire thing through. Besides, the fact was that I didn't want to make Sesha my consort; I wanted to choose Arko. Oh, why oh why had I let my tongue run away with me again? So I did what I did best: tried to bluff my way out. I cleared my throat. "Or me choosing Sesha might make it impossible for the snakes not to give the rakkhosh what they want—self-rule. It may just be the first step in having the snakes quit the Kingdom!"

Chandni didn't look convinced, but Sesha's smile seemed to grow at her hesitation. He raised his eyebrow in my direction, giving me a fake besotted look. "Oh, for sure, you keep thinking that, my demonic gumdrop!"

Chandni's eyes widened even more, getting a little hard and shiny. But she said nothing.

"Stop thinking you're some kind of serpentine Mr. Suave!" I put out my hand in front of Sesha's slimy face. "The consortship is a political alliance, not a romantic partnership!"

"Sure, of courssse," drawled Sesha. He was pretending to flirt with me, but I could tell his entire attention was toward

Chandni, trying to gauge how she was taking all this. "Whatever you say, my deliriously demented dumpling!"

"So are you going to tell me about the bee or what?" I demanded.

"What?" Sesha blinked, obviously having lost the entire train of the conversation in his attempt to get under Chandni's skin.

I sighed. "The bee? You said you would tell us where to find Professor Ravan's soul-bee?"

Sesha frowned, his eyes shooting from Chandni to me and back again. I could almost see the cogs in his brain turning, wondering if it was worth continuing this farce— pretending that he wanted to be chosen as my consort if I became Demon Queen. If he dropped the act, he could demand something different in exchange for the information about Professor Ravan's soul-bee. But if he kept up the pretense, he could continue to make Chandni jealous. What was worth more to him? I wondered.

In the end, as I could have predicted, he chose Chandni. Or me. Or rather, he chose me in order to bug the heck out of Chandni.

"As long as you give me your word, as a rakkhoshi, that you will indeed choose me as your consort, my little pinkalicious Pinki pie, I will indeed tell you where Professor Ravan's soul-bee is," Sesha said, his voice calculated and low.

To the left of me, I heard Chandni's hissing intake of breath.

But I didn't spare her a look. Instead, I stared at the serpent prince. He knew how impossible it was for rakkhosh to go back on a promise. Our promises bound us—to break one would mean near death. Sesha stared at me, his handsome face just as complicated, just as intriguing as the first day I'd met him. He was a bum. He was a jerk. He was a snake. But one thing he wasn't, I had to admit, was boring. You'd never catch Sesha following the path of nonviolence and trying to convince everyone to douse their inner fire.

"Well?" Sesha prompted in his oily way. "Do you promise?"

I hesitated. How could I promise to make my sworn enemy my consort? But then I noticed Chandni's face. Her features weren't wearing that prim and calm expression she usually had, but were marked with pain and a significant dose of confusion. I don't know for what twisted reason, but that look on her face fired up something illogical and vengeful in me. I guess, like Sesha, I still had a good deal of villain inside.

"Fine," I spat out through clenched teeth. My hearts

were hammering in my chest as I stared at Sesha. But through the corner of my eye, it was Chandni I saw flinch at my word.

"Fine what?" Sesha prompted. He flicked something invisible off his sleeve.

"I give you my word that I will choose you as my consort if I become Demon Queen," I said. Even as I said the words, I knew they were wrong, and was simultaneously, inexplicably, thrilled by their wrongness. "Now tell me where I can find Ravan's soul-bee!"

Sesha stared at me, like he couldn't believe that I'd actually promised to make him my consort. I could hardly believe it myself. Certainly, I couldn't let Professor Ravan die. But surely there was another, less reckless way to get the information out of Sesha? What in the multiverse had I been thinking?

"Okay, I'll tell you." Sesha grinned now, giving me a way-too-over-the-top gallant bow. "In exchange for one more thing."

"No more things!" I said, already feeling nauseated by my rash decision.

"What?" Chandni demanded, her hands on her hips.

"A kiss!" Sesha pronounced, making me want to both gag and punch him.

"Are you serious?" Chandni looked like she wanted to put both of us back in those moon domes. Or maybe turn back time to when Sesha and I were trying to kill each other, only a few minutes earlier. "What exactly is going on here, Pinki?" She sounded near tears. "Why are you doing this? This isn't what we're about!"

"I have no idea what you mean," I said huffily, even though it was a lie. Of course I knew what she meant. Why in the world *was* I behaving in this completely expected way, letting a boy come between us? And a horrible, villainous boy at that? The truth was, I had no real way to explain my behavior, even to myself.

"So it must bother you, Chandni, eh?" Sesha's eyes were hard, but I could see the hurt in them. "For me to transfer my affections to your demonic friend here? Or are you just wondering if they were never that strong in the first place when it came to you?"

Chandni turned away from me, looking upset, to face the prince of snakes. "Sesha, you once fought beside me in the resistance. We shared the same dreams for the Kingdom. I thought I knew you. We were friends." Her voice broke a little here, and Sesha made a low growl in response. I felt my own hearts squeeze painfully. "I thought you'd get over this phase of trying to please your father. But I guess I was wrong!"

With this, she turned on her heel and went stomping off toward the horses.

Sesha looked at her retreating back, his face full of shame and sadness. I'm pretty sure if I'd had a mirror, my face would have looked the same as well.

"Well? Where do I find the soul-bee?" I demanded, noticing with some irritation that the prince of snakes wasn't even bothering to look at me. Which only made me feel all the worse. I might have learned to control my fire power, but I hadn't yet learned to control the flames of my own impulsive behavior, which could be just as destructive as any inferno.

"You sure you don't want to find the crown too?" mocked Sesha.

I hesitated, but then remembered that terrible, burning feeling of the crown on my head. No, the longer that mukut stayed lost, the better.

"I just want to find the bee and save my professor," I insisted.

"You'll find what you seek with the transit officer." Sesha fiddled distractedly with his elaborately embroidered cuffs.

"The who?" I stepped in front of him, but he just leaned to the right so he could keep watching Chandni.

"The transit officer is a new post—he's the guardian of the transit corridor between our world and the multiverse," Sesha said in a loud voice so that Chandni could hear.

"So the rumors are true?" She whirled around. "The snakes have created a permanent wormhole between our world and the 2-D realm? Why? For what purpose?"

"You'll just have to wait and see, won't you?" Sesha raised his eyebrow, grinning wickedly. "You'll be impressed when you find out, I promise."

"I seriously doubt it," Chandni snapped. Without looking back again, she reached her pakkhiraj and began mounting up.

"Well, what about it, then?" Sesha turned finally to me.

"Well what about what, then?" I snapped.

"What about my kiss?" he said, taking a step toward me. He didn't come all the way close, I noticed, though. And I could tell that under all that bravado, he didn't really want to kiss me either.

"Keep dreaming, dude." I sent out a thin smoke ring that slapped Sesha briefly on the cheek, then dissipated.

"I will, my demented demonic dear!" Sesha bellowed,

obviously for Chandni's benefit. "I will dream of you, my dumpling-faced evil genius of a cruciferous consort!"

I had no idea what to say to that, and so I just turned and walked away, feeling refluxy.

When I got to the horses, I found Chandni in an uncharacteristically foul mood. "I'll let you go inquire about the transit officer? I imagine you can do that on your own?"

"Of course," I agreed. Inside, my feelings were doing somersaults—now delighted that I'd bugged Chandni so much, now appalled that I'd promised Sesha he could be my consort. What was wrong with me? Clearly, I was not cut out for do-goodery.

"I'll see you back at headquarters, then." Chandni barely looked in my direction as our horses leaped into the sky. "I have a lot I have to do."

I couldn't help but smile a little secret smile. Miss Purity and Perfection was getting a taste of her own medicine— what it felt like to have everyone like and want someone else, not her.

But then why did I feel so rotten about the whole thing?

CHAPTER 7

With Friends Like Mine, Who Needs Enemies?

The new transit corridor thing, according to that snake in the grass and my future consort Sesha, was at the edge of the bazaar that stood in the middle of the human and rakkhosh areas of the Kingdom Beyond. I didn't mind shopping in the dirty, open-sewered, stray-dog-and-cow-filled parts of the bazaar known for shady dealings and even shadier shopkeepers, but to get to the transit corridor I'd have to cross through the more upscale, human-frequented part of the market. And that made me want to light something on fire.

"Those weak-kneed humans are going to come after me with pitchforks and torches if I show my rakkhoshi face over on that side," I complained to Chhaya Devi, merchant of shadows. She specialized in selling dubiously obtained magical tree shadows and other black market goods, and so, her stall was in the more sketchy part of the bazaar. Which suited me just fine.

Chhaya Devi leaned over her counter and peered at me. Her voice was raspy and her eyes shifty. "So why not just disguise yourself as a human? You're excellent at human transformation, as we both know."

"I kind of want them to come after me with pitchforks and lighted torches," I confessed with a grin. "It would give me a good excuse to set some stuff on fire."

Chhaya Devi chuckled, and I could smell the paan she was chewing, the pungent smell of spices mixing with the green scent of the leaf in which they were wrapped. "Always itching for a fight, aren't you, my girl?"

I poked at a smoking and bubbling vial on Chhaya Devi's counter until she slapped my hand and pulled her wares out of my reach. "Today particularly. Surpanakha thinks I'm responsible for Professor Ravan's bee going missing! Not to mention ole Queen Hidimbi's crown of flames getting stolen."

She narrowed her rheumy eyes at me. "Why do you call it that? The crown of flames?"

I groaned inwardly. Chhaya Devi missed absolutely nothing. "That's the legend, right? That it's supposed to burst into flames if ever put on the head of an imposter?"

"And you're afraid that'll happen to you, eh?" Chhaya Devi put down the dirty cloth with which she'd been wiping her smudgy countertop. "Because you've decided to run for Demon Queen after all?"

"How did you know I'd decided to run for Demon Queen?" I demanded. Chhaya Devi really was too uncannily perceptive.

She shrugged, grinning with her betel-nut-reddened teeth. "I didn't. But I do now!"

I groaned, leaning my elbows on her counter. "It was mostly just to annoy my headmistress, but now I'm kind of stuck."

"Your mother must be over the moon," said Chhaya Devi.

"That's an understatement." I remembered Ai-Ma's unbridled delight at the thought of me being Demon Queen.

"I'm proud of you too." The old woman playfully grabbed my chin. "Look at little until-only-recently-antisocial you, putting yourself out there, taking risks!"

I shook myself free, putting my hands over my ears as if her words were burning them. "Stahhhp. I knew coming here was a mistake."

That made the merchant laugh. "On the other hand, your rakkhosh friends Aakash and Kumi can't be happy about it."

"They'll deal," I countered with a sniff.

"All that power's got to be a little tempting too," she suggested, raising her scraggly, sticky-outy eyebrows.

"I guess." Idly, I bounced a small fireball from one hand to the other. It glowed a bright red-yellow, spitting sparks. "Chandni didn't seem too keen on me joining the contest."

"Chandni and Arko have been spending a lot of time together since the raid," Chhaya Devi said, flipping casually through an old book of spells.

Without meaning to, I lost control of the fireball and the book caught on fire. Quickly, Chhaya Devi dumped some purple liquid from a bottle onto it, dousing the flames.

The merchant of shadows looked up, irritation flooding her features as her book smoked. "All right, then, spit it out."

"What?" I widened my eyes, the perfect picture of innocence.

Apparently, the picture wasn't perfect enough. Chhaya Devi snorted. "You're a terrible liar. Why are you here instead of already off looking for that transit officer? Is it that you're upset that Chandni and Arko freed your mother and didn't invite you?"

I slammed my hand on her counter, rattling her vials and mixtures. "You knew about that too?"

"You can't blame your friends for something like that!"

Chhaya Devi shook a skinny finger at me. "Although I guess you are."

"That's not the only thing," I sniffed, feeling very attacked. "What about those green cuffs around her wrists and ankles? They seem mighty suspicious! Like the snakes are up to something!"

"The snakes are always up to something!" the old woman said with a snort.

"My point exactly!" I muttered, not sure for a second what my original point was, after all.

"Well, what is it that you wanted to ask me?" Then, narrowing her eyes, Chhaya Devi continued. "Or is it that you've done something and wanted someone to confess it to?"

I put on my best show of outrage. "What are you talking about? I haven't done anything! Confess? To you?! Even the thought makes me laugh." Then, to emphasize my point, I let out a "Ha! HA!"

Chhaya Devi collapsed with mirth. "Oh, that's a good one!"

"Rude!" I shouted. "Why are you laughing?"

"For a rakkhoshi, you really are a terrible liar!" Chhaya Devi wiped her streaming eyes with the edge of her sari. "All right, girl, don't get all huffy, just tell me what happened already."

I realized the merchant of shadows was being literal; there were streams of smoke coming out of both my nostrils. But I had no one else to talk to and really needed to get something off my chest.

With a smoky sigh that made Chhaya Devi cough, I asked, "What do you know about the tradition of Demon Queens or Kings choosing a consort?"

"Two consorts," Chhaya Devi corrected me with a hacking cough. "If they're following the old system."

"What?" I straightened up with a jolt. Maybe having given my word to Sesha didn't have to mean that I couldn't pick Arko too. "No one told me about two consorts."

"Two potential consorts," Chhaya Devi said, coughing again. "In the time before the Serpent Empire, that's the way it went. The Demon Queen or King picked two potential non-rakkhosh consorts and then, well, the elder rakkhosh either chose between them, or sometimes, the two consorts battled to the death."

"Really?" That didn't sound good.

"Except that one time." Chhaya Devi looked speculatively at the ceiling of her stall, like the history of the Kingdom Beyond was written up there for her to read. "I believe the Demon Queen chose one consort and then publicly killed the other. It was pretty gruesome now that I think about it."

"Huh. Interesting." Now that was an option I could live with. To choose Arko and kill Sesha sounded good to me. And I wouldn't have to break my promise to the snake boy either. I mean, I'd promised to choose him as a consort, not refrain from murdering him.

"Who did you promise to make your consort?" Chhaya Devi hacked and spat on the ground. "Someone you're fantasizing about murdering now?"

"Why do you say that?" But even as I asked, my voice wobbled a little.

Chhaya Devi gave a little snort. "Must I point out the obvious?"

"All right, fine. It's Sesha," I admitted with a groan. "I was mad, or temporarily insane, or something. I promised before I really thought it through."

"The prince of snakes?" Chhaya Devi spat out some paan juice from the side of her mouth. The betel-nut liquid hit the earthen floor with a little splat, staining it red. "You promised to make the prince of snakes your consort if you become Demon Queen? Did you forget you were just locked in a life-or-death battle with him? A battle in which you came very close, need I remind you, to dying?"

"No?" I buried my head in my hands.

"So what are you going to do about it, my demonic genius?" The merchant of shadows gave me a scathing look.

"I could always make sure to lose the royal competition?" I suggested. "Or quit?"

"And break your mother's hearts? Not to mention mine?" she scoffed even as I groaned aloud. "Anyway, your giant ego would never allow you to lose, or quit!"

"Then I could choose two consorts and kill Sesha?" I suggested, as if it were the easiest thing in the world.

"Prince Arko wouldn't be too impressed. Killing Sesha isn't consistent with his whole nonviolent philosophy, no?" The merchant of shadows grimaced, displaying her reddened teeth again.

"I never said I would choose Arko as my other consort," I retorted.

"You didn't have to." Chhaya Devi poked her bony finger into my shoulder. "Now, stop thinking about boys already and go get Professor Ravan's bee before the poor man dies."

"You're the worst sort of friend," I groused, rubbing my shoulder. "You know way too much about everything."

"Who said we were friends?" cackled Chhaya Devi as I walked away.

I could hear the pleasure and pride in her voice, and it

seriously gave me hives. But it was her last comment that made me send up a shower of sparking fire.

"And don't worry about that crown of flames, eh?" she called. "It'll only burn you to a crisp if you're an imposter, right? And what are the chances of that?"

Along with my shower of fire, I made a rude gesture without turning around. The chances of me not being the rightful heir to Hidimbi's crown were pretty darn high. And that was exactly what I was afraid of.

CHAPTER 8

In Which Various Human Beings Annoy Me in Various Annoying Ways

I was too grumpy to transform myself into a more human-appearing form before I walked through the human-frequented parts of the bazaar. Here, the roads were wider, the stalls set up at even intervals, with the goods sold tending to foodstuffs and household items, as opposed to the black market weaponry available on the other side of the market. There were fewer criminals, fewer strays, and fewer shady deals. It was positively disgusting.

As I passed by in my full rakkhosh form, shoppers scattered. A vegetable seller screamed and pulled her children close, while multiple fishmongers shouted obscenities. Someone actually had the audacity to throw a fresh fish, which hit me with a splat. When I spun around, growling, to see who had done the deed, they were all hiding behind their piles of pungent silver-scaled ilish, catla, and rui fish.

"Cowards!" I snarled, brushing the fishy scales from my arm. Great, now I smelled like my water roommate, Kumi.

"Monster!" shrieked a grandma with a baby on her hip.

"Hey! Who are you calling a monster, lady?" I whirled around, causing the woman who had yelled to run away, her grandbaby bouncing beside her. I didn't mind the fish throwing and frightened screaming, but this was a step too far. "This is the same monster who saved those human children who had been taken by the snakes! If it wasn't for this monster, those kids would still be voiceless, all right? I don't expect parades, but I'd appreciate a little decency. And less projectile seafood!"

There was silence in the marketplace after that, although people were still giving me shifty looks as I turned to walk on. I hadn't gone but half a dozen steps, though, when I heard a number of fast footsteps running after me.

I whirled, ready to fight my attackers on the dusty market road. Only, no one was there. Not at my eyeline at least. When I adjusted my line of vision, however, there were at least five little market urchins crowded around my feet. They were shoeless and poorly dressed, in patched clothes, with ill-combed hair and dirty faces. Under the Serpent Empire's rule, there were few humans who could afford to keep their families any better. And these young ones looked loved, at least, skinny but not starving, smiling and bright-eyed.

"Aren't you afraid of me?" I growled, showing off my glowing fangs and sharp talons.

Inexplicably, the little snot-nosed humans actually giggled. "No!" blurted out one of the braver ones, his finger scratching unmentionable (although apparently itchy) areas of his anatomy.

I saw their parents and grandparents walking cautiously toward us, and ignored them. Instead, I bent down to meet the children eye to eye. "Why not?" I asked, but a little less scarily.

Another little one, a tangle-haired girl holding an even-more-tangle-haired doll by one naked leg, walked boldly up to me. At first I wondered if she was going to give me her doll, or maybe try to bash me with it. Instead, she put her grubby little hand up to my cheek.

"You thaved us," she whispered in a lisp that reminded me of my cousin Kawla.

And that's when I saw them: the identical scars on each of their soft little necks. It was the same scar my cousins Kawla, Mawla, and Deembo had, the magical scar through which the snakes had somehow stolen the children's voices.

Seeing those scars, it made me want to burn something up. Sesha, for starters. It was his fault these children had been kidnapped and traumatized. I relished the thought of choosing him as one of two potential consorts, only to incinerate him in a swirling inferno of fire. It was the right thing to do, honestly. Just the thought made me feel deeply satisfied.

The worried elders had caught up to the children now and were crowding behind them, trying to pull the little ones closer, but I ignored them.

"You children were in the cages—in the undersea

serpent retraining school?" I asked, my voice gruff. "You were with my cousins Kawla and Mawla?"

"Yes, but we're home now, because of you." A small person with sticky-uppy hair launched himself into my arms, almost toppling me over. I heard a gasp from the adults, but the child held on and didn't let go. After my initial surprise, I hugged the little human back. It felt squirmy and small, like some kind of warm-blooded, squishy animal, only weaker and with fewer survival instincts.

I cleared my throat, pushing the child from me and abruptly standing up. There was something alarming happening in my throat and my eyes were leaking liquid.

"Are one of you disgusting vegetable sellers cutting onions?" I growled, and to my annoyance, the adults started to laugh.

"No one is cutting onions, lady rakkhoshi," said one of the children's grandfathers, a tough-looking old gent with a warm smile.

And then he and the other elders urged their children forward, and all the children touched my feet, one by one, each giving me their respectful pronam.

I sniffed and grumbled and felt like lighting something on fire, but managed to hold it together as the little squishy humans touched my feet with their tiny squishy hands.

When their guardians started forward, looking like they were about to offer their pronams too, I had to draw the line.

"Have you all gone mad?" I shouted. "First grown-up who touches my feet gets eaten!"

At that, the parents and grandparents straightened up, putting their hands together in namaskars instead. To my chagrin, despite the whole announcement about eating them, all the adults, like their children, were smiling at me with disgusting pleasure.

"Thank you, Lady Pinki!" they chorused. "Thank you for saving the future of humankind. Thank you for giving our children back their voices."

And then I seriously almost puked because one after another, the adults began loading up my neck with flower garlands, and the flower sellers began pelting me with rose petals.

"Oh, of all the low-down, dirty tricks . . ." I grumbled, trying not to smile. It was humiliating, yes, but also just a little satisfying to finally get the thanks I so richly deserved.

And so I was off, sneezing from the pollen of the flower malas, eyes itching from the falling petals, with the thanks and gratitude of the humans chorusing behind me.

I would have so much preferred it if they'd just chased me with pitchforks. But I suppose we can't have everything we wish for.

CHAPTER 9

What with All the Acne and Ennui, Giant Teenage Monsters Are So Gross

I'm not trying to show off when I say that I've met a lot of different types of monsters in my time. Rakkhosh, khok-kosh, daini, doito, bhoot—you name a ghoulie or goblin or three-horned, toad-faced demon, I'm familiar with them all. So when I tell you I'd never seen a monster like Sesha's transit officer, you can appreciate how unusual the creature was.

After I walked past the rikshaw pullers and bangle sellers who occupied the edge of the market, the crooked, multi-colored houses with their drying saris and other laundry, I crossed over a stone bridge that arced above the babbling stream with leaping golden fish. On the other side of the bridge was a green meadow covered in wildflowers, buzzing with honeybees. The sound reminded me of the terrible scene when Professor Ravan had fallen ill. I quickened my steps.

I marched on, past the meadow, to the rocky path leading to a slightly elevated hillside. It was then I saw the signs pointing toward the newly established dimension-to-dimension transit corridor.

Newly Established Dimension-to-Dimension Transit Corridor
Passports Required, But Will Not Be Accepted Unless You Are a Serpent
Other Forms of ID Will Be Accepted Only If Edible
Have a Good Day
#ComplianceOverDefiance

"Fair enough," I muttered. "I mean, no accounting for differences in taste, I suppose." The next sign was even weirder.

This Is a Serpent-Controlled Space.
Our Eyes Are on You.
(Yes, You With Your Finger in Your Nose!
Gross! Wash Your Hands Already!)
Have a Good Day
#ComplianceOverDefiance

That was offensive. My finger wasn't in my nose, or any other orifice. The sign didn't just irritate me, it made me seriously self-conscious. I looked around, trying to find any spying gadgets lurking in the grasses, rocks, or sparse trees. Were the serpents really watching me walk toward the transit corridor?

The final set of signs were the most disturbing yet. What made them even more bizarre was that they appeared to be freshly painted, with some of the letters smudged and dripping. Plus they had a *lot* of goofy misspellings.

**If Bringing Yur Elders fur Intrgalaktik Sakrifice,
You Muss File An Intergalaktik Sakrifice
Form in Triplikate
With the Re-kwired Signatores and Seels
and Approopriate Fees**

Underneath this, on a smaller sign in smaller letters, it read:

**Teers Will Not Be Eccepted as Currenci
Under Ani Cirkumstances
Have a Gud Day
#KomplianseOverDefianse**

"Elders for intergalactic sacrifice?" I wondered out loud. What the heck were those snakes up to now?

I was facing the entrance of a dark cave from inside which came the ground-shaking sounds of someone—a very large someone, from the volume—snoring. I made my way quickly to the little podium in front of the cave. In front of the podium was another sign. This one without the hurried, sloppy, and misspelled look of the previous:

Ring Here for Transit Officer
Be Not Afraid (If You Can Help It)

Despite the instructions, there was nothing on or around the podium to "ring" with: no bell, no buzzer, no gong anywhere in sight. Man, if there was something I hated, it was false advertising. Irritated, I pounded on the podium, shouting, "Ding-a-ling! Ring-a-ding-ding! Get up, you lazy napper! I want to talk to the transit officer!"

There was an abrupt halting of the snoring. And a groaning, creaking, cracking sound like someone was getting up and stretching. Then the ground shook even more as the snorer stomped out of its cave to meet me.

The creature wasn't as tall as a fully-stretched-out rakkhosh, but he was tall, I'll tell you that. He was muscled, but what concerned me more was the sharp-spike-covered club he dragged behind him. Beneath an enormous crown and three curved horns was the face of a half rooster, half lion. He had a giraffe's neck, a human being's arms and chest, and a porcupine's spiny tail. His googly eyes spun this way and that until they finally focused on me. He seemed to pause, maybe a bit concerned at the sight of a flower-garlanded rakkhoshi waiting impatiently outside his bedroom door. He cleared his throat, like he was about to spout off some rules and regulations, or maybe launch into some kind of eloquent speech, but instead just said, in a surprisingly squeaky voice, "Hey, why'd you wake me up? I was having a nice nap."

The whiny tone and cracking voice made clear to me that this monster was young—a teenager, maybe. And obviously new on the job.

I straightened myself up, cracking my neck and shaking my hair off my horns. "Are you the transit officer?"

The creature scratched his hooked, pimply nose as if the answer to his identity would fly out of a nostril on the wings of some phlegm. "You were supposed to ring," he finally said, pointing to the sign by the podium. "It says it right there, ring for the transit offer."

"Yes, I can read," I said impatiently. "But there's nothing to ring with."

"Whatcha mean?" The creature stopped scratching and stared at me.

"If you ask people to ring, you've got to leave something they can ring you with," I explained. "It's not like people carry their own gongs around these days."

The creature looked a bit defensive. "Well, they should! Who knows when you'll have the need for one?"

"Beyond the point!" I was starting to get a sinus head-ache from all the flowery malas around my neck and threw a few of them off. "Now, are you the transit officer or not?"

"Be not afraid of me!" pronounced the creature, widen-ing his sleep-red eyes and waggling his chicken's wattle. He waved his arms like an overdramatic children's magician at a very iffy, thrown-together-at-the-last-minute birthday celebration. "If you can help it!"

I studied the guy. It was a decent enough attempt at being scary, I supposed. Red eyes, neck outstretched, teeth flashing and nails showing. But honestly, that whiny, crackly voice! Who could be afraid of this poser?

"Yes, yes, I saw that part of your sign, very nice touch," I said. "But I'm certainly not going to be afraid of some kid with his first real job. How did you get it anyway? What, did you know someone? Is your uncle in with the snakes or something like that?"

"How did you know about my great-uncle? And how did you know it was my first job?" The acne-covered creature pouted. "What gave it away?"

"You're obviously an amateur," I pointed out. "You didn't think to try and scare me before we'd already talked about your missing bell. Second, I'd never heard of a transit officer in the Kingdom until now. And besides, your last set of signs are wet."

"They're wet? Why? Did you spit on them?" The creature bared his yellow teeth.

"No, ding-dong!" I said impatiently. "They're dripping with wet paint!"

That seemed to deflate the fellow a little. "It's not my fault. I just finished painting them." He showed me his paint-covered hands and a pail he'd put to the side of the podium with wet paint within and a brush sticking out.

"Why're crying families bringing their elders here for intergalactic sacrifice?" I demanded, advancing on the officer with my eyes narrowed. "What do the snakes have planned?"

The creature tried to look like he didn't know what I was talking about. He doubled down on the dumb act first by whistling, then by picking at a pimple, and finally by saying, totally unconvincingly, "I don't know what new snaky policy you're talking about."

"So there's a new snaky policy, huh?" I said triumphantly.

"Wait, no! I mean, how'd you figure that out?" The transit officer's giant throat bump bobbled as he gulped.

"You just said so." I blew out a little fireball from my nose in irritation. The creature jumped back a few feet from me as I did. The fireball burned a little edge of the officer's podium. "I mean, you just told me so yourself."

"Hey! No firearms at the transit corridor!" He frantically patted out the fire with one of his giant feet.

"That didn't come out of my arm," I said, grinning evilly. "Besides, you don't have a sign to that effect, do you?"

"Then I'll have to paint one!" the officer said huffily, blowing at his now-singed foot.

I was getting bored of this conversation. And if there's one thing I don't enjoy being, it's bored. I put my hands together above my head, generating a giant fireball. "Are you going to tell me what's going on with these intergalactic sacrifices or are we going to have to get it hot up here? Believe me, I have no problem if that's the way this is going to go down." Just to show him I was serious, I shot some mini fire streams at his feet.

CHAPTER 10

What? An Intergalactic Sacrifice Program? I Mean, What Will These Snake Jerks Think of Next?

H ey, cool it! No need for that!" the rooster creature clucked, dancing around to avoid getting burned. "It's a new policy coming online soon from the Serpent Empire, something about grandparents, sacrifice, the galaxies, I'm not one hundred percent sure about all the details."

"Aren't you the one who painted the sign, whose job is guarding the intergalactic portal or whatever?" I pointed behind him while still shooting flames toward his feet.

"Have you ever stayed awake through an entire one of those Serpent Empire policy meetings? They're the worst!" The teenage transit officer continued to dance around to avoid my flames. "Profit margin, blah, blah, blah, sacrificing oldies to keep the economy going, yada yada, breaking the spirit of the citizenry so they never dare rise up again, whatever, whatever. No video game breaks, no snacks, a total nightmare!"

"The Serpent Empire wants to break our spirit by . . . what? Forcing people to sacrifice some of their dadus and didimas into the ether?" I demanded, finally dousing my flames.

"Not just some grandparents," clucked the creature way too gleefully, rotating his reddened eyes. His bloodthirsty nature was showing, and it was so not cute. "They're drawing up a centralized monthly schedule so that eventually, every family in the Kingdom Beyond must send all their elders through the intergalactic portal. All very efficient and organized."

"A centralized monthly schedule?" I repeated in horror.

"With an automated reminder system, a tracking device, thank-you letters to your home after you've sent your elders out through the galaxies, the works, very advanced." The transit officer looked inordinately pleased to report all this.

"What if the families refuse?" I demanded, thinking of the granny with the twinkling eyes I'd just met in the market. "Why would they sacrifice their precious elders?"

"Ah, that's the brilliance of it! Sacrifice your grands voluntarily or else you have to sacrifice your kids too!" the transit officer clucked. "What grandparent wouldn't willingly be sacrificed to save their grandkids? It's a brilliant plan—and yet, it also keeps all the families who remain mourning, scared, and weak."

"And even worse, demoralized, because they've sacrificed the very people they should be most revering? The keepers of their family stories, traditions, and dreams?" I thought of the hardworking grannies and granddads I'd just met in the market, the ones who helped in family businesses, raising kids, keeping everyone together. I thought of my own Ai-Ma, who had sacrificed so much in her lifetime, and still had energy to love on Kawla, Mawla, and Deembo. I thought of Chhaya Devi and even long-dead Hidimbi, and the connections that bound the present to the past.

"How can the snakes do this?" My voice rose in anger, but apparently the transit officer thought it was approval.

"Totally wicked, right?" The teenager tapped on the side of his head with a crooked finger. "Wicked cool, I mean. Disconnect a people from their past, and they don't have a sense of how to move into the future."

I felt like snapping the twit's spindly neck in half. I thought of my baby cousins, who had been taken to the serpent retraining school in the not-too-distant past. And now, to think that elders—like Ai-Ma, like Chhaya Devi—were expected to somehow launch themselves into the multiverse to protect their families? If someone asked me to do that to Ai-Ma, what would my answer be? To fight, to flame, to burn, obviously. But what if I couldn't? What if I was one of those weak-limbed human parents back in the marketplace with nothing more than vegetable knives and wet fish to fight with? Would I be forced to do such a horrible thing?

"That's the cruelest thing I've ever heard!" I was steaming, curling out smoke through my teeth. "Elders stabilize a family, a society! They have perspective, expertise, and maturity that no one else has! They're not just expendable!"

"Awesome, right?" the transit officer agreed, gurgling with happiness. "Cruelest thing I ever heard too!"

I couldn't believe this piece of news. Then it struck me. I was hearing all this because none other than Sesha had sent me here. Not to warn me, surely. To taunt me? To scare me? Or did he still have some of his old revolutionary spirit left alive somewhere deep inside him? Did he want me to spread his information and warn the resistance? I rubbed a talon to my temple.

"I'm actually here for something else," I said abruptly. I had no idea what to do with the information I'd just learned about the Intergalactic Sacrifice Program, and I wanted to talk to Arko and Chandni about it as soon as possible. Well, if Chandni was still talking to me, that is. Suddenly, I was aching to just finish my business with this nincompoop of a transit officer and get back to the rebel headquarters. "I'm looking for a rakkhosh soul-bee."

"Wait a minute." The transit officer snapped to attention and frantically began rummaging through his own pockets, then some papers piled under the podium. "Wait a parsec. Wait a googli!" he shouted as he threw papers here and there.

"What?" I leaned over the podium, to where the creature was now on his hands and knees, digging through what looked like pages of business memos.

"Here it is!" The teenager looked down at the paper in his hand and then up at me again. "If you're asking about a bee, then you're Pinki, the fire demoness!" His eyes got round, and he started eating the memorandum in his agitation. "Oh, this is bad. This is really, really bad."

I yanked a half-eaten paper out of the creature's beak. "What's bad?" I demanded, trying to see if I could read anything written on the paper. I couldn't, as it was all smudgy from being in the transit officer's mouth. But I could make out a faint picture of myself on the page.

"You were warned I'd be coming?" I pointed an angry talon at the officer's face.

"And asking about the bee!" wailed the officer, pulling at his horns. "I wasn't supposed to tell you about the elders-being-sacrificed thing! That overdressed oily-haired snake dude told me specifically! I wasn't even supposed to put up the new signs until you were gone!"

Well, that answered my question, I supposed. Sesha had sent me here but had forewarned his incompetent transit officer not to spill the beans about the Intergalactic Sacrifice Program. Which Mr. Employee of the Year had clearly goofed up on.

"I'm gonna get fired!" the officer yelped. Giant tears were flooding down his acne-pocked cheeks and dripping from his weak chin. "I need this job, I really do. I mean, the pay is terrible, but jobs are hard to come by that match my talents, you know? The local brute squad's on a hiring freeze! Piracy pays great—but I get seasick. I mean, what's a fellow to do?"

"Don't worry, I won't tell," I said, gingerly patting the crying creature.

"You won't?" The transit officer grabbed the edge of my sari and started blubbering into it. "I really wanna make a career out of this, you know? Work on my craft, be a path breaker guarding this liminal space, a respected professional of torture and terror."

I pulled my now-soaking sari edge away from the blubbering goon. "You could improve your presentation, you know. You're really not very scary the way you first come off. Rhyme always worked well for us rakkhosh until the serpents banned us grown rakkhosh from speaking it."

"I do enjoy a threatening verse. I mean, I have a few slam and punch poets I really like," the officer mused, snuffling.

"Fantastic. So you have some source material, some inspiration," I enthused. "Now, how about telling me about that soul-bee?"

The teenager wiped his boogery nose with the back of a clawed hand. He narrowed his eyes, adopting a menacing stance. "Only if you answer my riddle!"

I snorted embers of fire in impatience. Really, where had Sesha found this nincompoop? "Fine, if you insist. But hurry up!"

Little did he know that I was excellent at riddles. I'd had to become so, hanging out with Toto the bird as much as I had during the last rebel raid.

"I reach for the sky, I touch the ground, sometimes I leave, but I'm always around!" The transit officer cackled in glee.

I sighed. The kid really did make it too easy. Just to spare his feelings, I paused for a second, as if I was thinking hard.

"Do you give up?" he cackled. "Do I win? Oh, kik ri gee!"

"A tree," I said blandly, studying my talons.

"Wait, that's not fair," the little twerp whined. "Let me tell you another—"

But I cut him off. "No, you said one. One riddle. Which was easy, and which I have solved. Now *you* have to solve *my* riddle. If you get it right, I'll leave you alone. But if you don't, you have to tell me where that soul-bee is!"

The transit officer stared at me suspiciously, rubbing at his runny nose. "What is it?"

"The ocean's pearl, a grain of sand, more precious than all the gold in the land," I said, recalling Toto's riddle. "Life would be flat, life would be bland, without this diamond in your hand."

"A diamond!" shouted the pimply teenager almost as soon as I'd finished speaking.

"No . . ." I began, but the transit officer kept shouting.

"A star! A pearl! A dove!" he shouted in rapid succession.

"No!" I shouted.

"A brass band! Pani puri! Fake teeth! Butt powder!"

"Stop!" I roared, throwing a fireball at his head for good measure. He ducked out of the way just in time. "What is wrong with you? Do you not know how riddles work?"

The fellow plunked himself down on the ground and began wailing, long trails of tears and strands of snot rolling down his face and puddling on the rocky ground. "You're mean!" he cried. "Also I'm very hangry!"

I should be given a serious medal for refraining from

throwing a firestorm at the annoying creature. "Then just tell me where that rakkhosh soul-bee is, and I'll stop bothering you!"

The transit officer stopped crying long enough to peer up at me. "Did you bring any snacks? I need to eat regularly or my blood sugar drops."

"I don't have snacks!" I snapped impatiently. "Just tell me where that bee is already!"

The creature narrowed his eyes at me, and for a moment I thought he was going to refuse, or at least force me to answer more riddles. But instead he just sighed. "Okay, fine."

"So where is it? The bee?" I demanded. I had kind of been hoping the officer would refuse. If there was a monster I'd ever met worth incinerating, it was this one.

"You sure you don't have any snacks?" he asked hopefully.

"Tell me what I need, now!" I tapped my foot impatiently. "Unless you want me to tell the snakes you let the cat out of the bag!"

The transit offer jumped up, peering around. "Cat? What cat? Demon butts, I hate cats!"

I huffed out a frustrated flame. "It's an expression. There's no actual cat. I just meant that you told me the secret you weren't supposed to tell."

"Secret?" the teenage monster repeated vaguely.

"About the new policy? Sacrificing one elder per household through the portal?" I reminded him. Really, this guy probably *should* be fired. If I actually cared how the serpent bureaucracy functioned, I would tell Sesha exactly that. But, in a sense, more incompetent imperial employees was a good thing for the resistance.

"The new policy, right!" the transit officer said, shaking his head. "Sorry, there's a lot I have to remember at this new job. There wasn't an orientation or a handbook or anything. It really hasn't been the easiest transition. Promise you won't tell that Sesha guy I told you all that stuff? I'll tell you, he's even meaner than you!"

"I can't disagree with that." Unable to resist, I asked, "So why'd you take the job at all?"

"Oh, the benefits to being an oppressor are great, and imperialism comes with awesome stock options," the transit officer said. "Plus, you know, my mom said I had to get a job. I couldn't live in her cavement anymore."

There it was, the truth.

Finally, the transit officer said, "Okay, I'll give you the soul-bee as long as you don't say anything to that snake dude about the fact I told you about the Intergalactic Sacrifice Program."

He had the bee! "Absolutely!" I declared eagerly. "Mum's the word!"

The transit officer frowned. "Don't tell my mum either!"

Then the creature went into his cave to fetch me the little golden cage with Professor Ravan's soul-bee inside. I took the tiny treasure with an enormous sigh of relief.

"You know, he seems like he's so cool, but he's kind of a jerk," said the transit officer conspiratorially. "That snake guy Sesha, I mean."

I looked over my shoulder as I walked away, Ravan's soul-bee safely in my hand. "You honestly have no idea."

CHAPTER 11

I Am Not Nearly as Selfless as Arko Thinks I Am

I stopped by the rebel headquarters to return the flying horse and pick up my baby cousins. I also knew I had to tell someone what I'd discovered before I headed back to school. So I was super happy to see Arko coming out to meet me as I dismounted Raat at the mouth of the cave complex. Toto the bird was, annoyingly enough, on his shoulder.

"Well, hello, Your Demonic-ness!" squawked the parakeet. "Did you get the information you did seek?"

Wordlessly, I held up the bee's cage, and the bird whooped his approval, spinning around in a midair somersault.

"I have something I need to talk to Prince Arko about," I added pointedly. Toto, who was never one for subtle hints, settled onto on Arko's shoulder and just watched us.

"Chandni came back here in a mood," Arko said, helping me tend to the horse.

"Did she tell you what happened?" I bit my lip, hoping the moon girl had kept the whole Sesha-as-my-consort business to herself.

Of course she hadn't. Arko nodded slowly. "She told me. I was surprised you entered the demonic royalty competition. But even more surprised by who you promised to be your consort if you won."

My next words tumbled out of my mouth. "I can explain. It's not what it looks like!"

"No, you're wrong, Pinki. What you did is exactly what it looks like!" Arko took my hand, his eyes soft. "Chandni didn't see it at first, but what you did was an act of bravery, selflessness, and sacrifice. Something only someone as strong as you could do. You did what you did for the greater good."

Arko was looking at me with an expression of such trust and admiration I felt like throwing up.

I laughed nervously. "How's that?"

"You offered Sesha the consortship with an eye to destabilizing their rule over the Kingdom, making them see the error of their ways, or at least being in a position to have their power undermined." Arko arched an eyebrow. "What you did, in a certain way, can be seen as a nonviolent act."

"I certainly didn't feel very nonviolent when it was happening," I admitted with another brittle laugh.

But inside I felt like crying. Arko thought I was so upstanding and noble; how could I explain that part of what motivated me wasn't noble at all? That I'd mostly been thinking about making Chandni jealous? How could I admit I wasn't half as good as Arko thought I was?

"I'm sure you didn't feel nonviolent." Arko laughed as well. "That Sesha guy is the worst!"

"And how!" I agreed. I felt such a jumble of emotions inside me. "Arko, I still don't really get the whole satyagraha thing, you know."

"Well, the way I see it, we've got to walk our own path to freedom. Not allow the snakes—or any enemy, for that matter—to determine our decisions." Arko peered at me intently. "The opposite of violence isn't passivity; that's an artificial either-or situation that the oppressor set up for us. Ahimsa, active nonviolence, is a third path, a new way."

I shook my head. "I'm trying to understand, Arko, I really am."

"I know you are, Pinki." The prince gently touched my hand, making all three of my hearts do a loop the loop.

"So how was dealing with the transit officer?" Arko asked, obviously sensing I wanted to change the subject. He knew me so well. A flower of gratefulness blossomed inside my rib cage.

"It was fine. The transit officer is basically an incompetent teenager." I removed the saddle from Raat's back. "I mean, a dangerous incompetent teenager, but nothing I couldn't handle."

"Teenage monsters are the worst!" squawked Toto, shooting out a yellow tail feather into the air. "I mean, between the smell of zit cream and ennui!"

Arko and I both laughed. Then Arko glanced at the bee cage in my hand. "You should probably get the professor's bee back to the Academy as soon as possible."

"I'll go soon, but I wanted to talk to you first about something I found out about a new serpent program," I said.

"Let's go find Chandni, and you can tell us both," Arko said, but I put a hand on his arm.

"I'd rather tell you first." I was feeling protective of the opportunity to talk to him away from Chandni. Was there space for me anymore in the space of Arko and Chandni's new tight friendship? I was ready to find out, and, if the answer wasn't to my liking, take a crowbar to make some room between them.

"All right." Arko nodded, his brows furrowed. Toto imitated the prince's expression, crossing his wings over his chest and squinting his beady eyes.

We settled Raat in the makeshift stalls the rebels had constructed for their animals and I gave him a grateful pat. Then Arko and I walked a few paces together, the buzzing caged bee like a lantern in my hand, the squawking bird on Arko's shoulder like an annoying pest.

"Hey, Your Demoness!" said the bird. "What does a bee wear to the beach?"

"I don't know, what?" I asked, trying to humor the feathery comedian.

"A bee-kini!" he shouted, rolling with laughter on Arko's shoulder.

"That was a good one," Arko said encouragingly. Which was a mistake, because the little bird only kept going.

"What kind of bee can't make up its mind?" asked the parakeet.

"Toto, this is really—" I began, but the bird cut me off.

"A maybe!" Toto squawked. "Get it? A may-bee?"

"Very good, Toto. Now, give us a second, will you?" Arko lifted the bird from his shoulder. "Maybe find a nice worm? There's a good boy."

"Toto knows when he's not wanted," sniffed the bird,

stretching his wings and flapping away. "But even you must admit those were some good jokes!"

"Sorry, birdie!" I called to him. "Just grab a grub and come back!"

As soon as Toto had gone off into the trees, searching for his dinner, Arko turned to me. "So what's up?" His handsome face was etched with concern. "Does it have to do with Sesha?"

"Not in the way you think, but yes," I admitted. "It's something I learned by mistake, from the transit officer."

We walked a few steps into the trees, away from the entrance to the cave complex, and sat on two rocks on the edge of a forest stream. I threw off my shoes and dunked my feet into the water, letting the cool liquid ease the heat in my limbs. There was an evening breeze that rustled through the leaves and my hair. I breathed out for what felt like the first time in forever, the smoke in my fiery breath making shapes in the air.

"So what is it that you have learned?" Arko had thrown on a kurta made of the same homespun moon threads of his dhoti, and the dying sun pouring through the trees illuminated his head like a halo. To put it mildly, the sight of him looking all windblown and earnest in the evening light was really not difficult on my eyes. I thought of what Chhaya

Devi had told me, about rakkhosh in the olden days being able to choose two consorts, and my hearts lifted like they were rising on the heat of a bonfire. How would Arko feel, though, if I chose him to be my consort after I'd already chosen Sesha? The question was too overwhelming to think about right now.

"The transit officer let slip there's a new initiative in the works," I explained, absentmindedly splashing my toes about in the stream. "It sounds pretty horrific. I think the serpents are planning another family separation policy."

Arko frowned, studying a flat gray stone he'd picked up from the ground. "The surest way to break a community down is to take its children, its future. You think they are going to try and take children to those awful 'retraining' centers again?"

"This is even worse—I think those scummy snakes are planning to force families in the Kingdom Beyond to sacrifice their elders into the newly created wormhole up there in the transit corridor." I stared out over the river, remembering how in small print the sign had said that tears would not be accepted as payment. And if this policy really came to be, there would be tears, a lot of them. "The officer said the Intergalactic Sacrifice Program would be a way to keep families afraid, and that if they refused to sacrifice their grandparents, their children would be taken away too."

Arko whistled, sending the rock to skip over the water. It bounced once, twice, then three times before disappearing. "Are you sure about this? Our informants haven't told us anything of this kind."

"The sign was wet; the officer had only just painted it. So maybe he'd only just gotten the orders about it." I kicked at the water, making ripples. "And the transit officer is seriously an unprofessional twit; he blabbed the whole plan to me before he remembered he was supposed to keep it a secret."

"This is horrible." Arko closed his eyes for a moment, his expression pained. He leaned his head back for a moment to tilt his face toward the sun. "Without our elders, a community loses its wisdom, its history, its stories."

"And if families refuse to send their grandparents, the snakes will force them to send their children too," I added.

Arko's eyes opened with a snap. "If they know their grandchildren are at risk, most grandparents will willingly sacrifice themselves. The snakes must know this."

I had a pang as I thought about how much Ai-Ma adored Kawla, Mawla, and Deembo. Would she willingly sacrifice herself for them. Or me? Yes, I was sure she would.

"Those green shackles," I muttered, a feeling of dread creeping over me. "The snakes probably allowed Ai-Ma and the other elder prisoners free because those magical shackles will give the snakes power over them. Power to yeet them out into the universe."

Arko chewed on his lip. "I was worried about those shackles, but I couldn't understand what they would be used for. Hearing this, I'm afraid you might be right."

"So what are we going to do about it?" I demanded, my voice rising.

"We've got to negotiate with them somehow, get Sesha and his father to stop this monstrous policy," Arko said.

"Negotiate? How do we negotiate with evil?" I was astounded at his suggestion, and immediately felt flames of frustration roiling within me. "Arko, we've got to fight them. What is it with you and this nonviolence thing?"

"Pinki, please try to understand." Arko was staring at me, his dark eyes boring into mine, making my skin feel flushed with heat. "It's not just the place we're going that's important; it's how we get there. Remember, we're creating the path for those who come after us too."

"This isn't some theoretical goody-goody exercise, Arko; these are real lives we're talking about. Freedom is freedom, however we get there." I stood up from the rock, unable to name all the contradictory feelings mixed up inside me all at the same time. The sun was setting fast now, and the waning light danced across Arko's handsome features. Was he really ensnared by such goofy ideas he couldn't see what was important? "These snakes have had their feet on our necks for too long. It's time to rise up. I mean, isn't liberty something worth fighting for?"

"There are different ways of fighting, is all I'm saying," Arko insisted as he stood up himself. "Think about what you just did with Sesha—you negotiated with him, instead of fighting him!"

I felt so frustrated I wanted to scream. Why couldn't he hear what I was saying? "That's different! Anyway, the snakes will see nonviolence as weakness!"

"Pinki." Arko's face was patient but his voice firm. "I know it's hard to understand, but ahimsa, the principle of not hurting anyone or anything, is not weak. It requires incredible strength."

"What do you actually *do*, though, except not fight back?" I argued. "It sounds pretty reactive to me, not proactive at all!"

"Well, I'm so glad you asked," said Arko, finally smiling at me again. "Meet us at sunset in the market on Friday and I'll show you how proactive nonviolence can be!"

"Fine," I muttered, not knowing why I felt so angry. "Just think about what I said, though, okay? Think about all those broken families, those scared elders shot out through the wormhole to who knows what part of the multiverse, never to see their families again!"

"I will, I promise," said Arko, touching my hand. The way he smiled at me then did something seriously disruptive to my brain circuits.

I'm not going to lie, I felt like I was melting. I felt like swearing I'd follow the path of nonviolence forever and ever. I felt like singing, and shouting, and hugging him. But I didn't do any of that, not in the least because Toto chose that very moment to fly back to us, a fat worm in his beak. So I simply said goodbye to them both, then went to collect my baby cousins from Ai-Ma.

The process of saying goodbye to Ai-Ma was all sorts of emotional. What with her grabbing me and boo-hooing some more about how proud she was I was taking risks and how I'd make a perfect Demon Queen. The worst was when she said how I deserved to wear Hidimbi's crown. I felt my stomach sink. There really was no way I could quit the royalty competition without breaking her hearts. I was stuck in the competition. Which meant, unfortunately, I was also stuck with Sesha.

I was still sorting out my confusing feelings as Kawla, Mawla, Deembo, and I traveled on the school helicocroc back to Ghatatkach Academy. We flew through the evening sky, the kids chattering excitedly about the time they had spent at the rebel headquarters. I was a little annoyed at how much of Arko and Chandni's nonviolence prattle they seemed to have ingested.

"Injustice anywhere," began Mawla.

"Is a thweat to justice everywhea," finished Kawla with a cheer.

"The time is always right to do what is right," said Deembo in between bites of egg.

I tried not to roll my eyes too loudly. It was just too much for me right now. I was going to have to tell Arko and Chandni to keep their nonviolence nonsense to themselves and not poison impressionable young minds with it.

By the time we landed, night had fallen as it always did in the Kingdom Beyond—dark and sudden, like a curtain. I was eager to get Professor Ravan's bee up to the infirmary, but as soon as we landed, I realized that Surpanakha seemed to have been waiting for us.

"Where have you been, fire demoness?" shouted the headmistress, dragging me from the helicocroc by my ear.

CHAPTER 12

I Am Asked to Do Something Awful and Refuse to Play the Game and Therefore Reestablish Myself as the Awesome Rebel I Am

Ow! Headmistress! Let go!" I protested, yanking myself free. "I was searching for Professor Ravan's soul-bee, like you asked!"

"Well, did you retrieve it?" she asked me, narrowing her eyes. "Or did you fail?"

"Nevah fearw! The bee is herw!" announced Kawla.

"Didi found the bee! All for thee!" added Mawla with a low bow.

Deembo, for her part, kept quiet, simply handing to me the cage with Ravan's soul-bee in it. I held up the cage but was a little startled by the headmistress's expression. Did I imagine it or did she look disappointed I'd found her brother's soul?

"Here it is!" I announced, but as soon as I said the words, one of her jackals snatched the cage out of my fingers. "Hey, watch it!"

The jackal took the cage as Surpanakha sat down on some kind of a judge's throne at one end of the banyan grove. With a wave of her fingers, the headmistress shouted, "Welcome to your first test!"

"My first test?" I repeated, confused. "Don't we want to make sure Professor Ravan is okay?"

"There will be time for that!" As the headmistress lifted her hands dramatically in the air, torch lights all around her flared to life, and I realized that what looked like the entire student body was gathered around us in the previously dark banyan grove. I could also see that before Surpanakha was an elaborate standing maze—kind of like a huge glass-enclosed ant farm. In the maze were two other golden cages just like the one in my hand, and in those cages were two other loudly buzzing soul-bees. With an elaborate gesture, the headmistress put Ravan's soul-bee inside the three-dimensional maze.

My fellow students were all staring at me, hooting and

clapping. They pointed enthusiastically to the maze before me, but I couldn't make out anything they were saying.

"This is your first test of the Demonic Royalty Contest!" Surpanakha's eyes were gleaming over her spectacles. "And it should be a simple one!"

"Shouldn't I get the soul-bee back up to Professor Ravan in the infirmary?" I looked around, desperate to find Kumi's and Aakash's friendly faces somewhere in the crowd, but I couldn't see them. If this was the first test to become Demon King or Queen, wouldn't they be taking it too?

Surpanakha ignored my question, instead waving her hand dramatically in the direction of the maze with its three caged bees. "You must save one of these bees!"

"One? Why can't I save them all?" Soul-bees were sacred; they were where we rakkhosh kept our inner essence. Why had Surpanakha even brought out two additional soul-bees when she knew how her own brother's bee disappearing had affected him?

The headmistress laughed—an awful, cruel sound. "Because the moment you save one, the others will die!"

"What?" My eyes widened and I studied the maze. Each bee was positioned below a chute of a sort, with a stopper I could pull out. Each bee also had a kind of trap positioned on top of them. One bee had what looked like a gallon of water, which, if released, would drown them. Another bee had what looked like a swirling tornado positioned on top of their cage, while the third bee had a pile of soil on top of it, which, if released, would crush it. The chutes were connected in such a way that opening one to save one bee would activate the others.

"Oh no, Didi, that's not wight!" Kawla wailed, her tiny hand upon the glass of the maze.

"Don't give up those bees without a fight!" Mawla concluded.

Deembo gripped my hand hard, as if she knew how awful I must be feeling. "Injustice anywhere is a threat to justice everywhere," she whispered in a low voice.

As if they could hear her, the bees in their maze cages buzzed.

"Remove these children from the arena!" Surpanakha demanded, and some rakkhosh students came to lead my baby cousins away. They wailed and reached for me, but I nodded with what I hoped was an encouraging gesture on my face.

"You go back to the lower school dorms!" I had a smile plastered on my face. "It's past bedtime for you little ones! I'll come find you afterward!"

"Wise advice!" the headmistress said as the kids left the

clearing. "You don't want them to have to watch you murdering your so-called friends!"

My head whipped around to face Surpanakha. "My friends? What do you mean *my friends*?"

"Why, hadn't you guessed yet?" the headmistress drawled. "One of those bees is my brother Ravan's soul, the one you miraculously found. But the other two are your little competitors, the water rakkhoshi Kumi and the air rakkhosh Aakash!"

"What? Why are you doing this?" I demanded. I looked around, hoping for a friendly face in the crowd who I might call upon to help me, but everyone was just staring back at me hungrily, like I was an experimental bug they wanted to see squirm. An ant in a maze, as it were.

"Well, fire rakkhoshi! I'm sure this will be an easy choice! Do you want to be Demon Queen or not?" Surpanakha stood up dramatically from her chair, her sari anchal flowing behind her.

"Y-yes," I stammered. "I mean, I guess . . . but not like this!"

"With great power comes great sacrifice!" bellowed the headmistress.

"I'm not sure that's how that quote goes—" I ventured, but she cut me off.

"Save your professor's bee, the one who so believes in

you, and in doing so, kill off your competition's soul-bees! It should be an easy choice, because your status as Demon Queen will be guaranteed!" Surpanakha's eyes gleamed weirdly from behind her glasses. "Isn't that what you want? Or is it that you may suspect you're not Hidimbi's true successor at all?"

I stared. First, at my headmistress, wondering what had gotten into her, and then at the maze, wondering how I could get out of this mess. A few weeks ago, I probably wouldn't have had a problem killing off Kumi's and Aakash's soul-bees. Or at least, I wouldn't have allowed myself to have a problem with it, or even think too much about it until it was over. But over the last rebel raid, my frenemies had become, well, my friends, and I wasn't ready to sacrifice either them or the one teacher in this school who believed in me.

"Choose!" The headmistress looked practically crazed, her eyes wide and bloodshot, little bits of spittle forming at the sides of her mouth. What had gotten into her? "Or maybe it's easier to simply quit the competition? No one will blame you if you decide to do that. In fact, it's probably the braver thing to do, sacrifice your spot in the Demonic Royalty Contest in order to save your friends."

I looked up at her, realization dawning on me slowly. The headmistress *wanted* me to quit the competition! She had never thought I was Demon Queen material, after all. She'd sent me on the quest to find Ravan's soul, assuming I'd fail. Now she'd set up this test in such a way that I'd fail no matter what I did. I'd never realized she hated me so much as to go to these extraordinary lengths to get me out of the running for Queen. What she didn't know was that if I didn't win, it would break my mother's hearts. And not that I liked to admit it in public, but I couldn't do that to Ai-Ma. She'd already faced too much disappointment and loss in her life.

So I refused to quit, and I refused to fail. I refused to play by these limiting rules with which Surpanakha was trying to hem me in, these either-or, black-or-white, good-or-bad decisions. As Arko had said, I had to come up with a third choice, a third path. I just had to figure out a way not through the test, but around it.

"So I have to save at least one of the bees in order to pass this test, is that it?" I licked my dry lips, my brain trying desperately to come up with a plan.

All around me, people were murmuring and rustling around with impatience. "Hurry up!" someone muttered. "It's past time for dinner!"

"Choose which one to save already!" someone else hissed.

"Or better yet, drop out of the competition! You don't deserve to be Demon Queen!" a third voice growled.

I spun around, exhaling clouds of smoke from my nose, but couldn't catch anyone in the act.

"Choose, rakkhoshi!" bellowed Surpanakha. "Choose to kill, or choose to leave!"

"Give me a moment, please!" I begged. My mind was whirring, but I couldn't think of a solution.

"Kill or quit! Kill or quit!" the crowd around me was starting to chant.

I tried to block out their distraction and study the maze. There was no way around it; any of the chutes I chose to activate would save one bee but kill the other two. There was no way to play this game and win—that is, if winning meant avoiding murder. But was there a way to win without playing the game at all?

In a flash, I saw Arko's calm face floating in front of me, telling me that it took courage to choose nonviolence. I wasn't sure if I really bought all that, but still, this moment certainly seemed to call for a bit of ahimsa philosophy.

"I know what I choose!" I finally shouted out, making the crowd go wild, as if I were some midair helicocroc wreck they couldn't help watching.

"Kill or quit! Kill or quit!" they shouted, their voices

taunting. To be perfectly honest, all their bad-natured chanting was kind of hurting my feelings. Not that I'd ever admit it, or show them.

"What have you decided, fire rakkhoshi? Who will you save? Who will you kill?" Surpanakha asked. "Or will you just walk away from the entire competition like the quitter that you are?"

People around me laughed uproariously. My ears burned and nose tingled with fire.

"Isn't being Demon King or Queen about being a leader for *all* rakkhosh-kind?" I asked. "Protecting the well-being and interests of *all* rakkhosh?"

The headmistress narrowed her eyes. "Yes, of course."

"Then my choice is clear," I announced.

"Which chute? Which bee? Which chute? Which bee?" one part of the crowd yelled, while the other kept up with the "Kill or quit! Kill or quit!" chant. The night air thrummed with their cruel taunts and the sound of their stomping feet, keeping rhythm to their mockery.

"What is it? Hurry up, then!" Surpanakha spat out, but her expression was wary.

"I choose to stay in the competition, and save them all!" I announced. "If I chose to kill any of these bees, I would disqualify myself from this competition; I would not be looking out for the well-being of all rakkhosh. But I'm no quitter either!"

"You have to save one of them!" The headmistress's eyes were bloodshot and she was heaving out breaths of irritation. At her feet, her jackals whined eagerly. "Otherwise the test isn't over! Make a choice!"

I breathed in and out, harnessing my energies, hoping I'd be able to control my fire in just the right way. I breathed in and out, blocking out the demands for violence, the jeering and egging on of my classmates around me. I breathed in and out, trying not to wonder why the headmistress thought so little of me that she would set me up in this lose-lose situation. In and out, remembering how Arko had said that we couldn't play by the rules that were given to us by our enemies, but had to get to our goals by maps we drew for ourselves.

I wasn't going to play by Surpanakha's game of her false choices—I wouldn't kill, but I also wouldn't quit. She wanted me to choose one of only two paths, but instead, I would navigate and traverse a different way all my own.

Taking in one last big breath, I let out three narrow strands of fire from my mouth. They were thin and malleable, like three small whips—which wrapped around the framework of the maze holding the bees, melting all the

chutes, drying up the water, dissipating the tornado, blowing up the dirt. But because I'd finally learned to control my
fire, I did this while leaving whole all three bee cages.

There arose a shocked gasp or two from the audience.

"I choose to save all three bees because I know that's
what a true queen would do," I said as my fire whips deftly
caught each cage, bringing them back to me. "I won't
quit just because you don't think I deserve to be Queen,
Headmistress, but I won't kill my kind either."

The crowd booed, but Surpanakha narrowed her eyes,
a hint of a smile on her face. "All right, Pinki, I'll admit I'm
impressed."

I was furious with her. How could she be smiling at a
time like this? But instead of losing my temper and setting
fire to the entire banyan grove, something I might have
done only a few weeks ago, I actually managed to keep my
anger in check.

"Would you have let me go through with it? Kill my
friends? Or Professor Ravan?" I demanded.

The headmistress shrugged at my question. "If you
killed them, you would have disqualified yourself from the
competition—as you say, Demon King or Queen must look
out for the well-being of all our kind. But I was hoping you
would just quit and make it easier for all of us."

"Why?" I felt stunned. "Why would you do that?"

"Because you don't deserve to be Demon Queen, Pinki. You're not Hidimbi's true successor," Surpanakha said, her eyes flashing. "And if we hadn't lost that darned mukut from the sanctum, then the moment you put that crown on your head, you would know that. But since there is no crown, for now, I'm going to have to be the one to tell you: You're not the leader we so desperately need right now—the one who will lead our country to freedom. And the sooner you admit that to yourself, the better."

CHAPTER 13

I Assume Everyone Is Plotting Against Me, Which Is Most Likely True and Only a Little Bit Me Being Paranoid

I tried to go directly from Surpanakha's ridiculous "test" to the Ghatatkach infirmaries. I had been told by some fellow fire rakkhosh that Aakash and Kumi were now up there along with Professor Ravan. Apparently anyone who had their soul-bee removed from the honeycombs didn't feel too swift afterward. Which made me all the more shocked that our own headmistress had done this to my friends.

But when I ran up the winding stairs of the main building to the infirmary wing, I found my way blocked.

"Sorry, fire rakkhoshi, visiting hours are over," said the land-rakkhoshi nurse sitting at a desk outside the main doors. She had a giant pile of charts in front of her but was reading a well-worn rakkhosh romance book with a swooning heroine and a very chesty, long-haired, and horned hero on the cover.

"But my friends, they'll want to see me," I began, but fell into silence when the nurse put down her paperback and began to laugh.

"They're your competitors, no?" She adjusted her nose ring and sniffed loudly. "You really think they'll want to see you?"

That made me pause. I'd assumed Kumi and Aakash were just victim of this situation, like me; that Surpanakha had taken their soul-bees and made them sick without their knowledge. But what if this nurse was right? We'd only been friends for a few weeks, really. What if Aakash and Kumi resented me now that I'd become a competitor for the crown they both wanted? What if they'd willingly agreed to go along with Surpanakha's plan to humiliate me?

"But how are they doing? Did they say anything about me? Did they know this test was going to happen?" My voice rose sharply with each question.

The nurse stood up and physically began to shoo me out, making the ground beneath my feet ripple and sway with her land magic. "You're going to need to keep your voice down. And your temper too! I don't need you burning down the infirmary with an out-of-control flame! I've heard about you and your fire, girlie!"

"I'm not going to burn down the infirmary!" I protested. "That was a long time ago! I have total control over my fire now!"

Even as I said this, of course, a few huffs of smoke escaped my nostrils, making the nurse cough impatiently, waving her hand in the air in front of her.

"Watch it! Enough now! It's late and these patients need their rest! Come back tomorrow during visiting hours!" She was shutting the main doors in my face.

I whirled around, trying to make her open the door to me again. "But please, can't I just speak to them for a second, I want to ask them—"

"Go back to your dorm room and get some rest already!" The nurse finished shutting the door and shouted at me through the glass window. "Come back tomorrow!"

I walked back down the long stairs, my mind racing. If Surpanakha had devised a test to make me either look bad or drop out of the royalty contest, had she included my competitors in her planning? I thought Aakash and Kumi were my friends, but had I been wrong? The thoughts swirled around my troubled mind, making me feel restless and ill-tempered. I burped. Ugh. Paranoia always gave me heartburn too.

When I got to Kumi and my shared dorm room in the east tower, I found no rest. In fact, what I found was a bunch of official Ghatatkach Academy guys moving all my roommate's things out.

"Hey, where are you going with all that?" I demanded, trying to block the door.

"Miss, this is on direct orders from the headmistress's very own wart-covered lips," said a bumpy-nosed mover with about a thousand horns growing directly out of his head. He was wearing a unitard-type coverall thing, and read from a piece of paper attached to a clipboard, his voice bored and monotonous. "We are instructed to move the personal belongings of one water rakkhoshi, Kumi, to tower two while she is recovering in the hospital wing from having her soul utilized in an event of a tournament-like nature."

"Why?" I demanded. "Why are you moving her things?"

"I would think it would be obvious to a scholar such as yourself, Your Fire-ship." The mover smacked the gum in his mouth as he tucked a pencil behind one of his horns. "Yous two are individuals of the competition-inclined. In other words, yous are what we like to call in vernacular parlance—bosom enemies."

I didn't bother arguing with this gum-smacking buffoon that Kumi was not, at least from where I sat, my enemy, bosom or otherwise. "So we can't live together anymore because we're competing against each other to become Demon Queen?"

"You have hit the nail right on the proverbial nose of the hammer, as it were," the mover agreed, nodding to his fellow movers. "All right, fellas—" he began, but I cut him off.

"I don't understand. Does the headmistress think if we live together, we're going to share secrets, help each other in the contest?" I asked, looking around Kumi's already half-vacated side of the room with some panic.

The mover guffawed, almost hitting himself in the head with his own clipboard in his apparent mirth. "Quite the opposite, Your Fiery-ness! You cannot live with said water rakkhoshi Kumi anymore because the headmistress is quite sure you might commit something of an underhanded, explosive, and also possibly dismembering nature."

"Dismembering nature? As if!" I squawked in outrage, huffing steam from my ears.

"No offense, Your Fire-ship." The mover rakkhosh and his buddies all edged back a few feet. "But perhaps maybe like setting your roommate's wardrobe on fire?" He indicated the scorch marks on both sides of Kumi's closet, from the previous few times I had lost control and set all her clothes on fire.

"That was in the past, and by accident! And she was never actually *wearing* any of the clothes I lit on fire!" I protested as the moving guys started up their collecting of things once again. "I've totally learned how to control my flames since then!"

"Who's to say, my lady of fire, when our actions are intentional and when at the guidance of our elusive subconscious?" the mover asked with surprising psychological insight.

All this talk of me scorching my enemies was really getting me down. "I suppose the headmistress would think that I'd do something dastardly to Kumi, just to win." I sat down on my bed with a sigh. "She's wrong, through."

"Well, it's quite good of you to be so understanding, I'm sure." The mover bobbed his head at me and continued to direct his team in packing and transporting Kumi's things from my now-single room. When they finally left, he popped back in briefly to give me a cheeky smile. "Good luck, Your Flame-ship!"

It was a rough night in my half-empty room. I kept

tossing and turning, and finally I got up to read one of the
thick tomes of rakkhosh history that I had on my shelf, flipping right to the rules about demonic consorts. Even as I
put down that book and picked up another, I was careful
not to pull out the old copy of *Thakurmar Jhuli*. I had no
intention of time traveling back to Hidimbi's court tonight.

When I finally did fall sleep, near dawn, my dreams were
a mixed-up jumble of Kumi and Aakash yelling at me to be
more nonviolent, and Chandni and Arko turning into bees
and trying to lead the resistance in that form. And then,
from a distance, I saw two figures, one a girl with a bow and
arrow, luminous like Chandni, but also very much with her
feet planted on the ground. The other figure was a boy, who
made something twist painfully, lovingly, in my hearts. He
reminded me so much of Arko, but he wasn't Arko. He was
dressed all in blue and his name came to me, fully formed,
in the dream: Neel. The name that Queen Hidimbi had
asked me about! But Neel and his kurta and combat-boot-
wearing friend were not from my time, or from Hidimbi's;
they were from the future, walking the path we ancestors
had laid down for them.

And then, in my dream, I saw Sesha and an entire snaky
army approaching my friends, overtaking the boy and girl,
but I couldn't warn any of them. "Fight!" I wanted to yell,

or even "Run!" But my mouth didn't seem to work and all I could do was watch the snakes destroying the future world that the boy and girl had come from.

Then Hidimbi was there—or was it Surpanakha?—a flaming crown in her hands, her eyes swirling like galaxies. "Kill or quit! Kill or quit!" she yelled as I tried to get out of the maze she'd locked me in. I couldn't go back to the past, I couldn't see forward to the future, and I couldn't even save our present. "Will you burn with the crown's power?" she asked, lowering the flaming crown once again upon my head. "Or will you let its power burn you?"

The crown exploded in fire, just like it had last time, a searing pain that reached across time and space. I opened my mouth to scream, but no sound came out, only fire and more fire. And just when I thought I was about to burn up entirely, I woke with a start, covered in sweat. Like before, my neck and jaw ached from the weight of the magical mukut. My ears buzzed. I put my hand tentatively to my head, but once again, there was nothing there.

I lay down once again, too upset and exhausted to sleep. I may have been alone in my room in Ghatatkach, but my mind and soul still burned with the memory of that crown of flames.

CHAPTER 14

Everyone's Grossed Out by the Whole Sesha Thing, and I Really Can't Blame Them

I slept through my alarm, and was running into combat class right as Surpanakha called out Kumi's and Aakash's names. Looking more tired than usual, but otherwise okay, they got to their feet and climbed to a central platform in the middle of the banyan grove classroom.

"Ah, Pinki! How *kind* of you to join us!" the head-mistress drawled, obviously less than pleased to see me. "I had thought after yesterday's performance, you might be ready to quit the competition once and for all!"

"But I won the test you set up for me!" I desperately wanted to check in on Kumi and Aakash but couldn't catch their eyes. "And I didn't harm any of the soul-bees!"

"You broke the rules!" Surpanakha snarled, but not

without some grudging admiration. I was pretty sure that, when she was my age, the headmistress must not have been a big rule follower either.

"I bent the rules. You said I had to save at least one of the bees, and I saved all three." I heard Arko's voice in my mind as I added, "After all, if the rules are unfair, you have to make your own."

Obviously irritated, the headmistress narrowed her eyes at me, and the jackals at her feet spat and growled. I decided to ignore them. You can't make deemer dalna without cracking a few eggs, after all.

"Congratulations, roomie. Er, ex-roomie," said Kumi, turning toward me as I climbed up to the platform. "You passed the test."

I studied her face. She looked worn-out, but not angry at me. But then again, if she was plotting against me with the headmistress, would she be obvious about it?

"Thanks also for not killing our soul-bees in the process," Aakash added. He too had dark circles marring his normally perfect face. "That would have been a serious bummer, yaar."

"I would never have allowed that to happen!" snapped Surpanakha. "As I told you two, this was a test to see *if* your fire-rakkhoshi competitor here would be willing to sacrifice you in her quest for power. She may not have done so yesterday, but I still wouldn't put it past her."

I felt myself steaming under the horns. I couldn't believe what I was hearing. I mean, what the actual heck was wrong with our headmistress? How much could she possibly hate me?

"Unlike some others who shall remain nameless, I don't betray those I love!" I snapped. Okay, it was probably not the wisest thing to say, but I couldn't help it; my temper was very literally on fire by now.

"Is that so? You don't betray those you love?" snarled the headmistress. "What's this I hear, then, about you promising to make Sesha, the Prince of Serpents—representative of the very empire that's oppressing us—your consort if you become Demon Queen?"

The entire classroom let out a collective gasp. The jackals even yelped, as if they'd been bitten.

Kumi and Aakash whirled on me, their faces horrified. "You didn't!" Kumi exclaimed, spitting water at me.

"Did you, like, forget that he's the same snaky dude who almost killed all of us?" Aakash asked. Then he echoed the words that Arko had just said to me. "Sesha's the *worst*, man!"

The other students in the grove were now whispering excitedly, pointing and hissing. I felt right back to where I'd been a few weeks ago, a friendless outcast mocked by her classmates. I must admit, it didn't feel very good.

"And you call yourself a revolutionary!" Surpanakha was frothing at the mouth a little as she shouted at me. She turned to the classroom. "Freedom is a debt we owe to our revolutionary ancestors—who fought for a better tomorrow they may not be alive to see; it is a promise we make to the young ones who come after us, so that their lives may be better than ours! But you, all you can see is yourself in the now!" Surpanakha was practically ranting now. "Do you all see why I said that this fire rakkhoshi is not worthy of being Demon Queen? She'll side with the snakes, undermine rakkhosh-kind the first chance she gets! She is not the leader we need to light the way to freedom!"

I couldn't help but begin to see her point, at least a little. But that certainly didn't explain how she'd found out about the deal I'd made with Sesha. I thought for a minute about denying the whole thing, lying about my promise to the prince of snakes, but I knew I wouldn't get far with such a falsehood. The headmistress probably had spies everywhere. Or was it Chandni who had somehow betrayed me and told her?

"I don't know how you heard about that, Headmistress," I said, drawing even more hissing and booing from my classmates. "Or are you the one with friends among the snakes?"

Surpanakha rose to her full height, her eyes and tongue red with fury. "How dare you, you smelly goat dropping!"

"So it's true?" Kumi asked, her mouth agape. "You asked Sesha to be your consort?"

"Yo, way nasty, yaar!" Then Aakash's expression changed as he added, totally unnecessarily, "Also, mad props, Pinks. I mean, that's kinda freaky!"

"Wait!" I begged my friends. "There's a completely reasonable explanation for why I promised Sesha that. I didn't want to, but I had to!"

"Oh, really? You *had to* promise to make our oppressor your consort?" Surpanakha rounded on me, practically screaming in my face now. "Forget weaseling your way out of yesterday's test! I have half a mind just to kick you out of the Demonic Royalty Contest anyway!"

"You can't do that!" I shouted before I even thought about it. This made me pause, and I suddenly realized something surprising. It wasn't just about Ai-Ma, or Chhaya Devi, or anyone else. I really wanted to be in this demonic royalty competition. I did actually want to lead rakkhosh-kind! I was just worried about whether I could do it. I was worried about being caught out as an imposter.

I cleared my throat, trying to explain. "Listen, I made the deal with Sesha to make him my consort because it was the only way to get him to tell me where Professor Ravan's soul-bee was being kept!"

"Likely story!" screeched Surpanakha, but Kumi and Aakash looked at me with new understanding.

"Wait, Headmistress, if that's the case, shouldn't we be thanking Pinki rather than punishing her?" Kumi asked, edging closer to me until she was close enough to bump my elbow. "I mean, last time I saw her and Sesha together, she came pretty darn near to dumping him over the side of a balcony and turning him into a snaky pancake. I can't imagine Pinki was happy about having to make that promise to the snake!"

Aakash too sidled up next to me, throwing an arm over my shoulder. "Plus, Pinki did find that soul-bee. I mean, ole Professor Ravan was looking like he was feeling a lot better this morning when I left the infirmary. Where would he be now if not for Pinki?"

I felt something easing inside my hearts. I looked at Kumi's and Aakash's smiling faces and felt buoyed up with joy. My friends weren't trying to trick me, and they actually were still my friends, no matter what Headmistress Surpanakha, or any of the other students, thought of me. No matter how Chandni had changed, Aakash and Kumi hadn't. It felt good to know I wasn't alone.

"You two are too gullible!" Surpanakha grumbled.

But her tone was less furious. I could tell she was thinking of her brother.

"Are you going to let me stay in the competition?" I asked. "I'm sorry I had to promise Sesha the consort thing, but maybe it can be something we turn to our advantage. And besides, isn't there that tradition from before times where a Demon King or Queen could name two consorts?"

"Two consorts?" repeated Kumi and Aakash at practically the same time.

"There was once such a tradition," said Surpanakha grudgingly. "A long time ago. But a long time ago isn't now!"

"Then it's high time we reinstated it!" I exclaimed. I ran to my bag and produced the giant book of history I'd been reading the night before. I flipped open to the section outlining consort choosing practices. "Especially since, as I've discovered here, by our traditions, a duly elected Demon King or Queen can choose one of the two consorts and then kill the other!"

"That would solve your little snaky problem pretty nicely!" Kumi grinned slowly.

"It would be better than that fink Sesha deserves," grumbled Aakash.

Surpanakha was studying me with a strange, impressed expression on her face.

"Well, Headmistress?" I asked. "Does it mean I can stay in the competition?"

The headmistress grunted, then nodded rather grumpily. "I suppose you may."

All righty, then, that wasn't an enthusiastic statement of support, by any means. But I'd take whatever I could get at this point. Still, I was a bit nervous when, later that afternoon, we all got called to the banyan grove for the first of the demonic royalty competitions.

"Shouldn't we give Aakash and Kumi more time to recover before we start the combat competition?" I asked Professor Ravan. He was sitting on a judge's chair at the top of the banyan grove next to his sister. He still looked kind of pale and weak from his recent ordeal, as did, honestly, my air- and water-clan friends.

"They are young rakkhosh!" snapped Surpanakha before Professor Ravan could answer me. "Unlike my brother here, their souls were only caged for a brief amount of time. They'll be fine. And if not, maybe they shouldn't be in the running!"

For a second, I was seriously confused. I mean, if Surpanakha wanted me to lose the competition, it would make sense for her to wait until Aakash and Kumi were back to their full strength before she had us fight, right? In their weakened states, I could beat them both to a pulp, I was sure. Or, rather, burn them both to a crisp. Regardless, from the circles under their eyes and the slower-than-normal way they were both moving, it was obvious I'd win this combat competition. How could that be a part of the headmistress's plan to stop me from becoming Demon Queen?

But then I realized what our headmistress's twisted imagination had cooked up for this competition. And it was too diabolical for words. As Aakash, Kumi, and I walked up to the platform before the judges' chairs, Surpanakha stood up with a dramatic surge. Waving her arms before her, she announced, "Bring in the three combat competitors!"

"We're not fighting each other?" Kumi asked, giving words to what I was thinking. "If we're not fighting each other, who are we fighting?" Aakash looked around in confusion. I could tell he still wasn't back to his normal self by the way his hair was slightly less coiffed and poofed than normal. If there was one thing I knew about my air-clan friend, it was that he took his hair styling very seriously.

The three of us stared at each other, not understanding what the headmistress intended for our competition. But then, when I saw who came out from behind the judges' chairs, I practically erupted in uncontrolled flames.

CHAPTER 15

In Which I Make Use of Arko's Whole Nonviolent "Choose a Third Way" Philosophy. Or Try To, Anyway.

I couldn't believe it. This was shocking even for Surpanakha. Because who should our combatants be but my goofy cousins, Kawla, Mawla, and Deembo.

The teenage rakkhosh around us began tittering and laughing. Obviously, no one could believe that this was actually happening.

"Hi, Dada and Didis! You see us, right?!" Mawla announced, sticking out his little barrel chest. He, like his sisters, was wearing a new Ghatatkach Academy tunic and some kind of sash across his chest. "We are the foes that you must fight!"

"That's ridiculous! They're just kids!" Kumi let out a small rain shower in her surprise.

"Yo, that's uncool! I don't wanna fight no babies!" Aakash exclaimed.

"Don't be afwaid! Don't you cwy!" Kawla grinned, showing her crooked teeth. She, like Mawla, had her hands on her hips like she was a superhero. "We are hewre to help you fly!"

Deembo grinned, handing each of us older rakkhosh an egg from her pocket, which Aakash, Kumi, and I took from her in a kind of stunned silence.

Our classmates sitting around the banyan grove kept whispering and giggling. What in the multiverse was going on here? I felt my anger boiling to the surface, like lava. This was obviously just another part of Surpanakha's scheme to have me quit the demonic royalty competition. When she couldn't kick me out with her soul-bee trick, she must have come up with this ridiculous plan.

"Headmistress! Professor Ravan!" I exclaimed, whirling on them. "How can you expect us to fight . . ." I searched for a word that wouldn't hurt my baby cousins' feelings too much. "These snot-nosed mealy-mouthed pipsqueaks who are practically still in diapers?"

Okay, I admit it. That probably wasn't the nicest way for me to phrase it.

"Hey, fool! That's way uncool!" Mawla, who'd always had a bit of a tendency to the grumpy, ran up to me and kicked me in the shin.

"Yo! Watch it, munchkin!" I groused, rubbing where he'd kicked.

"I'm not chicken, I'm not meek!" he protested. "Don't you call me a snotty pipsqueak!"

"We're throng and fiewce even though we're wee!" Kawla pouted, her eyes suspiciously shiny. "Didi, why you tho mean to your cousthins thwee?"

"I'm not trying to be mean!" I began as I fended Mawla off from kicking me again. "But even you must see it's ridiculous for you three to be assigned to fight with us in this competition!" I turned to the judges' chairs again. "The headmistress is trying to make me quit the competition by bringing my own little cousins in to fight! It's obviously a dirty, rotten trick!"

"What did you say to me, fire rakkhoshi?" snapped Surpanakha.

"It's our honor, Didi, don't be mean!" Deembo said, sticking out her little chin in my direction. "We want to help you become Demon Queen!"

"Come on, short dudes!" Aakash bent down on one knee

so he could look at my cousins eye to eye. "You've gotta see that we can't fight you little ones! It would be, like, unchivalrous, way not gallant. Like, super uncool!"

"This is ridiculous, Headmistress!" Kumi protested. "You can't expect us to have our combat competition involve . . . babies!"

The headmistress narrowed her eyes. "Do you refuse to fight, water rakkhoshi? Is that what I'm hearing?"

Kumi gulped, her face and hair drenched with raindrops. "No . . . I mean . . . but . . . isn't there another way? Couldn't we fight each other? Or like"—she indicated our other classmates in the banyan grove—"someone our own size?"

Professor Ravan, I noticed, wasn't saying anything but was fidgeting uncomfortably in his seat. He couldn't think this was a good idea, could he? I knew she was headmistress, but why couldn't he challenge his sister's decision?

"Why would you want us to fight these little kids, Headmistress, if not as some kind of mental game?" I demanded. I was speaking to Surpanakha, but included her brother as well. "You knew I wouldn't want my cousins to be hurt, and so, what, you wanted to come up with a new way to get me to quit?" I looked at my overeager, ridiculously clueless baby cousins. If they fought us almost-grown rakkhosh, they'd be hurt, seriously injured, or possibly worse!

"Either you fight the combatants I have chosen for you, or you will forfeit this combat round, receiving a zero for this part of the demonic royalty competition," Surpanakha said smoothly. "That is the only choice before you."

And then I knew that this entire thing was about me. Whether or not Kumi and Aakash were ultimately willing to fight little kids, Surpanakha guessed that I would rather quit than risk injuring my own kin. Especially after all the lengths I went to in order to save my cousins from the serpents' underwater retraining school, the headmistress knew full well that I'd sacrifice anything to stop from hurting them. I felt that shock of disbelief again. Did Surpanakha feel like I was such a bad candidate for Demon Queen that she was willing to risk injuring some little kids at her own school in order to get me out of the competition?

I cast my eyes around, desperate to find a solution to this ridiculous, and possibly deadly, situation. I couldn't let Aakash and Kumi fight my baby cousins, not for real. And I couldn't fight them either. But how could we fight, but also somehow not fight? It was a contradiction that made no sense.

That's when it occurred to me—even though I didn't entirely understand, or agree with, Arko's whole ahimsa thing, his philosophy had helped me out of a seemingly impossible situation the night before. Surpanakha had thought she'd trapped me in a no-win yes-or-no situation—that I'd have to kill two soul-bees in order to save the third. But instead of playing by her rules, and using the tools she gave me, I'd abandoned the rules of her game entirely and walked a third path—neither killing any bees nor quitting the competition. I'd just have to do something similar again now. But this time, I'd have to convince Aakash and Kumi to go along with me too.

"The best offense is defense!" I said in a low enough voice that only Aakash and Kumi could hear. "We'll fight them by protecting them!"

"Well? Can we start the combat competition or not?" snapped Surpanakha. "Or do all of you forfeit?"

Kawla, Mawla, and Deembo looked super upset at this suggestion, giving me three sets of disappointed puppy-dog eyes.

I groaned to myself. Were my cousins trying to rip each of my three hearts out from my chest? "No, fine, Headmistress, you've got us. We're in! The fight's on!"

At this, my baby cousins jumped and cheered, Deembo scattering eggs from her pockets that rolled all over the competition floor.

"We're tough!" announced Mawla

"We're mean!" added Kawla.

"We're a three-rakkhosh fighting machine!" finished Deembo.

"This ain't going to be easy!" muttered Aakash, flexing his wings. In front of him, Mawla was adopting some kind of dramatic fighting stance, cracking his little knuckles, his expression equal parts mean and adorable.

"I don't wanna hurt these little kids!" Kumi said in a strangled voice, even as Kawla growled at her, crouching down before the water rakkhoshi like a bull getting ready to charge.

"We're not going to," I assured my friends, hoping against hope my plan would work.

"Let the combat competition begin!" announced Professor Ravan, clapping his hands dramatically.

As if they had planned it beforehand, Kawla, Mawla, and Deembo crouched down in unison, placing their little hands upon the ground. As land clan, what little magic they had managed to develop was only amplified by them working together. Their faces fierce with competitive spirit, my baby cousins made the ground quake and shake beneath our feet.

"Whoa!" Aakash lifted up from the ground with a quick bat of his wings, but in her surprise, Kumi let off a huge wave of water. It wasn't big enough to knock a normal-sized opponent off their feet, but it was certainly big enough to drown three little lower-school rakkhosh.

"Watch it!" I shouted, sending a flaming fireball to counteract Kumi's wave. I hit the wall of encroaching water just before it got to my baby cousins, making it dissolve into a hissing cloud of steam.

Surpanakha's whistle blew, loud and sharp. "Ten points off for you, Pinki! You're fighting the land rakkhosh! Not defending them! You can't interfere with Kumi's offense!"

Kumi, Aakash, and I exchanged worried glances. This was going to be harder than we'd initially thought.

"Come down from the air!" shouted Mawla, moving his little hands to magically generate a dirt bomb that flew up to hit Aakash square in the face. "So I can fight you fair!"

"Hey, that's not cool, little man!" Aakash protested, wiping the soil from his eyes with two hands even as he floated back down to the ground. "My face and hair are, like, off-limits!"

Kumi burst out in guffaws at the spectacle of vain Aakash looking like a grubby mud monster. But Kawla screwed up her face like she might cry.

"At me do you laugh?" snapped the little rakkhoshi. "Well, sthee what you think of my mighty sthtaff!"

With this, Kawla did a bit of magic I'd actually never seen her do. With a wave of her tiny hands, she generated a staff created from dirt, which she flung at Kumi with a mighty heave. To stop the staff from pummeling her, Kumi created a small rainstorm, which made the magical stick disintegrate and turn into mud.

"Didi, aw dip!" Deembo cried, pointing at me. "Watch it or you'll slip!"

"You're not fooling me, little warrior!" I cried, assuming that it was all a part of some trick. Little did I realize that Deembo was being sincere, trying to stop me from tripping on the small bevy of eggs she'd spilled out of her pocket before. Which, of course, was exactly what happened. Not looking where I was going, I slipped on the rolly eggs and landed painfully on my back, the wind knocked out of me. The crowd roared in laughter.

"Looks like the little kids are kicking some butt!" I heard someone shout.

"Or maybe none of these three bozos deserve to be our new King or Queen," someone else countered.

That got my back up, and I could tell from the murderous looks on Aakash's and Kumi's faces that they'd heard too.

"Don't deserve, huh?" snapped Aakash, sending a whirl of a tornado in the direction of my cousins, sweeping all three of them off their feet. But then his expression changed, and I could tell that he regretted his actions. All three little rakkhosh let out earsplitting yells.

"Watch it!" I bellowed, mistakenly singeing Aakash with a spark of fire that shot out of me mostly out of fear. I was seeing visions of my little cousins being reduced to pancakes.

"Hey, what's the big deal, yaar?" complained Aakash, even as Kumi sent a rainspout his direction to douse his burnt arm.

"The kids!" I shouted, even as my little cousins fell through the air, now bereft of the force of Aakash's tornado winds.

"Hey, take that, you pesky kids!" Kumi snapped, sending a wave of water that looked vicious, but actually cushioned the three small rakkhosh as they fell back down to the ground.

Aakash sent Kumi a grateful look, but nowhere as grateful as I was. That was some fast thinking on my water-clan friend's part! Not to mention good acting—since we didn't hear Surpanakha's whistle for any kind of infraction.

Okay, it was clear we were going to have to do this with some sincerity now. I sent a dramatic fire to encircle the kids, blocking them from everyone's view. They screamed in fear, but I concentrated hard, making sure that I contained every spark, every piece of ember from the wall, keeping them away from the kids in the center. It was hard, though, and took tons of energy and concentration.

Kumi, always sharp, picked up on what I was doing and shouted, slightly overdramatically, "I'll drown those pipsqueaks in there!"

Unfortunately, she killed the whole "murderous demon on a rampage" vibe by giving me a big open-mouthed wink after she said it. I really hoped neither Surpanakha nor Ravan had seen. She sent a big wave arcing over my flame wall, making it shoot around the inside of my fire circle, so that the kids were now in very little danger of being burned by any errant sparks. I gave her a grateful look as I was able to ease up a little on my level of concentration.

Aakash, always a bit sharper looking than thinking, gave us both a shocked look. "Yo, that's super not okay, guys! Those are little babies in there!"

He shot up into the sky with a rapid beating of his wings and, before either Kumi or I could stop him, dived down into the fire-and-water circle, lifting all three kids out in his muscular arms.

Surpanakha's whistle sounded again. "Ten points off from Aakash for rescuing all three of your opponents!" she snapped.

The crowd booed, much to Aakash's shock. One of the most popular rakkhosh in school, he wasn't used to being booed. "Uncool, my fellow students, way uncool!" he groused, even as he tried to hold on to a squirming Kawla, Mawla, and Deembo in his arms.

As soon as he put the kids down on the ground, they joined forces again, and started pelting us with magicked clods of dirt.

"Hey! Watch it!" I yelled as I ducked out of the way of one giant dirt clod only to get pelted in the back with another. That hurt! I sent a few quick flames to explode the clods flying at me, reducing them to smaller pieces before they could hit their mark.

"This is the least fun game of dodgeball I've ever played!" complained Kumi as she caught a dirt clod hard in the shoulder. She hissed, shooting water spears out through her teeth, which impaled some of the flying dirt balls but then changed into harmless rain before they reached my little cousins.

"I hate dirt!" shouted Aakash, flying around to avoid getting hit. "It's terrible for my complexion, and total murder on my hair!"

Giggling, the three young rakkhosh sent the biggest blob of dirt yet right at Aakash's head.

"Incoming!" I yelled. But instead of looking where I was pointing, Aakash got distracted by turning toward me, giving my baby cousins plenty of opportunity to pummel him with not just one but multiple clods of dirt right to the head.

Aakash landed with a not particularly nice curse back to the ground. "Not the hair!" he cried, looking truly distraught. "Not the hair!"

And then, even though he was clearly a whole lot older

than Kawla, Mawla, and Deembo, Aakash completely got into it with the little ones. "You think you can ruin my hair and not pay for it?" he roared. "You're so, so wrong!"

For a second, I was worried he was really going to hurt them, but then I saw that he was just getting in on the act, picking up some of the now-broken down clods of dirt the kids had pelted at us and throwing them back. He hit Mawla with a piece of dirt, but it was so small, I could tell my cousin was more annoyed than actually hurt.

"Eat dirt, kids!" I yelled, joining Aakash. Abandoning any pretense of magic, I started picking up the dirt balls they'd sent our way and chucking them back too. One nailed little Deembo on the cheek, making her laugh and roar rather than cry.

"Why make 'em eat dirt when we can make 'em eat mud?" shouted Kumi, making it rain right over all our heads so that our tournament space was a muddy, sloppy, disgusting mess.

Surpanakha's whistle was screaming. "Stop! This is supposed to be combat! Not a mud-slinging fest!"

But her warnings were useless because now, all our classmates jumped up, getting in on the act, flinging mud at each other, us, the kids. Aakash slipped, howling as his hair got even muddier than it had been before. Gleefully,

Kumi rubbed a handful more of messy mud into his coiffure, twirling his hair into a sloppy pompadour with her hands. A bunch of my fire-rakkhosh clans-folk were dousing me in gloppy mud, but you can believe I gave back just as good as I got, pelting them until they were head-to-toe filthy. Kawla, Mawla, and Deembo giggled and shrieked as they kicked mud on each other, ending up looking more like little goblins or trolls than rakkhosh. Even Professor Ravan got in on the act, throwing handfuls of mud at all his students.

Headmistress Surpanakha's whistle shrieked again and again, but everyone was having way too much fun to pay attention.

"Ten points!" she yelled. "Twenty! You're all an embarrassment! A travesty to rakkhosh-kind!"

It was, therefore, a bit of poetic justice that she then slipped, falling face-first into a ginormous pit of slimy mud.

We all tried very hard not to laugh. I'm not promising we succeeded.

CHAPTER 16

Peace, Love, Unicorns, Blah, Blah, Blah

The next day was Friday. I was so furious at Surpanakha's nasty trick from the day before that I didn't bother asking for permission before leaving the school grounds at sunset. I grabbed Kawla, Mawla, and Deembo and hopped on one of the school helicocrocs, heading for the market. They were still giddy from the combat competition the day before, of which they had been declared the winners. Among us three royalty contestants, though, Kumi was the one with the fewest points taken away, so she was now in the competition lead.

But I didn't care about any of that. I wanted to get away from Ghatatkach, our vengeful headmistress, and the pressure of the competition altogether. I wanted to see Arko and find out what it was exactly he'd wanted to show me in the market.

"Where do we go?" asked Kawla as we flew through the air, hanging on for dear life to the helicocroc's back. "To join the fweedom show?"

"What freedom show?" I turned around to look at my cousin.

"Ai-Ma and Chandni Didi told us to come," elucidated Mawla. "A freedom march with peace, not guns!"

"There's going to be a march?" I gulped a little as the helicocroc banked a hard left. "That's why Arko told me to meet him in the market today?"

Deembo nodded, pointing down. And sure enough, as we landed the helicocroc by Chhaya Devi's stall, we saw an enormous crowd all clad in white. I couldn't help but feel annoyed. Why hadn't Arko told us we were coming to join a peace march? I was still pent up with irritation from the day before. I wanted to break something, not hold hands and sing harmony in the round or whatever.

As we approached, I could hear the sounds of voices. We turned a corner, and I was stunned to see the market road packed with marchers. Their fists were raised in the air and they held flickering candles that lit up the night. There were hundreds on hundreds of rakkhosh, khokkosh, humans, and others with signs that said things like "Quit the Kingdom," "Self-Rule, Not Snake Rule," and "Freedom

Now!" Some of the non-humans didn't believe in traditional spelling, so there were also signs that read "Get Ooot You Snaki Boo0ts" and "Le$s Serpants More UnderPants"— which I wasn't exactly sure how to interpret but seemed in the general vein of freedom from the Serpent Overlords. The atmosphere on the market street was electric, and everyone seemed giddy with excitement. Bodies filled the area as far as the eye could see, most dressed in white clothing, if not the moon-thread homespun that the rebel leaders wore.

At the front of the line, clapping and singing, were Arko and Chandni, linked arm in arm with Arko's brothers and some of the other rebels I'd seen at the secret head-quarters. In the next line behind them were Ai-Ma, Chhaya Devi, and the merchants and children I'd met on the other side of the bazaar. I rushed forward through the crowd toward them.

"What's going on?" By my feet, my cousins were squirming and jumping, excited by all the noise and people.

"It's a freedom march!" announced Chandni. "One of many we have planned to show the snake empire that we have all the people's will on our side."

I felt a surge of irritation. Surpanakha had placed my cousins in danger the day before, but now, for my own friends to do it? I whirled on Arko, "You should have told me not to bring the kids! This isn't safe."

"We aren't flakes!" announced Mawla, boogeying a little. "We wanna kick out those snakes!"

"Oh, my darling Pinki shona, ré! If they are old enough to get kidnapped by the serpents, they are old enough to march for freedom and justice," said my mother from over Arko's and Chandni's heads, smiling toothily. "It's for them we march, isn't it? They represent the future we are fighting for, after all!"

"We march for fweedom! We march for peace!" announced a beaming Kawla.

"We are our ancestors' wildest dreams!" finished Deembo.

I scowled at the little rakkhoshi. "Eh, linear time is a colonial construct anyway!" I groused, pointing to Ai-Ma. "And anyway, you come from a long line of pretty radical and revolutionary elders. What if they're *our* wildest dreams?"

I was just being grouchy, but Deembo seemed to like this idea because she gurgled with glee. Then, like precious gifts of respect and reverence, she started handing out eggs to all the elders in the crowd she could reach.

I let out a frustrated sigh, then caught and held Arko's gaze. "You knew this march was today? That's why you asked me to come?"

"Of course." The prince smiled. "You asked me what active nonviolent protest looks like, and I wanted to show you. Don't worry, the children will be fine. This is their future too; they all have a right to march with us."

Easier said than believed, I thought grumpily, even as Kawla and Mawla scrambled over people's heads to launch themselves at Ai-Ma. She grabbed my cousins and plunked them, one each, on her bony shoulders.

"Join us, Pinki." Chandni linked her other arm through mine. "Can't you feel the energy, the force of change in the air?"

I wanted to argue with my clueless friend, remind her how violently the snakes had responded to our previous efforts at change. But they all seemed so dedicated to this new nonviolent philosophy. I guess if I really wanted to be Demon Queen, it was worth giving all types of leadership a try. As much as I didn't want to admit it, Chandni and Arko's nonviolent ideas had helped me to pass not only Surpanakha's test with the bees but the combat session with my cousins as well. Sighing, I plunked Deembo on my shoulders, then linked arms with Chandni and Arko and started walking along with the crowd.

Around us, the marchers were singing that song that Arko had once sung to his poor patshala students, back when he was still disguising himself as a village school-master. "Jodi tor dak shune keu na ashe, tobe ekla cholo re!"

If there is no light, if the path before you rages with
dark, then light your own heart on fire. Be the
beacon. Be the spark.

The meaning and beauty of the song rang out as we walked, filling the air of the now-empty market. I could hear Ai-Ma and Chhaya Devi behind me, Arko and

Chandni next to me, Kawla's and Mawla's voices ringing in the air. And, filling my hearts, I could hear Deembo's voice from right above me. Deembo, who had for so long not even been able to speak due to the serpents' cruelty. Soon, everyone around us was singing, our voices rising and falling together. I got a little chill up my spine. It reminded me of the night we had rescued the children from the undersea training school, when their voices raised in song was a part of the magic that freed them.

Despite not being at all sure about this nonviolence thing, I couldn't help but join my voice to the song of the crowd. Like our footsteps, our voices moved with each other in harmony. We walked along the market path, arm in arm, young and old, human and rakkhosh, singing our song of freedom and letting our voices ring throughout the air. We were singing the song the rebels had been singing for me in the resistance hideout, "Byartho Praner Aborjona Purie Phelo," when it happened.

As the stars bloom in the dark fabric of night,
lightning changes darkness to light. So listen for
destiny calling your name. Light your soul on fire
with freedom's flame.

Just as these words left my lips, the snakes arrived.

At first, they silently lined up on either side of the street. But despite being still and quiet, theirs was an ominous presence. They stood in their half-human forms, their red regimental uniforms loaded with shoulder fringe and medal-covered sheaths, their scaly heads topped by pointed helmets. Their faces were impassive, save for the flash of a serpent tooth, the occasional whipping of a tongue. Bayonets rested threateningly on their shoulders, and pistols sat visibly holstered in their belts.

The marchers, for the most part, ignored the snakes, and kept on walking and singing. But I noticed a few of the merchants swiveling their heads nervously at the sight of the snaky soldiers, and pulling their children and grandchildren closer.

"What's the plan?" I muttered through clenched teeth to Chandni. "How do we protect all these people if the snakes attack?"

"The plan is we keep going," Chandni said firmly. "We don't engage verbally or physically. We don't play by their rules, remember?"

I was starting to feel sparks of anticipation rising up my spine, and my stomach warmed with warning flames. I mean, not playing by the rules had gotten me out of Surpanakha's traps these last few days, but she hadn't been pointing a weapon in my face.

"They look like they're here to do damage," I whispered. "Do you remember our last confrontation with them in the market?"

This time it was Arko, leaning across Chandni to say, "Have faith. We are walking a different path now, Pinki."

I rolled my eyes. "I don't think this will work, Arko. Violence is the very language of the snakes! You think they'll just let us walk peacefully by?"

But Arko just smiled at me and kept on singing.

As the stars bloom in the dark fabric of night, lightning changes darkness to light. So listen for destiny calling your name. Light your soul on fire with freedom's flame.

He sang it like a call and response, him singing a line and letting the crowd sing it back to him. I knew his voice. His presence was giving courage to the marchers, the courage they needed to keep marching toward their destiny, toward freedom. Still, I could smell their anxiety in the air, and I knew it was well founded. The serpent soldiers were just waiting for an excuse to answer the marchers' peaceful-ness with violence.

"Steady, everyone. Steady." Arko said it in a normal voice, but the message passed back row to row, from person to person. "Remember, no matter what they do, we walk on. We don't resort to their tactics. We don't use violence. We don't show fear."

It was easier said than done, because with each passing moment, there were more soldiers lined up by the side of the road. The stray dogs of the marketplace, who had been up until now trotting happily alongside us marchers, scat-tered, whimpering, back into their safe warm hiding spaces between and among the market stalls. Clearly, they knew what they were about, which was more than I could say for Chandni and Arko, who made a gesture to some of the pro-testers. A row of fairy paris flew forward from the peaceful crowd and began garlanding the gun-toting soldiers with flower garlands like those the market merchants had given me. Some fairies even stuck flowers in the barrels of the snakes' bayonets.

And then it began. One of the soldiers threw a fiery torch into a nearby merchant stall. A cry went up from the marchers as the stall burst into flame.

"They're looting, sir! These criminal marchers are

looting local businesses!" shouted the very same soldier who had himself lit the fire.

"No respect for property! No respect for business!" shouted some other soldiers as they used heavy bats to smash all the displayed bottles in a drink merchant's stall. The glass shattered everywhere.

With a gesture from Arko, a small band of marchers broke off and formed a bucket brigade bringing water up from the river. In almost no time, the fire burning in the stall was put out. But still, the soldiers kept up their systematic destruction of stalls and smashing of property.

"Stop!" shouted the marchers, many of whom were merchants themselves. "Those are our stores, our property!"

"Then you better go protect your property from these thug rebels who only seek to make chaos!"

When I turned to see who was speaking, I groaned out loud. Oh, great. Just great.

CHAPTER 17

Consorts Schmonsorts

Sesha was standing at the head of one of the battalions of soldiers, slapping a thick baton in his hands like he was weighing which of our skulls to crack first. As the flood of marchers approached where he and his soldiers were standing, he yelled out a call, and all the snakes marched forward in formation, blocking the road before us. We protesters had no choice but to stop as we approached them, barely an arm's distance from their bayonets and batons. The street was chaos, covered in glass and destroyed property, with multiple stores now burning on both sides of us. At first, our ranks were noisy, some calling out insults to the soldiers. But Arko frowned, raising his hand, and all the rows of marchers quieted down so much, you could have heard a pin drop on that silent market street. The only sound was the crackles of the few still-burning flames.

"This is an illegal gathering, an activity of a seditious nature," Sesha called out in a loud voice. "I command you thugs to disband this march immediately and return to your businesses and homes like good subjects of the Serpentine Empire."

"The only thugs I see here are your soldiers destroying these good people's property." Arko raised his head, and without breaking the chain of linked arms, he asked in a calm tone, "Will you please part so that we may pass?"

Sesha blinked at Arko, like he was seeing him for the first time. He looked the human prince up and down, as if studying his simple clothing, then sneered, showing his teeth. "No. I won't part my soldiers, you pathetic princeling. What's with the way you and your brothers are dressed? Did Daddy Raja cut off your clothing allowance? I barely recognized you; you look like a beggar!"

The soldiers around Sesha snickered, and I felt my blood begin to heat up. What I wouldn't give to smash that smirk off Sesha's arrogant face.

"We are all beggars under the heel of serpent rule," Arko answered evenly. "Please make room so that our peaceful march may continue."

Sesha batted his baton in his hand some more in a

menacing way, eyeing both Chandni and me. "Come on, girls, you're smarter than your little noble friend here. You don't want me to unleash my soldiers on all these innocent humans—these grannies and little children! Tell them all to go home now and I'll tell my soldiers to stand down."

I hated to admit it, but Sesha was right. I didn't want to see him unleash his soldiers on this crowd of grandparents, parents, and children. I didn't want to have these weak and underfed humans hurt, or my own Ai-Ma and cousins. As if she could sense my sentiments, though, Chandni squeezed my elbow tight, cautioning me not to speak. I let Deembo crawl down from my shoulders and grab on to my back, like a little monkey.

"Hold on tight," I whispered to her, and felt her grip solid around my neck.

"We are not bothering anyone. This is a peaceful and nonviolent protest," the moon girl said in her tinkling, bell-like voice. I could see how Sesha's eyes softened as she spoke, and I knew he still loved her. "Please let us pass."

"I can't do that!" Sesha said, his voice louder and more frustrated. "Come on, Chandni, don't make me do this! Don't make me hurt all of you!"

Ugh. Such typical gross villain talk, I couldn't even stand it.

"You are responsible for your actions and decisions, Sesha, no one else," Chandni replied. "And you can still choose to let us go!"

"I can do no such thing, and you know that perfectly well." Sesha's voice was laced with so much frustration, I knew he was thinking of his father, the Governor-General. I wondered what punishment Sesha's father would dole out to him if he failed to break up the march. I'd seen the old serpent hit Sesha right in front of all of us and his soldiers. What more violence was he capable of in private?

"Chandni, Arko . . ." I muttered in a warning voice. My hands were starting to itch from the desire to break a few serpent heads.

Of course Sesha heard me. On locking eyes with mine, his expression and demeanor entirely changed.

"Pinki, my dear darling demented dumpling! My murderous and dangerous future Demon Queen!" he said in an oily way, now coming to stand before me. To my shock and revulsion, Sesha lifted a multi-ringed finger to stroke my cheek. And darn it, because my arms were linked with Chandni's and Arko's, I couldn't even slap his hand away. I heard Deembo growl in warning from her position from my back.

Ignoring the little rakkhoshi, Sesha continued, grinning.

"Oh, my future killer of a consort, why don't you talk some sense into these nonviolent knuckleheads?"

Arko made a noise in his throat but said nothing.

Chandni shot me a look, and I could see how annoyed she still was by what had happened in the Thorny Woods. "Pinki may have promised you to be her consort if she gets elected Demon Queen, but that doesn't mean you have to be gross about it."

"My darling daughter, is this true?" Ai-Ma cleared her throat, noisily rattling a bunch of phlegm. "While I'm still very proud you're running for Demon Queen, we really must talk in private about your choice of consort. Maybe at some later, slightly less dangerous time."

Oh, this was not the time for any of this. "This is not the time for any of this!" I snapped at my friends and relatives.

The snakes were about to make serpent chow of all these nonviolent protesters. I really didn't want to explain to my mother about my choice of consort right now.

"It's always time to speak of our impending union!" said Sesha with what felt like an extra-super-duper helping of sliminess. I caught him sneaking a look at Chandni's face, and I knew he was overdoing all the "I'm so excited to be your consort" stuff just to annoy her and make her jealous.

"By the way," I blurted out without even thinking about

it, "I'm going to pick two, not just one consort when I'm elected Queen, you know."

"Oh?" asked Sesha, raising a dark eyebrow in that maddening way. "You didn't mention this little fact before. What if I'm not willing to share you, my delectable tart of demonic-ness?"

"Really? Two consorts?" Chandni whipped her head around to face me.

"In the before times, this was our custom," agreed Ai-Ma from behind us.

"Yup! It's true! Two consorts!" I said in as cheerful a tone as I could make it. "Still figuring out who that would be, but definitely have some good candidates."

I couldn't help but look over at Arko as I said this. Sesha caught my look and widened his slimy grin. "Oh, goody. A love triangle," he spat out. Then he gave Chandni a little glance. "Or quadrangle, should I say?"

I seriously wanted to wipe that smug look off Sesha's face. "Enough, you total weirdo!" I shouted. "Friend-forts before consorts!"

Chandni grinned, giving me a little fist bump that I grudgingly returned. "Right on!"

Arko gave me a startled look but soon gathered himself. "Enough of this. There are more important issues at stake in the Kingdom—like the merchants who work here in this bazaar being able to earn enough to decently feed and clothe their families. Like protecting our ability to collectively protest serpent rule."

A cry rose up behind us from the marchers: "Self-rule! Not snake rule!" Next was a call and response begun by a winged and sari-clad pari wearing a pink hat of some sort. She banged on a bongo while shouting: "Show me what nonviolence looks like! This is what nonviolence looks like!"

But that very cry was the straw that broke the serpent's back. "You treasonous twerps!" Sesha shouted. "I'll show you what obedience to your masters looks like! Compliance over defiance!"

And the snakes took up the cry "Compliance over defiance!" as they ran forward in a lathi charge, wielding their sticks to crack heads, bones, and spirits. Many of the merchants in the back rows, especially those with little children, scattered, screaming. All was chaos as the serpent soldiers pushed down anyone in their path, raising the dust of the road as they brought down the force of their violence. I pushed Deembo into Chhaya Devi's arms.

"Take my mother and the babies to your shop safely!" I shouted over the rising screams and chaos. "I'll meet you there!"

"No, Didi, that's not right!" shouted little Mawla bravely. "We want to stay! We want to fight!"

But Ai-Ma and Chhaya Devi understood the danger the children were in and nodded grimly to me, bustling the little ones along somehow through the crowd. Even as they began their escape, however, Sesha pointed his baton in their direction, yelling, "You're next, old women! You can run now, but your time is coming soon!"

My hearts gave a lurch as I watched my two elders take the young ones away from this scene of slaughter and toward safety. What did Sesha mean by that?

I whirled back to the scene, wanting to defend my friends with my fire, only to meet Arko's already-bloodied face. "No, Pinki, no violence. Please." His voice broke a little as he said this and I paused, two fireballs roiling in my palms now, unsure if I could bear to betray his noble dream.

"That family!" I screamed, pointing. There were a grandmother and her grandchildren about to get beaten by the soldiers before them. Throwing an arm out, Arko sent out a beam of his sun magic, creating a shield before the family. The soldiers battered ineffectively at the shield, allowing the family time to run.

"I thought you believed in getting beat up!" I said, both pleased and surprised.

"I said I would not wield a sword," Arko said, the twinkle back in his eye. "I did not say anything about not using a shield."

As I looked around, I realized that Chandni had had the same idea. She was throwing up shields of moonbeams to protect various humans and other creatures, giving them time to get away from the charging serpents. What she wasn't doing, however, was using her moon magic the way she'd used it on Sesha and me in the Thorny Woods.

"Why not just encase the soldiers in one of those domes?" I shouted at her as I sent out a fire rope, pulling some fish merchants out of the way of the attacking soldiers.

"No!" Arko replied, even as he used his sun magic to shield some frightened fairies cowering by a market stall. "We protect our own, that is all."

It looked like we might actually win. Our magic was giving the human and other marchers a chance to get away from the bulk of the serpent violence. I wondered how long we could keep at it like this, only protecting and never attacking, when Sesha made the decision for us.

The Prince of Serpents looked up and grinned. Then he cried, "Arrest them!" as several hissing, horrible helicocrocs swooped down from the sky. Ridden by snake soldiers, the ferocious animals proceeded to scoop up my friends in their claws and fly them away. First Arko and Chandni, then the other princely brothers!

A cry went up from the crowd. "They've gotten our leaders!"

And that's when everyone lost it, running this way and that in panic.

"Let them go!" I yelled, but it all happened so fast. By the time I even had the ability to generate more fireballs to throw, my friends were already beyond my reach.

When one of the animals came to grab me, I shouted, "I don't think so!" and let my fire fly. The helicocroc who had been aiming at me screeched, flying off sideways with an injured wing, as it dropped its rider ungracefully to the ground.

"Get back here, Pinki!" Sesha snarled. He was at a distance now, hardly visible through the dust and haze of all the chaos, the felled bodies of protesters returning violence with dignity. He clearly didn't feel the need to fake his romantic feelings for me anymore since Chandni was out of hearing. "I'm going to kill you!" he yelled, letting go some green lightning in my direction.

I ducked and rolled, sending back a sword of flames in his direction, which blazed and turned in sharp fury. I didn't have time to see if it hit the mark, however, because more and more soldiers were closing in toward me, the only person fighting back on the entire street. I threw flame, ash, and smoke, not trying to injure any of them, but rather to create enough cover and chaos to help the remaining protesters run away. Even a few weeks ago, I might have chosen to stay and fight, but all my friends were captured and I was vastly outnumbered. It was far more important to get all these innocent, foolish, noble protesters out of the market safely.

"Run! Go!" I shouted to the scattering marchers. "Fly! You fools!"

And then I took my own advice and ran for my life.

CHAPTER 18

A Comportment Contest?
A COMPORTMENT CONTEST?
I Mean, What in the Trifling
Nonsensical Superficialness?

After I met Ai-Ma and my cousins at Chhaya Devi's stall, I flew as quickly as I could back to Ghatatkach Academy, taking Kawla, Mawla, and Deembo with me. Ai-Ma returned to the rebel headquarters, to tell the others what had happened at the march.

All the way back, I worried about Chandni, Arko, and his brothers. Would Sesha's fondness for Chandni keep them from being treated too badly? Or would Sesha fold, as usual, to his father the Governor-General's cruelty?

My reception back at school was not exactly what I was expecting. I was expecting Surpanakha to lose her mind with fury that I'd left school grounds, but instead, at the sight of me, the headmistress merely snapped, "Where have you been? Hurry up and get dressed!"

I frowned, not understanding at all what she was saying. "Dressed?" I repeated.

She frowned, now focusing on me over her glasses. "Wait a minute, how did you not hear the change in schedule announcement? Did you leave school without permission?"

"No. Yes. I mean, maybe," I stammered, not sure which answer would stop her from trying to kick me out of the competition again.

"Well, I don't have time to worry about that right now." Surpanakha patted her very elaborate high coiffured bun. Now that I looked more carefully, I realized that she was wearing a brilliant multicolored silk sari instead of her usual block-printed cotton, and there were strange animal shapes and figures tucked into her hairdo. "If you missed the announcements about the schedule changes to the Demonic Royalty Contest, you'll have to get caught up by Kumi and Aakash."

"The what?" I felt like I had traveled through a wormhole and landed in an alternate time and space. What in the multiverse was going on here?

"The next part of the competition is about to start," explained Aakash, flexing a bicep. "The combat competition was only the first event."

"She knows that, genius," snorted Kumi with a laugh.

My head was spinning from all that had just happened in the market. That had been initially inspiring, then terrifying. Now I felt like I'd been thrust into something completely absurd. Both my rakkhosh former-frenemies-now-friends were dressed differently than they normally were. Aakash was in a sparkling white panjabi-dhoti with his elaborately airswept hair even more sweepingly styled. Kumi was in a heavy silk sari the color of water, pearls at her throat and ears, corals and seaweed in her hair. And wait a minute, were they both wearing *makeup*?

"Why are you dressed like that?" I asked, peering around the banyan grove. There was a long walkway set up among the roots, with seats all around.

I lowered my voice, leaning in so that only Aakash and Kumi could hear me. "Listen, we don't have time for whatever this is happening right now. Chandni and Arko, not to mention most of his brothers, have been captured by the snakes!"

"We gotta break 'em out?" asked Aakash, eagerly rolling up his sleeves. "Come on, where are they?"

I sighed, frustrated. "That's the problem. I don't even know."

"So how are we going to rescue them?" asked Kumi, frowning. "Are we just going to break into the snake palace, demanding we be allowed to see them?"

"I'm not sure," I admitted. "It was kind of a chaotic scene. There was a peaceful march, but then the snakes showed up, and things got decidedly *not* peaceful."

"Are you three even serious about competing to become Demon Queen or King?" snapped Surpanakha. "Stop yammering already and get ready, Pinki!"

"Get ready? Get ready for what?" I asked.

"Now!" The headmistress pointed me toward a changing area before stomping off.

I turned to Kumi and Aakash, who seemed equally enthusiastic about bustling me off toward the changing area. I swatted at their pushing hands. "Who is going to tell me what's going on?"

"Look, it's a total bummer about Chandni and Arko getting captured, but we've got to figure out where they are before we can do anything about it," said Aakash, unrolling his sleeves and smoothing his kurta. "So we might as well go ahead with this competition thing, amirite?"

"What is 'this thing' that I almost missed?" I asked even as Aakash again pushed me toward the dressing room.

"You practically missed the most completely trifling event in this demonic royalty brouhaha," Kumi explained, her face twisted in disgust. "The evening comportment competition."

"Comportment?" I asked. "What does that even mean?"

"It's kind of a beauty competition." Aakash fluffed his hair with pride. "I mean, how graceful we are, how we carry ourselves, that sort of thing."

"You've got to be kidding." I couldn't think of something that felt less important, less relevant in light of all I'd just experienced. My friends were in trouble! I didn't have time for a beauty contest! "Do we really have to do this? Why don't we just say Aakash won and move on?"

Aakash puffed out his chest, pretend-humbly checking out his thick forearms. "Look, no one's expecting either of you to win or anything. It's not like comportment is exactly what either of you are known for."

"Rude!" I crossed my arms in irritation.

"Also, sadly, true," snorted Kumi.

"But if you don't participate in the comportment competition, Pinks, you'll be disqualified for the next ones— poisons, battle strategy, the works," Aakash pointed out.

"Look, ex-roomie, I'm not excited about this comportment crap either, but we've got to do it." Kumi generated a wave that pushed me toward the changing tent. "There's a sari in there for you; hurry up and put it on and we'll help you with your hair and stuff. All the official dressers and hairstylists are already gone."

As I undressed out of my dusty cotton clothes and began wrapping the twelve yards of fire-colored silk sari around myself, I explained all that had happened at the march. I stepped out from behind the screen, repeating, "We've got to go rescue our friends from the snakes!"

"Like I said before, we've got to find out where they are first." Aakash had been doing pull-ups on a low-hanging banyan branch and dropped down to the ground.

"They're super high profile, so the snakes won't keep it a secret for long," Kumi assured me as she tried to fix my sari pleats. "They'll make some big, braggy announcement and then we'll go kick some snake butt and rescue our buds."

"I just feel so helpless waiting." I ground my teeth. "Besides the fact that I feel really ridiculous dressing up while our friends are probably being tortured."

"They're strong, they'll be okay," Kumi said even as she helped me pin my sari in a few strategic places. "Anyway, that slimeball Sesha's kind of got a thing for Chandni, right? He'll keep her safe."

"True dat," said Aakash, "and if he doesn't, we'll just have to pulverize him into snaky polenta."

Kumi grinned and high-fived Aakash.

"Are you ready?" It was a small air-rakkhoshi stage manager who was flying around with a headset over her ears and an overstuffed clipboard in her hands. She shrieked at the sight of me. "Your hair! Go do your hair! It's almost time to begin!" she cried before flying away again on her pixie wings.

"Okay! Okay! Way to make a girl feel bad!" I complained as Kumi tried desperately to tame my curls with some pins and ribbons. I, in the meantime, poked myself in the eye with the eyeliner that Aakash handed me.

"You two really are hopeless! Give that comb to me!" Aakash shooed Kumi away and began twisting my hair into an elaborate braided and bunned design. His fingers flew over my locks, rubbing cream here, crunching in some gel there until it actually started to look decent. "Hopefully we'll get some word from Ai-Ma and the other rebels by the time we're done with this competition."

"Airhead boy actually makes a lot of sense," said Kumi grudgingly. She was smearing my cheeks with some rouge that made me look like a clown. "We can't just run around the countryside in our silks, willy-nilly, no idea of where

Chandni and Arko are. The only thing that will do is get us arrested alongside them."

I sighed as Aakash finished my hair and took over my makeup too. I knew my friends were right. But I cannot express how much I hated the fact that instead of rushing off to break my rebel comrades out of jail, I was instead going to be competing in a comportment contest.

The competition attracted all the students of the Academy, so that by the time I was finished getting ready— Aakash really did know his stuff when it came to hair and makeup—the students were all crowded into the banyan grove. The evening was lit by fire-clan torches and the natural light of fireflies, and each clan gathered under their own tree to watch the show. Someone had spread a multicolored runner down the long platform so that it became a runway decorated with all the colors of the Ghatatkach clans, and on our way toward it, the school newspaper's reporters mobbed us like real paparazzi.

The lights from their flashbulbs shone bright and glaring as I tried to hold a smile and look graceful, resenting every moment of it. Every reporter seemed obsessed with asking Aakash, Kumi, and me the same questions.

"If you were elected, who would you choose as your consort?" they called out, their pens poised above their notebooks.

Kumi and Aakash each exchanged a laughing look, and I knew they were both thinking of the same person: Chandni.

"Wouldn't you like to know who we'd choose?" said Kumi coyly, slicking back her wetted hair from her angular face.

But I turned their question on the reporters. "Why are you asking about a consort; why not consorts?"

I noticed the headmistress, who was seated in a special judging chair at the end of the runway, lift her head as I said this.

"In the before times," I said, parroting Ai-Ma's phrase, "the Rakkhosh King or Queen got to choose two consorts."

"Two consorts?" whispered the reporters, scribbling furiously.

At my words, Surpanakha made her way down to where we stood. "That is an old custom, and we have not talked about reinstating it."

"But there's no reason we couldn't," I pressed.

Surpanakha narrowed her eyes at me. "We can talk about it after the comportment contest."

"Are any of you worried about Hidimbi's crown being missing?" It was a land-clan girl named Harimati sticking a microphone in our faces.

"We already have some leads on that," Surpanakha said, giving me a stinky side-eye. "No thanks to anyone in the present company."

I felt acid rise in my stomach. What leads did Surpanakha have? I wondered in passing if it was she who had taken the crown herself—but that didn't make sense, did it? She probably wanted to find Hidimbi's mukut as soon as possible to prove to everyone how I was the wrong candidate for Demon Queen. Knowing her, she was probably daydreaming about making me burn up in a fiery explosion.

"Well, are any of you nervous about what might happen when it's found?" persisted Harimati. "Do you believe the legends, that it will burn on the head of any imposter to the demonic throne?"

The reporter's question hung in the air as Aakash, Kumi, and I exchanged worried glances. But there was no time to respond, because just then, Professor Ravan, who was seated in another judge's chair, waved his arms. He looked weak, but pretty much like his usual self otherwise. "Let the competition commence!"

And so the contest began, with music and flashing strobe lights, and a ridiculous amount of hooting and hollering from the audience.

First was Aakash, who sashayed his way down the runway, turning, waving, and posing like a pro. He paused, hand on his hip, swishing his hair with his hand, and then, as if by accident (but obviously not by accident), flexing his giant muscles. He was such a ham, grinning and posing, turning and winking. The student crowd went wild, some even throwing roses and love notes shaped like hearts at him.

"And now for my talent!" exclaimed Aakash. He flexed his beefy arms and made his biceps and triceps bounce in time to "Happy Birthday." Then, unnecessarily ripping open his kurta, he made his pecs bounce to the music too. It wasn't the most amazing talent exhibition I'd ever seen, but it was certainly something.

One of the reporters stepped up on the runway for the interview portion of the competition. "What would you say is the biggest problem facing rakkhosh-kind in this millennium?" she asked eagerly, sticking her microphone in Aakash's face.

If she was waiting for an insightful answer from my air-clan friend, I'm sorry to say that the young reporter would be waiting a very long time.

"It's really hard to get good hair products, you know? The ones that give you that solid hold when you crunch and plop your hair," Aakash said in a not-particularly-profound way. He was bare-chested, having gotten rid of his torn-up kurta, and still busy flexing for the crowd. "As an air-clan rakkhosh, I can tell you, good wind-resistant products are very difficult to come by."

When the reporter frowned and the judges furiously scribbled on their ballots, Kumi and I exchanged a look of concern. He might be our competition, but neither of us was ready for our friend to look bad just because people didn't understand his deep and abiding love for hair mousse and curl-activating gel.

"Is the problem with hair product availability because of the Serpentine Empire? The limitation on goods like that on the market?" I called from my position offstage.

"Right, of course it is," Aakash agreed, completely sincerely. Then he paused, engrossed in thought, his eyes wide and earnest. "So I guess the biggest problem facing rakkhosh-kind is really the fact that we're a colonized people living under the thumb of an empire unwilling to give us freedom of choice in our hair products, or, in fact, our very lives."

There went up a big cheer from the audience. Kumi and I high-fived. At least Aakash had been able to save himself, with our help.

Next came Kumi's turn. She was a near disaster on the runway, walking too fast, glaring at everyone around her, not pausing for any poses or photo opportunities. She dripped water on the audience from her fingertips, making it rain on a small crowd of spectators when she tripped on her sari. Kumi answered her interview question fine, talking about the abuses of the Serpent Empire, including their proclamation that we rakkhosh couldn't rhyme, but her struggle was with the talent portion of the competition.

"What's your talent?" asked Professor Ravan.

"My talent?" Kumi interlaced her fingers menacingly, tucking her sari anchal tightly at her waist. "My talent is cracking skulls, of course!"

"A talent you can show us here onstage safely!" Surpanakha's eyebrows shot up with irritation, and if she'd had nostrils, they would have been flaring.

"I didn't know we had to have a talent. I thought this was just about not tripping over yourself or, like, drooling," complained my roommate.

Again, the judges began scribbling comments while frowning. Aakash, who had just stepped offstage, looked desperately at me. "Can murder be a talent?" he hissed.

"No it can't!" I whispered back. Then I slightly increased my volume. "Weren't you going to water juggle?" I asked in a voice pitched low enough just for Kumi to hear.

She whirled around, her face scrunched up in confusion. "What?"

"Water juggle!" I said only slightly louder, pantomiming juggling hand motions from offstage.

"I don't know what you're saying," said Kumi loudly from the middle of the stage. Several people in the audience laughed. "What are you doing with your hands?"

"I'm juggling!" I shouted in frustration. "Water juggling!"

Kumi made a scoffing noise. "You're not a water rakkhoshi! You can't juggle water!"

The audience was now falling over themselves laughing, and the judges were still scribbling furiously.

"I know I'm not!" I hissed, glaring at her. "But *you* are!"

"Oh, I get it!" Kumi's face finally lit up with understanding. "Like my talent, right? Wow, okay, thanks!"

Finally catching on, Kumi produced balls of water that she began juggling. As they moved through the air, she transformed them into colorful spouts and raindrops and swooshing waves. Soon, her act became like a dancing water show with leaping jets of water changing into misty clouds, then rollicking droplets. The audience oohed and aahed and Kumi looked so graceful as she juggled, now in front of her, now behind her back, I thought she might make up for her inelegant performance on the runway. To my relief, the judges actually looked approving as they scribbled some more.

"Pinki, the fire rakkhoshi!" Professor Ravan announced.

And so it was my turn. I managed to walk without tripping on the runway, although I was nowhere as elegant or posey as Aakash. Then I did a fire show for my talent, making fire scenes appear in the sky and animal-shaped firecrackers shoot out over the laughing and clapping audience.

"You've finally learned to control your fire, I see," said Surpanakha in a tone of grudging approval.

"And now it's time for the interview," said one of the reporters. It was Harimati again, with her huge, old-fashioned tape recorder and a giant microphone.

"What do you think is the biggest problem facing rakkhosh-kind today?" she asked, her warty face eager and way too close to mine.

But before I had a chance to answer, there was a commotion from the audience. Students were whispering, running here and there to share some kind of juicy news. Even the reporters were distracted by all the action.

"What is this disruption?" shouted Surpanakha. "Silence during the competition!"

"But, Headmistress!" shouted out one of the reporters. "We've just heard that Prince Arko, Chandni the moon maiden, and many other rebel leaders are going to be tried by the serpents in an emergency tribunal right now!"

"Tonight?" I exclaimed. "In the middle of the night?"

Professor Ravan, a look of concern on his face, stood up from his judge's chair. "An emergency tribunal? That's a farce of the law."

"Not just that!" the same reporter continued. "If they're

found guilty, they'll be banished from this dimension—shot out through a new wormhole the snakes have constructed into a parallel galaxy!"

"The transit corridor!" I breathed, catching Kumi's and Aakash's eyes. "Let's go!"

CHAPTER 19

A Travesty of a Joke of a Setup of a Farce of a Bogus Fakery of a Trial

I don't know how Aakash, Kumi, and I convinced Surpanakha to let us attend the trial. Honestly, she probably wouldn't have let us go if Professor Ravan hadn't intervened on our behalf. In fact, I'm sure he would have come with us if he wasn't still recovering from his illness. I think it was something about us being the three royalty contestants as well. That said, no one else from the school was given permission to come. So my fantasy of storming Arko and Chandni's trial with an army of angry, chanting Ghatatkach rakkhosh students demanding my friends' freedom didn't exactly come to fruition. In fact, I kind of got the impression Surpanakha was just trying to get us to stop bothering her when she let us go.

"I can't believe the headmistress didn't want to come help herself," I said to my friends as we flew toward the market. Kumi and I were on helicocrocs, Aakash was flying on his own power, and I was providing flame lamps to guide our way. "I mean, with all her big-big talk about the revolution."

"Remember, she asked us specifically to keep a low profile, disguise ourselves in human form when we get there," said Kumi from the back of her flying monster. "The headmistress is responsible for keeping all the kids at our school safe, so I'm not sure she's ready to declare some kind of all-out, open war against the Serpent Empire just yet."

"Why not?" I griped. I was feeling extra edgy because of how much I hated to fly. Flying in the dark only made that hatred worse. "I mean, they almost killed Professor Ravan only a minute ago."

"We don't know for sure that was the serpents who did that. It could have been a weird fluke," Aakash argued as he flapped his wings against the wind. "Anyway, they've pumped up the magical protections around the school soul-bees now, so we should be good to go."

"If you say so, man." I hung on for dear life, feeling seasick, as my helicocroc took a sharp turn and angled down toward the ground.

"I just hope that the headmistress doesn't penalize you for not finishing the comportment contest." Aakash widened his eyes with fake sincerity.

"Don't even!" snorted Kumi. "You know you won it anyway. It wouldn't matter how fire girl here answered the interview question. You are the undisputed beauty queen, all right, bud?"

Aakash smiled, fixing his hair even in mid-flight. "Beauty king, but thank you very much."

After we landed, and parked the two poison-spitting animals near Chhaya Devi's deserted stall, I led the way through the eerily empty bazaar.

"Where is everyone?" Kumi hissed, nervously shooting water from her fingers. "I mean, I know it's late, but shouldn't the shops still be open?"

It was true. Night shopping was a popular activity for human families, especially when the days were hot and long. But now there were no humans, rakkhosh, or other beings in the market to be seen. No vendors hawking their wares from their stalls, no stall-less sellers wandering around with baskets on their heads, no rikshaw-wallahs calling for customers. In fact, every stall seemed closed and dark. Rikshaws stood idle one upon another at a side of the road. Even the stray street dogs who usually ran up for pets and snacks had vanished.

"This is giving me the creepy-yeepies." Aakash kept lifting up canvas storefronts and peeking inside. "Where is everyone?"

"I don't know," I whispered. "But maybe we should change into human form just in case?"

The three of us said the incantation of transformation, turning in place until we became hornless, fangless, talonless versions of ourselves. In other words, we all looked incredibly dull and boring, which was a drag, but it would at least allow us to blend into a human crowd.

We only began to see signs of life as we crossed over to

the other side of the bazaar, then over the bridge that ran over the stream at the edge of the market. As we headed up toward the transit corridor, we heard a low rumbling. Only as we walked on did we realize what the noise was— hundreds of people gathered outside the transit officers' cave. As we made our way closer, we jostled for space in the crowd—hoping to blend in as slightly tall and strong-looking humans. All around us, people were mumbling and looking worried. There was an atmosphere of scared anticipation. Then, to my complete shock, I saw someone very familiar. Someone very familiar, with bright yellow wings and a terrible sense of humor, who flew over to land on my shoulder.

"Toto? What are you doing here?" I hoped he wouldn't blow our cover. But none of the humans around us seemed to think it too strange that I was talking to a bird on my shoulder. I guess it just goes to show that there were a lot stranger things in the Kingdom Beyond than a tall girl and her talking parakeet.

"Ai-Ma sent Toto to keep an eye on the proceedings," the annoying bird squawked in my ear, annoyingly referring to himself in the third person as usual. "Toto didn't want to come, but she said I was the least likely to be recognized by the snakes."

"She's right." It figured my mother had become a de facto leader of the rebels now that Arko and Chandni had been captured. She couldn't just leave well enough alone, could she? "Ai-Ma would be recognized right away."

"Toto doesn't want to be made into mince-bird pie," moaned the not-particularly-brave bird, discharging several yellow tail feathers from his bum.

"Where are Arko, Chandni, and the others?" I peered around over the actual humans' heads. All I could see were the rows of snake soldiers at the edges of the human crowd.

"Over there!" Toto indicated the transit officers' podium with his wing.

"Where?" I eyed their guns and bayonets, feeling like it was a repeat of the scene during the march.

"Look!" hissed Kumi. I saw what she was talking about. Next to the podium was an empty judge's chair. And in front of the chair was a giant empty prison cell just waiting for some captives.

"Hear ye, hear ye, the serpent tribunal is now in session!" It was Sesha, dressed in some kind of old-fashioned lawyer robes with a fancy neckerchief, thumping a giant cane thing on the ground. "All you pesky humans, rise to your feet to sing our national anthem!"

"Toto hates the snaky anthem," moaned the bird in my ear. "So many confusing stanzas! Such terrible alliteration!"

"I know, right?" agreed Aakash. "Like, no sense of rhythm or musicality!"

"Well, you have no choice," I whispered back. "Just shut up and sing!"

We, along with all the humans around us, began an unenthusiastic chorus of "Snake save our glorious snakes, Snake bless our noble snakes, Snake save the snakes." It was clear no one knew all the words, and everyone was singing half-heartedly, but no one dared disobey.

When we finished, Sesha called out again, "The honorable Governor-General of the Serpent Empire will be presiding today as the judge and jury!"

"Seems kinda shady not to have a separate jury," observed Aakash in a low voice.

"Super shady," I muttered.

Sesha's father, the Governor-General, came out, dressed in dark, flowing robes with an ornate white wig on his head. The thing looked dusty, with all sorts of curls over it and a hanging, ribboned ponytail. Heavily, he took a seat on the judge's chair. He looked a bit more red-faced and bloated than even the last time I'd seen him.

"You could buy a whole lotta groceries with the Governor-General's eye bags!" squawked Toto. A few humans around us looked over, and I took the parakeet off my shoulder to cradle him in the crook of my elbow.

"Quiet, bird!" I ordered.

"That was a shoddy job of an introduction!" the Governor-General growled up on the stage. The older snake stood up from his judge's chair, lifting an arm as if he was about to strike his son. "Is that any way to introduce a leader of such infinite power as me?"

Even from where I was standing, I could see Sesha flinch away from the expected blow, and then, when it didn't come, redden with humiliation. He took a nervous look out at the human audience, which was shifting around uncomfortably now, and swallowed hard. He cleared his throat, shouting out, "All of you dirty humans, bow down now for the infinitely powerful Governor-General of the entire Serpent Empire! The ruler of the sky above your heads, the master of the ground beneath your feet, the owner of the water you drink and the very air you take in with every breath! Bow down and thank him for your lives! Bow down and tremble in fear!"

Most of the human crowd obeyed immediately, but a few shifted around, making scoffing sounds. I heard someone mutter, low but loud enough to carry, "Just like you bow down and tremble before your daddy, snake boy?"

Sesha whirled on the audience, his eyes blazing. "Who said that? Who *said* that?" he screeched, letting go some green lightning above the crowd, forcing everyone into low, subservient bows.

"Yo, I hate that Governor-General dude," Aakash muttered from his crouched position.

"Not as much as his son does," returned Kumi, equally low.

They were right. Sesha looked so furious I thought he just might unleash some of that green lightning on his own father.

"Enough! Thisss isss boring me!" snarled the ruler of the Snake Empire from his throne. "Bring out the prisonersss!"

Sesha turned away, seeming to swallow his anger. In the meantime, the transit officer and some of the snaky soldiers led out our friends from the depths of the transit officers' cave. Chandni, Arko, and his brothers were blindfolded and handcuffed, linked together in a long line.

"Get in the cage, you dirty beasts!" the transit officer huffed, his eyes huge and wattle wobbling. "Or you better bet I'll eat your feets!"

Oh, great, the incompetent teenager had decided to take

my advice on rhyming his threats. Why had I even told him that? I really had to start making better choices.

"Oh, he's an ugly, scary, toothy fellow!" Toto moaned from my arms. "You won't let him eat poor old Toto, will you, Lady Pinki?"

"Only if you don't stop talking!" I snapped, which shut the bird right up.

As I watched my friends get roughly pushed into the cage, I winced, hoping they weren't too hurt. Finally, inside the cell, Chandni, Arko, and his brothers were unlinked from each other and their blindfolds taken off. But their hands were still bound before them. Blinking against the fiery torchlight, Chandni almost fell down. Someone in the crowd gasped with sympathy. Someone else in the crowd was softly crying. Arko gently helped the moon girl to her feet before silently standing again.

"Why are you sssilent at the sssight of these criminalsss?" the Governor-General admonished the crowd with a click of his yellowish teeth. "These are enemies of the peace, rebel enemies of the ssstate! You should be booing them!"

Some of the humans in the crowd obediently booed, but you could tell their hearts weren't in it. They shot each other nervous "what else can we do?" type looks. The

Governor-General glared at Sesha, making an angry hand gesture, to which his son blanched a little.

"Louder, mongrels!" Sesha snarled. "You heard what your Governor-General said! Boo them louder!"

At this, some of the snake soldiers around the crowd brandished their weapons, and more people began to boo. Some of the soldiers began handing out baskets of spoiled food and encouraging the crowd to throw things at the prisoners. At first, the humans were hesitant, but then, at some threatening looks and gestures from the soldiers, they began half-heartedly throwing the spoiled food at our friends. A tomato hit Arko in the chest with a splat, staining his kurta red as if he were bleeding from a wound to his heart. An entire head of cabbage hit Chandni, sliding down her back, leaving an oozy trail. But neither of them, nor any of Arko's brothers, reacted with any animosity to the boos, the food being thrown at them, the humiliating position they found themselves in. Instead they just stood there, like the noble, pacifist fools they were. I felt my fury boiling inside my hearts. I longed for Chandni to zap that snake Sesha with a moonbeam to his traitorous butt. She was certainly powerful enough to explode that cage out. I'd seen more than once what her moon magic could do. And

Arko's sun magic too, for that matter. But with their hands bound before them, they couldn't summon their powers, even if they wanted to.

"This is horrible!" I hissed. The flames were roiling inside me, waiting to come out. "Why are we letting this go on?"

"Because we're three rakkhosh plus a talkative bird versus the entire serpentine army, that's why." Kumi placed her hand warningly on my arm. "Don't rush it, we're going to stick to the plan."

But what if the plan didn't work? my brain screamed. I didn't want to wait; I wanted to get my friends out of that humiliating cage, now.

"Your honorable judge-ness!" Sesha bowed low before his father, the rings on his fingers flickering in the torch-light. "These prisoners are accused of inciting a riot against the Serpentine Empire, of spreading false and malicious rumors about our rule, and of planning to overthrow the rightful rulers of the Kingdom Beyond. They are known rebels, and I suggest you make an example of Prince Arko— the leader of this ill-conceived revolutionary rabble."

"No!" Toto squawked in indignation, before I gave him a warning squeeze and he quieted down. A woman in the crowd let out a strangled cry. Prince Arko was beloved among the humans—not because his father was a Raja but because people knew he had once disguised himself as the schoolteacher Shurjo and taught their children. He cared for the common people in ways that his father and other human leaders did not.

"What do you suggest we do with this rebel scum, my princely progeny?" The Governor-General had his thick fingers tented beneath his chin. Although he didn't favor quite as many shiny rings as his son, there was a giant ruby on one of his fingers and an emerald on another.

Sesha smiled, pacing back and forth before the prisoners like he was considering his father's question with great seriousness. "I suggest the rebel scum Arko be the first to be expelled from this dimension through the newly formed transit corridor—that he be sent out into the galactic darkness, never to incite insurrection in the Kingdom Beyond again!"

Now more people in the crowd cried out, and others rumbled with discontent. But Sesha turned on them all with a fierce cry. "Silence, you pitiful peasants!"

I exchanged alarmed looks with Kumi and Aakash. We couldn't let them shoot Arko out through the wormhole, but we were seriously outnumbered, even with our magical rakkhosh skills. If only the headmistress had allowed us to bring more rakkhosh with us!

The Governor-General scratched beneath his dusty wig with a long fingernail. "And what if I don't want to send Prince Arko through the transit corridor?" he asked in a drawling voice.

I wasn't fool enough to think the Governor-General of the Serpent Empire was saying this because he wanted to spare Arko. He had some other devious plan up his sleeve. Some plan that probably had something in there about humiliating Sesha. I held my breath, waiting for the other scale to drop, as it were.

"What do you mean? He's the leader of the group!" Sesha looked a bit nervous at his father's question too.

"What if instead of Prince Arko I want to send someone else?" The Governor-General rotated his finger lazily, pointing at the prisoners. "Someone like . . . oh, I don't know, what about . . . HER!" He pointed at Chandni.

"What? No!" Sesha looked downright panicked. Man, his dad was still the meanest. The Governor-General knew about his son's feelings for Chandni and was basically torturing him in public.

"Or we send *both* the moon brat and your prince, how about that?" The Governor-General rubbed his hands together, like he was anticipating a tasty meal.

Aakash and Kumi looked like they were ready to jump

out and beat up the judge. I held them both back, pulling at their sleeves. "Don't be hasty," I hissed. "We stick to the plan."

Aakash snorted. "That's rich coming from you."

"Yeah, the Queen of Hasty," muttered Kumi. The two exchanged the tiniest of high fives. Toto cackled, fluttering his wings in my arms.

In the meantime, Sesha was fidgeting and flustered in response to his father's suggestion. "I don't think it's necessary to send them *both*," he said, trying to maintain his cool. "Actually, I think that sending Arko through the wormhole will absolutely be enough of a deterrent to the rebel forces."

"What if I disagree?" The Governor-General's eyes were narrowed. "Who is in charge here, boy, you or me?"

"You—you—" stammered Sesha nervously. But his eyes darted repeatedly to Chandni in her cage. Chandni, for her part, glared back at him. "Of course you, sir."

The Governor-General stood up dramatically from his chair and faced the prisoners in the cage. "Rebel scum! You have been found guilty of plotting against the rightful rulers of the Kingdom Beyond—the Serpentine Empire. You incited an unlawful riot, encouraging insulting slogans against the snakes and suggesting the common people engage in lawlessness, pillaging, and violence. Also, your posters about the snakes were downright rude!"

"I thought you said it was a nonviolent march?" whispered Aakash in my ear.

"It was. On the other hand, some of those anti-snake slogans did slap." I stared at Arko, willing him to look back at me from within his cage, but he didn't.

"I'm not letting that jerk yeet Chandni out through that wormhole," muttered Kumi. "No way."

"No yeeting!" agreed Toto with a squawk.

"We stick to the plan," I repeated to my friends, trying to convince myself the plan would work. It was based on a book of serpentine rules about honoring local customs I'd been reading, and so it had to work, right? Things based on books were never wrong, were they? I felt my nervousness starting to rise up in my throat, like bile.

"You resistance scum were witnessed firsthand by several hundred serpentine soldiers, whose testimonies we have already collected," the Governor-General was saying. "And so, unless there is any other evidence or witnesses to the contrary, we will proceed immediately and forthwith to the judgment and punishment phase."

There was a pause, a moment when we all seemed to hold our breath in the crowd, and then I jumped into the breach.

"We wish to introduce new evidence that will prevent

the Serpentine Empire from sending either Prince Arko or the Lady Chandni through the transit corridor and into another dimension!" I shouted loudly.

"Who said that?" Sesha's head whipped around, searching the crowd. I could tell from his wary expression that he recognized my voice.

All righty, then. There was no going back now. I just hoped my strategy would work.

CHAPTER 20

It Takes a Special Talent to Snatch Defeat from the Jaws of Victory

What evidence could a bunch of dirty humans have that could change my mind?" snarled the Governor-General, his beady eyes whipping around the crowd.

"We are the three rakkhosh competing this year to become Demon King or Queen," announced Kumi as we three shed our human disguises. As we once again became taller, more muscular, more horned, and more fanged, the humans around us shrieked and shrank back.

"Whoever wins the contest will choose, by ancient custom, their consort from outside the rakkhosh community." Aakash winked at some of the human ladies nearby us. At this, the human ladies in question shrank back a little less. In fact, they giggled and blushed. One even batted her eyelashes at him, squishing closer to my grinning friend. I wanted to groan. Aakash was such a cheesebucket.

"We know that by serpentine decree, all local customs pertaining to royalty and ascension to the throne will be honored, is that not so?" I shook out my hair and stretched, reveling being in my rakkhoshi form again. Toto flew back onto my shoulder, his chest puffed out proudly. I tried to keep my voice from shaking and my eyes fixed on Sesha and his dad. "To break that ruling would be to undermine the entire system of rajas, ranis, kings, and queens that have kept the subjects of this kingdom content and happy this long."

There was a murmuring of approval now from the crowd. They knew what I was saying was true. While royal titles held by humans and rakkhosh alike were relatively powerless—little morsels handed out by our snaky rulers to keep us docile—they were a key part of how the snakes continued to rule over us. The serpents themselves had made the laws about not interfering with local royal customs.

"How do you know about that?" the Governor-General snapped, narrowing his eyes at me. I could tell he was fantasizing about attacking me right there on the spot.

"I read it in this handbook of the Empire of Serpentine Overlords, entitled *Dealing with Annoying Subjects While*

Keeping Them Compliant." I held up the book, which had the serpentine hashtag #ComplianceOverDefiance printed on the back. "And oh, look, Governor-General! How interesting! I believe this book was written by you!"

"Yeah, written by you!" Toto repeated from my shoulder, tittering in that little birdie way of his.

I couldn't blame him. It was hard not to laugh from triumph. It felt good to win, for once.

"You rakkhosh rebel scum!" snarled the Governor-General. His bulging eyes were looking seriously bloodshot. "What are you saying?"

"I'm saying that if either Aakash or I win the contest, and

become Demon Queen or King, we will choose Chandni the moon maiden as our consort!" announced Kumi. "You can't send her through the wormhole without undermining the entire royal rakkhosh competition."

"Oh, Father, that's an issue we must examine closely," said Sesha eagerly. "Wouldn't want to undermine the quaint exotic customs of these locals!"

Then it was my turn to declare my intentions. "And if I win the contest, I will choose . . ."

"I know who you will choose!" said Sesha, cutting me off with an alarmed expression. Hmm, that was interesting. Snake boy clearly didn't want me to tell his father about my promise to him.

". . . Prince Arko as my second consort," I finished.

"Yeah, so suck on that egg, you snaky egg suckers!" shouted Toto.

I gave a warning tug on his wing.

"Too much?" he whispered in my ear.

"Way too much," I agreed.

"What do you mean second consort?" Sesha snarled. Clearly, even though he didn't want to tell his father I'd promised to make him my consort, he also didn't want me to pick Arko.

"Didn't you know?" I raised my eyebrow in imitation

of his gesture. "It's one of our quaint exotic rakkhosh traditions—that we can pick TWO consorts, not just one."

The Governor-General let out a guttural scream. "Consorts? Who cares about some monstrous consorts? I want to finish the trial! I want to punish somebody NOW!"

"Unfortunately, we must consider this issue, sir." A turbaned snaky minister came out from who knows where, muttering into the Governor-General's ear and gesticulating with some papers and law books. The crowd was muttering in low voices, but I could make out a few words the minister was saying due to my rakkhoshi hearing.

"Cultural traditions," I heard him say. Also "fragile peace with rakkhosh-kind," "not easy to control," and "all their power unleashed."

Over the last weeks, I'd learned that as unassailable as the Serpent Empire appeared, their rule was based on a lot of carefully placed pieces. Pull out one piece and the entire structure of their power might crumble. The snakes had made deals with different communities to keep them quiet, waved the stick but also handed out carrots like royal titles to keep those who could make trouble on their side. The question was, could we use all of that to our advantage?

Inside their cage, Chandni, Arko, and his brothers had turned toward us. They said nothing, but their eyes communicated volumes, and concern etched their faces. Plus, both Chandni and Arko seemed surprised at being named potential rakkhosh consorts. I couldn't help feel a little hurt that Arko wasn't happier at the thought of being mine, but that said, I was trying to save his life right now and couldn't really worry about other more minor issues like people's feelings.

"I hate this, but it appears my minister is right!" the Governor-General bellowed. "In light of some nonsense ruling I apparently wrote far too long ago, I'm not going to be able to send two of these prisoners through the transit corridor today!"

Toto let out a whoop and flew triumphantly around my head. "Which snakes are best at math?" he squawked. And without waiting for an answer, he howled, "Adders!"

Normally, I would have been annoyed with the bird for cracking jokes at a time like this, but I could smell the heady scent of impending victory and so I indulged myself a little. I glanced up at the flying parakeet. "Hey, Toto, what medicine do you give a sick snake?"

"A butt kicking?" snickered Aakash.

"A dung cake?" asked Kumi.

"No, I know!" squawked Toto as he landed back on my shoulder. "It's asp-irin!"

We all laughed, exchanging triumphant looks. We could afford to laugh. Our plan had worked!

Or so I thought, at least, until I heard what the Governor-General said next.

"Fine!" he bellowed. "I can't send two of these prisoners through the transit corridor today, so instead, I'm going to send the rest of the prisoners through the transit corridor!"

"What?" Arko yelled. "No!"

"Well, gosh, that didn't work out the way you thought, my lady," squawked Toto, plunking back onto my shoulder.

"We're getting really good at snatching defeat from the jaws of victory, huh?" muttered Kumi.

"Quiet, all of you!" I snarled. Oh no. This couldn't be happening. This couldn't be happening!

Arko's brothers, Aadil, Ishan, Uday, Umran, and Rishi, looked to their eldest brother, panic in their eyes. Finally, after all this time, Arko turned around and met my eyes. I felt my three hearts shrink in my very chest at the look of pain and betrayal on the human prince's face.

"Oh, this is too delicious! Aren't you lucky, you rebel losers! All five of you princely brothers are going to get to explore another dimension!" yelled Sesha gleefully as he had the soldiers herd the five princes out of the jail cell. They pushed Arko and Chandni away with the butts of their weapons.

"No! Please stop! Take me instead!" Arko cried, trying to pull his brothers back.

"Please, Dada, don't worry!" said Aadil.

"We'll be together!" added Ishan.

"We'll be fine!" said Umran, although I noticed the boy's voice did quaver a little as he said this. My hearts squeezed even tighter.

"We knew what we were getting into!" Uday took his brother Umran's hand.

"Shut up, all of you!" sneered the Governor-General. "Enough sniveling! I hate sniveling! Almost as much as I hate noble self-sacrifice! Ugh!"

"Brother, you must continue to fight for the cause!" yelled Rishi, the youngest of the princes save Rontu, his handsome young face full of faith at his eldest sibling. The expression of trust I saw there nearly made me keel over.

"Do something!" Arko yelled, and I knew his words were for me. I realized with a lurching of my digestive system that I hadn't entirely thought out this plan of mine. Sure, I'd saved Arko and Chandni, but in doing so, I'd effectively sealed a horrible fate for five honorable and brave young princes. They were going to be banished out of our dimension and through a wormhole to who knows where.

Oh, this was not good. Not good at all.

But then it seemed for a minute that fate might just be on our side. Even as the soldiers kept trying to put the princes in the wormhole, nothing happened. The intergalactic portal seemed to be broken. No whirling, no swirling, no changing of colors, no clang-clang noises, nothing that we would normally associate with a functional interdimensional wormhole.

"Why isn't the blasted thing working?" shouted Sesha, pointing at the transit officer. "You were supposed to make sure it was working! Did you drop the ball, you chicken-wattled nincompoop?"

The transit officer started to blubber, snotting and wailing all over himself. "I swear it was working before when I tested the diagnostics, boss! I ran the beta systems, and I cranked the compartment stabilizer! I swear, boss! Don't fire me, okay? I really need this joooooooob!"

I wanted to cheer. Of course the nincompoop of a teenage transit officer had goofed up! Maybe luck *was* on our side!

"Oh, for pity's sake, stop with the excuses!" shouted Sesha, handing the transit officer a giant handkerchief into which the creature noisily blew his nose. The teenager tried to hand the wet cloth back to Sesha, who looked like he wanted to punch him.

"What's going on?" whispered Aakash. "If they can't get the transit thingy to work, what happens then?"

"Sesha should never have hired that chicken kid to run his wormhole!" Kumi gleefully crowed. "Serves him right for not being willing to pay for skilled union labor!"

I shook my head, not wanting to believe the hope blossoming in my chest. "Let's not count our lizards before they hatch," I cautioned out loud, even as my three hearts were doing the do-si-do. I wanted to run up and kiss that pimply transit officer and thank him for being an incompetent lout. Thank the multiverse he was so bad at his job!

There were snake soldiers all crowded around the wormhole now, so tightly that we couldn't see the princely brothers anymore. That's when things started tilting a bit sideways for us again.

"If you can't fix the wormhole, then institute plan B!" shouted the Governor-General, and his snaky minions ran off in a million directions, everyone repeating, "Plan B! Institute plan B!"

"Help!" Chandni mouthed in my direction from inside the cage.

My hearts stopped dancing in my chest. Smelly donkey pits! Why did the snakes have a plan B?

"The snakes have a plan B!" squawked Toto. "What's our plan B? Do we have one? What about a plan C? Or D? E, F, G?"

My mind floundered. I had dug up that old handbook of serpentine rules and regulations and thought what I'd discovered within it was a foolproof plan to save Chandni and Arko. But I hadn't thought beyond that. Toto was right; why didn't we have a plan B? I stared at the doomed princes, willing something to come to me. The cogs of my mind whirred. Then it occurred to me. Of course. Why hadn't I thought of it before?

"I've got it!" I turned urgently to Kumi and Arko. "If I could declare two consorts, so can you guys!"

"I'm not really into . . . princes," Kumi said with a grimace.

"You're not asking them to a school dance; you're rescuing them from being punted across the galaxies!" I said impatiently.

"True that, true that." Kumi nodded.

"Hey, do you think there's going to be a school dance once one of us is crowned?" Aakash mused, looking thoughtful as he twisted a lock of his own hair around his finger.

I stared at him, wanting to pull out my horns in

frustration, but instead just scratched my head with both hands. "Not the time, my air dude. Not exactly the time to be worrying about that! We've got people's lives to save?"

Aakash looked at me intensely. "If you're itchy, maybe you should use a different hair care regimen? I've been meaning to mention it, Pinks, but I really feel you're losing some volume and shine."

Before I could answer, or bop Aakash in the nose in frustration, I was distracted by a sound. There was some sort of flapping noise coming from somewhere above us. What was that? Heavy wingbeats? I looked up but saw nothing.

"What was that?" squawked Toto. "That didn't sound good! A hawk, come to eat Toto? A hungry helicocroc? What was that?"

"Listen." Kumi stomped her foot. "Can we worry about random sounds, and, like, hair products, later, folks? Like after we stop those snakes from yeeting the Princes Champak out into outer space?"

"Gee, what a good idea!" I said sarcastically. "Okay, so you guys—hurry up and claim your second consorts!"

"Okay." Aakash frowned, counting off carefully on his fingers. "But there are, like, five princes, so if me and Kumi claim two more as consorts then that still leaves out . . ." He paused, recounting on his fingers.

"The other three!" Kumi finished for him.

Aakash frowned. "I was getting there!"

I bit my lip. Then I was distracted by that sound again. I looked up, but again saw nothing. Was I hallucinating?

"I can't think of any other solution that could save them all." I gestured to the princes now waiting purposelessly at the mouth of the dysfunctional wormhole. "But I don't think it matters anyway. From what I can tell, they're not getting that thing working anytime soon!"

"I don't know," said Kumi thoughtfully. "I'm kind of surprised we haven't been captured and killed already. The snakes kind of outnumber us here—by a lot."

"Whatever, yaar. That chicken dude's incompetence is, like, super lucky for us," said Aakash, rubbing his hands together like he was prepping for a big rickets match. "Let's do this thing!"

"I declare Aadil to be my second consort choice!" shouted Kumi over the hubbub. I was nervous about her being heard, but girl had a loud voice.

"I declare Ishan!" shouted Aakash equally loudly.

Unfortunately, just at that moment, I realized what the overhead flapping sound I'd been hearing was. I looked up to see the legendary, giant, human-faced birds Bangoma and Bangomee, flying around and around in a circle just behind the defunct portal that was the transit corridor. As they flew, they created between them a shimmering, whirring wormhole.

"Oh no, that's their plan B!" I shouted. I felt everything crashing around me. This was a nightmare.

"I knew we should have had a plan B!" Toto whined.

And then it happened. With an ominous whooshing, like some kind of intergalactic vacuum being turned on, the temporary portal created by the two magical birds activated. And before any of us could react, all five of Arko's brothers were sucked through to another dimension.

"No!" shouted Arko, his cry heavy and jagged with pain. He put out his hand and, despite his wrists still being tied, smashed the prison door open with a golden blast of power. The snakes, busy celebrating the jettisoning of the five royal princes, didn't even react. With a sneer, they let a sobbing Chandni and distraught Arko just step out of the prison cage.

"Go! You two are released!" Sesha raised a dark eyebrow, smiling at our sorrow. He untied the remaining two prisoners' hands. "But if you keep up this rebel nonsense, my prince, you'll be next! And I'll make sure the next portal doesn't send you anywhere near your brothers—wherever in the multiverse that is!"

Arko growled—his nonviolence forgotten—lunging at Sesha. Chandni caught his arm, pulling him back.

Before the snakes could change their minds, we three rakkhosh bundled our friends away from the transit corridor. Sesha's cruel laugh was ringing in our ears the entire time.

CHAPTER 21

Arko Totally Blames Me for Everything, Which Is Mostly Unfair and Only a Teensy Bit Justified

Remarkably, we reached the helicocrocs that we'd left parked by Chhaya Devi's stall without much incident.

"Let's get you two back to the rebel headquarters," I urged, pulling Chandni and a still-stunned-looking Arko onto the backs of the flying monsters. The cool darkness, normally so comforting, felt too dangerous right now. Plus, we needed to put some distance between us and Sesha, and pronto. For all I knew, the snakes would change their minds and decide to come after us at any second.

"How are you acting like nothing happened?" Arko's face was so full of fury, shining weirdly in the blinking streetlight, that I took a step back. He choked out the next words, his handsome face twisted in emotion. "You just got five of my brothers shot across the galaxies to who knows where! You should have left it and let me be sacrificed."

"Arko!" Chandni burst out. "They meant well."

To which Arko just glowered. "Meaning well and doing well aren't the same thing!"

I chewed on my lip. I'd never seen Arko so upset. But to his credit, I'd never inadvertently orchestrated five of his brothers being shot out through an interdimensional portal before either. All righty, then. Even if I won Demon Queen, I was sure he wasn't exactly going to be pleased about being my consort.

"It was the best plan we could come up with without more help," Kumi explained apologetically as she got on the helicocroc behind Chandni.

"Sorry we couldn't do more," said Aakash sadly as he flapped his wings, lifting off from the ground. "We tried to save two more of your brothers, but those slimy snakes yeeted them to outer space so fast!"

Toto just chirped faintly from my shoulder, uncharacteristically quiet.

I silently mounted the helicocroc behind Arko. He stiffened, muttering, "I'm sorry. I didn't mean to lash out at you like that, Pinki. I know it might seem like it, but I . . . I don't blame you. I know you were just trying to help."

For whatever reason, Arko saying he didn't blame me both made me feel worse and made clear that he *did* blame me. As we rose into the night sky, I felt my three hearts sink in my chest. I hated that I'd hurt him. I hated that I'd not been able to save the other princes. And most of all, I hated that snake in the grass of a snake, Sesha.

As we flew toward the rebel headquarters, I kept going over and over what had happened. At first, the breakdown of the portal had seemed like a gift. I was sure that our friends were all saved, or at least that we had bought some time to figure out how to save them. If only Bangoma and Bangomee hadn't been the Serpent Empire's plan B. Everyone knew those dratted birds would make an intergalactic wormhole for anyone who was willing to pay. That's when it hit me.

"Wait a minute!" I shouted to my friends. Chandni's mom, the Old Moon Mother, was shining now, and her light was bright this high in the sky. It bathed all of us in a silvery glow. "How much do you think it costs to buy a wormhole?"

"No offense, but definitely more money than you got,

Pinks." Aakash snorted, flaring his nostrils. "Oh, wait, that's right, you don't got any!"

"True that!" Kumi chuckled as Aakash flew over to high-five her in the air.

It was more than well-known at school that I was a scholarship student, and pretty much broke all the time. I ignored my two joker classmates, though. I didn't have time for their nonsense right now.

Chandni looked over at me from the other helicocroc, her skin luminous in her mother's moonlight. "Why do you ask, Pinki?"

"Wait. I think I understand." Arko turned around to look at me over his shoulder. "You're thinking about hiring Bangoma and Bangomee, right?"

"Exactly!" I nodded. "If the snakes could pay them to make a wormhole, there's no reason we couldn't pay them to make a second one to the same place. After all, if anyone knows where that portal jettisoned your brothers, it's those two magic birds."

"If we could find them, we could maybe bring them back!" Kumi said.

"It's brilliant!" Toto burbled. "I'm so glad you followed Toto's advice."

I gave the bird a glare, and he piped down.

"Well, if we're doing this, we're going to have to change our route," Arko said firmly. "We're going to have to go to my father's palace."

All five of us—Toto, Kumi, Aakash, Chandni, and I—stared at the prince from our respective spots in midair. "Why?" I finally asked.

"Because he's the only one with enough money to pay for those dratted birds. They're really expensive!" As soon as Arko said the words, the sky emitted a sickening ripping sound.

"What was that?" squawked Toto, discharging a few tail feathers in fear. "What was that?"

"Oh no, the partition is happening again!" Kumi shouted, looking around her with alarm.

"Yo, I hate that crap!" Aakash looked nervously around him, as did we all. "Partitions are the worst!"

"Do you see the rift? Where is it?" Chandni's voice was shrill with panic.

Once, Deembo, she, and I had almost been sucked into one of the rifts in the atmosphere caused by what everyone now called "partitions" and it hadn't been a very pleasant experience. In fact, it had been downright terrifying.

"I hate that the snakes are still doing this!" I shouted, wanting to wring Sesha's neck.

Because the serpents wanted to prove their authority over us, these shiftings of air, water, and land now happened at the most random and unpredictable times—moving land-masses and relocating rivers, repositioning mountains and transposing seas. They were scary, and dangerous—anyone flying during a shifting could easily fall into magical rips in the atmosphere, never to be seen again. The only non-serpents I knew who liked the partitions were the magical cartographers, creators of "moving maps" that could show you where landmasses were in relation to each other at any given time. They were making a bundle off the serpents' cruelty, let me tell you.

The ripping sound happened again, and this time, we saw the rift in the atmosphere form just below us, like a huge, dark gash in the sky caused by a pair of very sharp claws. With a noisy squawking, some ducks who had been flying near us were sucked into the rip in the sky even as the instability of the air pulled all of us closer to the gaping death hole.

"Yeeks!" I shouted, feeling my dinner rising toward my throat.

Toto impaled my shoulder with his claws. "Don't let Toto get made into bird chow!" he wailed. I pried the para-keet off my shoulder and held him tight in my hand.

And wouldn't you know it, just then, the shifting atmosphere made a cloud pass over the moon, dimming her light. My insides quaked. I hated flying at normal times, but flying in the midst of a possible deadly partition in the dark was really the pits.

"Do your thing, Pinks!" shouted Aakash even as I saw a gray outline of my air-rakkhosh friend tumbling headlong through the air. He tried to fight the waves of turbulent air, flapping his wings and waving his muscular arms, but he was clearly losing. "Hurry up already!" he yelled in a less-than-calm voice.

Both the helicocroc that Arko and I were riding and the one carrying Chandni and Kumi now lurched toward the gaping hole in the atmosphere as well. The flying crocodile creatures let out terrible guttural screeches, clawing at the forceful wind with their sharp-taloned feet. Both Chandni and Arko, who were sitting in the front, pulled at the animals' harnesses, but it was of no use. It was going to be up to me.

"It's too dark, I can't see what I'm doing!" I shouted, leaning to peer around Arko's back. "Tell your moon mother to shine more brightly, Chandni!"

"Like she listens to anything I say!" Chandni shouted back. She wasn't lying, of course. Even though Chandni was a resistance leader, her mother the moon was actually a serpent collaborator. If it hadn't been for her, the sneaky snakes could never have left their undersea realm and invaded the Kingdom Beyond in the first place.

"I'll try to get you closer so you can see better!" Arko yelled. His voice was firm and confident. It felt good to be on the same side again.

"It's too dark! I can't see the gap!" I yelled into the now-whipping air. I handed Toto to Arko, and leaned even farther around Arko's back. As I did, though, some duck feathers shot out of the midair rip in space, practically landing on my face. I coughed and spluttered, picking them out of my teeth. "I need to be a little closer!"

"I don't know how much closer we can get without getting pulled in ourselves!" Arko shouted. I could see he was trying to maneuver the helicocroc sideways so I'd have a better angle of approach to the now-practically-invisible rift. Even though we couldn't see the rip in the air, it didn't mean we couldn't feel it, of course. My eyes felt gritty and face sore from the force of air shooting out of the scar in the middle of the air. Poor Toto, now tucked into Arko's pocket, yelped and squawked.

"You'd get a better angle if you did the thing you did before—on Raat's back!" Chandni shouted. The helicocroc she and Kumi were riding was sliding even more precariously toward the sucking gap in the air. The animal was batting its wings against the onslaught of wind but failing to make much headway. It let out a horrible, metallic wail.

"Whoa!" Unexpectedly, Aakash lost his grip on the air and started hurtling, head over heels, toward the rift.

"Catch him!" I shouted.

Arko and I were too far away to rescue our air-rakkhosh friend. Chandni reached for him and missed. Kumi then lunged, catching Aakash's hand. Unfortunately, the pull of the partition was too strong—as Aakash got pulled more toward it, there was a horrible cracking sound as Kumi's arm broke and Aakash slipped through her grasp. Kumi screamed, both from the pain of her now-obviously-dislocated arm, and from the frustration at losing Aakash.

"Get him!" I shouted again, worried our friend was about to follow in the very unlucky footsteps of those ducks.

"Help me, yaars!" Aakash bellowed, trying to clutch at something, anything, as he fell through the air.

And then, just in the nick of time, Kumi and Chandni's helicocroc grabbed Aakash by the wing tip with two of his sharp teeth. We heard poor Aakash's wing rip, and his yelp of pain, but at least he was safe.

The wind was still swirling around us, like strong,

ghostly arms pulling us inexorably farther toward the rift in the sky. I couldn't let any more of my friends get hurt. I wouldn't. I would have to do the thing that scared the fangs of me.

"Don't let me fall, princeling!" I muttered, rising from a sitting position to a kneeling one on the helicocroc's back.

"What are you doing?" Arko's eyes shot to mine, wide in the dim moonlight. "In this wind, you'll fall!"

"I need to get a better angle on that rift if I'm going to have any hope of closing it!" I shouted. I gulped, already feeling unsteady. I gripped tightly on to Arko's broad shoulders, trying to still the jelly shaking of my legs as I stood up in the helicocroc saddle. The wind howled mercilessly around me, making my sari and hair lift and dance. I felt like a kite, unsteady and unsure. Could I do this? Could I aim my fire and stop the partition like this, way in the middle of the air, unmoored and in the dark?

Arko turned, looping one strong arm around my legs. "I won't let you go!" he promised.

I was still scared but felt a jolt of strength coursing through me, as if from Arko's hands, through my limbs, and straight into my three pounding hearts. I gulped, trying to moisten my dry throat. "Here goes nothing!" I roared, opening my mouth and letting my fire fly.

Even in the semidarkness of the half-shaded moon, I could see the midair gap enough now to aim accurately at it. My flames coursed into the space caused by the partition, filling it and healing the gaping wound in the sky, like glue poured into a three-dimensional tear. I sent more flames after, and then more still, all the while holding on to Arko's shoulders for dear life, and feeling his arm clamped around my legs as well. I filled the gap with flames of fire until it was healed and sealed. The wind died down slowly, and then all at once. Like a light switch being turned on, the cloud parted from in front of the moon's face, and we could again see our way through the darkness. I collapsed back into a seated position on the helicocroc, feeling shaken and nauseated.

"You did it!" Toto cheered.

"Good job," Kumi said, her arm at a seriously unnatural angle.

"I'm glad we'd already figured out that your fire was the only element not affected by the partition," said Chandni, looking wide-eyed and windblown. "I thought we were all goners there!"

Aakash was sitting on the other helicocroc now with Kumi and Chandni, his bent and broken wing obviously too injured to fly. "Good job, Pinks," he said in a gruff voice. "Thanks for saving us!"

I took a good look at my air-clan and water-clan friends. They were both pale-lipped, one holding his crooked wing and one holding her arm at a strange, painful-looking angle. "You're both really hurt! You three are going to have to go straight to Ghatatkach Academy."

"No, Pinks, I'm good, I can go on to the Raja, help you find Bangoma and Bangomee," Aakash insisted. Kumi, uncharacteristically, said nothing, but a soft groan escaped her lips.

Chandni gave our friends a critical look. "Pinki's right. I'll get these two to the Ghatatkach infirmary to get patched up."

Arko nodded. "Pinki and I will go and get the money from my father and then meet you at the rebel headquarters, Chandni."

"All right, that sounds like a plan," Chandni agreed as our two helicocrocs veered off in different directions from each other.

As our three friends flew back toward school, growing smaller in the moonlit sky, Arko turned to me. "Let's go get that money from my dad."

"Let's go rescue your brothers," I agreed.

"Can Toto maybe have a snack at the palace?" asked the little bird.

Arko and I both laughed. "Sure, birdie," Arko agreed. "All the birdseed you want."

"Birdseed? No birdseed!" Toto retorted as we flew on into the night. "I want some caviar, some ilish mach, a regular fourteen-course meal!"

"We'll see" was all Arko said, but from the warm tone of his voice, I could tell that he might actually be beginning to forgive me. And that was all I could ask for.

CHAPTER 22

Rontu the Raja Are Not Words I Ever Thought I'd Have to Say

It was just past dawn when we landed in the thick woods around Arko's father's marble palace. The filigreed turrets and archways gleamed in the sun, and lush flowers bloomed all along the high walls. We crossed the wide lawn where Chandni and I had once attended a fancy outdoor party. Now the green expanse was empty except for us and, at the far end of the green expanse, a cawing, dancing pair of peacocks, their mighty tails spread out in full splendor.

"Everyone will be asleep. We will have to wait again until nightfall," Arko said, kicking a bit of gravel on the paved path.

"I'm sorry we didn't get here sooner," I said, stifling a yawn. It was an incredible bummer that we'd have to wait for so many hours before we could approach the Raja about the money we'd need to hire Bangoma and Bangomee.

"Why's everybody asleep during the day?" Toto squawked, looking around.

"Don't you remember? Arko's entire household is under a sleeping spell during the days, a time when his brothers are all turned into champak flowers!" I explained to the bird. Toto really had the worst memory. "He's the only one not affected by the curse."

"Are you sure about that?" squawked Toto.

"Yes, of course, why?" Arko sleepily rubbed at his eyes.

"Well, that fellow coming over there sure seems like one of your brothers." Toto pointed with a feathery wing. "And he doesn't look anything like a flower!"

Arko and I turned, and actually both gasped. There he was, Arko's youngest brother, Rontu, meandering casually in our direction from the royal stables. He was whistling, and tossing some kind of jewel in the air as he did. He was dressed in fancy silk clothing, even though he was a little rumpled, like he was just coming in now from a long night of partying. And the thing is, Toto was right. Rontu looked fully human, and absolutely nothing like a champak flower.

"Rotting rakkhosh guts!" I muttered. Arko and I had

discussed me donning a human disguise once I got to the palace, just so as not to scare all the palace servants. But since I'd fully expected them all to be asleep, I hadn't bothered. Now I quickly spun in a circle, turning back into my disguised, human form. I only hoped that Arko's youngest sibling hadn't caught sight of me before I'd done so.

"Rontu?" Arko ran the last few steps over to his brother, embracing him. "How can this be?"

"Bor-da?" Rontu's beady eyes shifted left and right. Who was he looking for? "Are you okay? Should you be here right now? Aren't you under snake arrest?"

"How'd you know about that?" squawked Toto.

"Who's this?" Rontu laughed, putting out his hand for the yellow bird. Toto, that complete fink, flew over to land on it.

"This is Toto, a friend," said Arko briefly. "But tell me, how are you not under a spell right now?" Arko was still grasping his youngest brother's shoulders in a kind of stunned marvel.

Rontu opened his mouth, like he was about to explain, then caught sight of me. "You've brought the Lady Pinki with you!" He got free of his brother's embrace and ran eagerly over to me, grasping my hand in his own slightly sweaty one. "Oh, my lady! You are looking even more beautiful than the last time I saw you . . ." Rontu trailed off before he waxed poetic about my height and strength, which he'd been enamored with the last time we met. The prince had a confused look on his face. "It must be that I didn't sleep too much last night, because I would swear you looked different just a moment ago?"

On Rontu's shoulder, Toto cackled in amusement. I shot the bird a dirty look.

"Different?" I echoed, artificial amusement in my voice. I tried to pitch my tone higher and make myself sound more simpering and foolish, how I imagined real human ladies must sound. I cracked my neck, shaking my hair over my shoulders. "Like different how?"

"I'm not sure." Rontu frowned, looking both pleased and a little befuddled. His eyes kept going to my head, like he had somehow caught a distant sight of my horns before I'd transformed.

"Maybe you're stunned by seeing her full beauty in the light of day," Arko suggested, coming back over to stand next to me. I shot the older prince a dirty look.

"Sure, that must be it," said Toto snidely. This time, both Arko and I shot him warning looks.

"My poor eyes are stunned by this vision before me, like a parched desert traveler who doesn't know how thirsty he is until he reaches the oasis." Rontu smiled goobily, still staring at me. I could tell he was about to start kissing my hand, or laying on the slobbery admiration again, but Arko cut him off.

"You haven't explained how you're awake, little brother," Arko repeated. "Did you find a way to break the champak curse?"

Rontu looked shifty, and I couldn't tell if he didn't want to answer Arko's question or if he was embarrassed to be seen next to his rebel brother in the open. "Let's go inside and I'll tell you."

The young prince led the way to an open portico at the front entrance of the palace. Once we were inside the open courtyard with its burbling central fountain and draping, fragrant flowers, I realized that we weren't alone. There were servants bustling this way and that down an open-air hallway a few yards away, like they were busy with their morning chores. Which was pretty strange, since the curse that had caused all the brothers Champak to become flowers during the days made their entire household sleep.

"Spill it, Rontu," I demanded. "How'd you break the curse?"

Rontu grinned. He was sitting on the edge of the inlaid marble fountain and flipping the jewel in his hand up into the air again. He caught it with particular relish, smiling at the jewel in a way that felt creepily familiar. "There's always a way through any tough situation when you're the particular friend of the prince of snakes."

"You mean you're the particular friend of Sesha?" I frowned, flicking my hand through the cool, running water of the fountain. My inner fire made the water sizzle and evaporate a little, so before Rontu could notice, I removed my hand again. "Are you telling us the champak spell being broken has something to do with Sesha?"

"Oh, yes, my lady!" Rontu placed a sloppy kiss on my hand, which made me want to stick my hand back into the fountain. "Since my ever-so-noble brothers have gone off on their mad quest to become rebels, I've been doing things the smart way. I've been cultivating my friendship with those in power. There's no end, you know, to the favors that money and power can buy!"

"You got the snakes to reverse the champak curse?" Arko, who had been pacing around in front of us, now stopped, staring at his brother. He seemed as stunned as I. "Do they even have the power to do that?"

"Not the power, but the money! I got my very close friend Sesha to pay for the curse to be lifted off not just me but all of us—he's got no end of magical creatures and whatnot working for him, you know!" Rontu burbled, batting his stumpy eyelashes at me. If he thought that this was information that would impress me, he was sadly mistaken.

"You got that snake to lift the curse in exchange for what?" Arko demanded. "Rontu, you fool! Don't you see that you've played right into his hands?"

"Don't you call me a fool!" Rontu snapped, standing up. "I'm not a fool, unlike all my older brothers. I'm not the one who got myself arrested; I'm not the one who's abandoned my duties as a prince! In fact, I was selfless; I got the curse lifted from all of you!"

"I'm sorry for leaving you," began Arko, but I interrupted him. There was exactly zero reason, in my mind, for Arko to apologize to his baby brother. Especially now that we knew his baby brother was kissing up to that slimeball Sesha.

"Guess who just put all of your other brothers into a wormhole to jet them across the multiverse? Guess who is systematically trying to split up families, making people sacrifice their elders?" I pushed my finger accusingly into Rontu's squishy chest. "Your great friend Sesha, that's who."

Rontu looked stunned. "Well, that can't be right. He wouldn't do that to me. I mean, I just came from a great night playing pasha with him. He didn't mention anything to me about that. Are you sure that all my brothers are gone?"

"You just came from gambling all night with Sesha?" Arko thundered. "Little brother, what has gotten into you?"

"What's gotten into *me*?" Rontu looked like he was about to cry. "What's gotten into *you*? You deciding to become an anti-serpent rebel is one thing, but then luring our other brothers into your ridiculous schemes! If there's anyone to blame for whatever's happened to our brothers, it's *you*, Bor-da. You're the one who's forgotten your duties! You're the one who made them forget theirs!"

Arko's face twisted in shock and, if I was right, a good deal of guilt. "Fine, blame me if that makes you feel better. But you must see that you cannot continue this friendship with the snakes?"

"I see no such thing!" Rontu blustered, puffing out his chest.

"Enough!" I stepped in between the warring brothers, as this conversation was getting us exactly nowhere. "Prince Rontu, listen, we've come to speak to your father. We think we actually might have an idea of how to get your brothers back."

Rontu's face softened only a little when he turned from Arko and to me again. But then he started to look shifty again. "Well, unfortunately, you can't speak to my father. Not unless you know how to enter into dreams, that is."

I had a brief flash to how I'd spoken with Hidimbi, as if in a dream.

Arko frowned. "He's asleep? I thought you said Sesha lifted the champak curse."

Rontu said nothing, lowering his eyes. He suddenly became very occupied with playing with the water in the fountain, like a prince without a care in the world. He took Toto off his shoulder and held the birdie out on his finger so the parakeet could drink directly from the flowing water. Which, of course, Toto did, like the little kiss-up he was. The bird was clearly enjoying life in the palace.

"Little brother?" asked Arko suspiciously. "What have you done?"

"I haven't done anything." Rontu sniffed, his posture defensive. "Just that, as Sesha explained it, there's some costs involved with lifting such extensive curses. The magic of the escaping curse has got to find a place to go."

"So you lifted the curse from everyone else and dumped all that magic on your father?" I asked accusingly. Even Toto looked up from his water drinking in surprise. I felt a chill cross my skin. Just like Sesha, Rontu was clearly not that bothered by getting rid of his elders.

"I didn't realize . . ." began Rontu as Arko grabbed him by his lapels.

"Does he ever wake up?" the older prince snapped, shaking Rontu a little like he was a wet rag. "Or is he asleep all day?"

I gently disentangled Arko's hands from his brother. "Nonviolence, remember, Arko?"

My friend seemed to recollect himself, flushing under his brown skin. "I'm sorry, Rontu, I forgot myself there for a moment."

"I'll say!" Rontu sniffed, dusting off his sherwani. "You certainly did!"

I crossed my arms over my chest. "I notice you didn't answer your brother's question, though. Is your father cursed just during the days, like before, or does the extra magic somehow make him sleep all the time?"

"Well, the thing is . . ." Rontu hesitated, twisting a jewel-encrusted ring around a meaty finger. "He hasn't actually woken up yet."

"How long has Father been asleep?" Arko roared. Toto flew into the air, tweeting in fright.

"Since I lifted the curse on the rest of us," Rontu admitted. "Six weeks ago."

It struck me that the fact that Arko's brothers had been unaffected by the champak curse this whole time could be because of Rontu, not because of anything to do with sunlight not entering the rebel cave complex.

"Wait, are you telling me our father has been in a cursed sleep for *six weeks*?" Arko yelled, grabbing his brother's collar again. This time, he lifted the shorter boy a good few inches off the ground. As gently as I could, I disentangled his fingers from Rontu's clothing. Arko didn't even notice, but went on, "How could you do this? Besides which, who's been ruling the Kingdom this whole time?"

At this, Rontu seemed to stand up straighter, shaking himself off. He turned toward his older brother, his face haughty. I took in a breath. Rontu's arrogant expression reminded me very much of Sesha. And then the younger prince cemented the similarity by raising one dark eyebrow in a gesture that was so like Sesha's he must have copied it.

"Who's been ruling the Kingdom?" Rontu spat out. "Well, since you and all our other siblings have been out playing anti-snake rebel, big brother, I've been ruling the Kingdom."

Toto let out a little trumpet call of "toot-toot-toot-toot!" Then the bird flew in a circle around Rontu's head before landing on his shoulder. Toto puffed out his yellow chest, like he was some kind of royal minister. "All hail the Raja Rontu!"

Arko frowned, his face so furious, I was seriously worried for Rontu's safety. And for Toto's, honestly. I guess nonviolence only went so far.

The flames of anger were rising in my chest too. It was

glaringly obvious to me why Sesha, who had once tried to manipulate me into a deal with him, had agreed to seemingly help Rontu. It was definitely to the Serpent Empire's benefit to have incompetent Rontu in charge of things in this little sub-kingdom of the Kingdom Beyond. Not that Arko's father, the Raja, hadn't been a snake lover, but how much better to be able to control a young, weak-willed prince who was effectively king?

That snake Sesha had a lot of suffering to answer for.

CHAPTER 23

Rontu Asks for Something I Can't Refuse, but Really, Really Don't Want to Do

Where are my other brothers?" Rontu asked me.

He and Arko were giving each other a wide berth and exchanging some seriously barbed glances. We'd gone farther into the palace in search of a bit more privacy now that everyone in the palace was waking up. Everyone, that is, except the Raja, who slept on in a magical sleep of Sesha's cruel making.

We were sitting in a parlor decorated with low, lush divans and silver tables on which some invisible palace servant had already arranged a tea service and endless amounts of rasagolla, gulab jamun, sandesh, and mishti doi. Clearly, Rontu's sweet tooth was still going strong. The morning light filtering through the high windows crisscrossed the space, making it bright without being too hot. The room was high enough for Toto to fly around, making twirls and dips and dives among the marble pillars and through the filigree railings of the balconies. Toto even tweeted out a slightly off-tune song as he flew. The small bird was clearly living his best life.

I took a sip of my milky tea and gave Arko a warning look before answering Rontu's question. "I told you. Your brothers were sent through a wormhole into some other galaxy," I said, fixing a hard stare at the younger prince. "And it was all because of your good friend Sesha."

Rontu spat out some sandesh from his overfull mouth. "I can't believe that! Sesha must not have realized who they were! Why would he do that?"

Arko made a growling sound. "It doesn't matter if you believe it or not; it's true!"

Since my friend seemed about to lunge over the tea things to grab his brother, I intervened, placing a warning hand on Arko's arm even as I said to Rontu, "But we think there's something you can do to help get them back."

Rontu held up a bit of sandesh for Toto, who landed obediently on the young prince's ringed hand to nibble the sweet out of his fingers. "I want to help my brothers, of course," Rontu said, hesitating a moment before adding,

"But I can't do anything that will jeopardize my relationship with the Serpent Empire."

Arko made another growling noise, and this time I had to physically restrain him from leaping over the tea setting and jumping on his brother.

"I don't think it has to," I said, giving Arko a sharp, rebuking look.

Arko let out a big breath, obviously trying to calm down. He tossed back his cup of tea, swallowing it all in one big gulp, then spoke in a less-growly voice. "We just need to get some funds from the treasury, which, as eldest prince, should be my right to obtain anyway."

Rontu's nostrils flared in offense. I groaned. There was absolutely no reason for Arko to phrase it like that. For someone who apparently believed in nonviolence, my friend was really not great at diplomacy.

Rontu's face was flushed. "You may be the eldest prince, Bor-da, but you abandoned your duty and forfeited your rights the moment you became a resistance leader against our rightful serpent rulers."

"Such a bootlicker, as always!" Arko fumed. "How can you not see that self-rule is coming? The time of serpent oppression is nearing its end!"

"Who are you calling a bootlicker, you rascally resistance rebel?" Rontu alliterated, scattering spittle everywhere.

"Oh, for all the foul fairy farts!" I stood up, feeling extremely irritated at both brothers. "Enough bickering, boys! Let's worry about Aadil, Ishan, Uday, Umran, and Rishi for a moment as opposed to our egos, shall we?"

Both princes deflated, looking chastised.

"Sorry, Lady Pinki," Rontu murmured. He grabbed my hand with his free one, trying to kiss it again. I shook myself free with a frustrated sigh.

"Yes, I'm sure you are," I muttered, then, clearing my throat, went on, "Listen, this is the story—it was those human-faced giant birds, Bangoma and Bangomee, who created the wormhole into which your brothers were punted. And we thought if we had enough funds, we could hire them again, to maybe make a second wormhole that could bring the princes back."

I felt like this explanation required some sustenance, so I sat back down and shoved a sticky rasagolla in my mouth. I sighed, inhaling its fresh, rosewater-scented sweet goodness.

"Bangoma and Bangomee?" Rontu repeated, frowning. Then he copied me, jamming one rasagolla and then a second one into his mouth before continuing. "I wonder that Sesha didn't just use the newly formed transit corridor, like he'd been planning."

"You knew!" Arko roared. "You knew about the transit corridor! You knew the snakes were planning to use it against us, and you chose not to warn us?"

Rontu scooched back on his silk-covered divan, as if worried his brother was going to try and grab him again. "Of course I knew about the transit corridor! But I just thought our serpent government was going to use it against smelly ancient folks past their prime! You know, all those useless oldies!"

"Are you serious? Useless oldies?" I couldn't help blurt out, but Arko shouted so loud at the same time that Rontu didn't even register my comment.

"And all that sounded okay to you?" Arko snapped, shaking his head. "Because our elders, once they've brought us into this world, raised and supported us, educated us and been our role models, are useless, right? I suppose you do think that, since it was obviously so easy for you to get rid of our father and take his place!"

Rontu frowned, his mouth becoming a thin, angry line at his brother's words. "Well, tell me, who are they any good to?"

"Are you kidding me? It was our elders who showed us the way to revolution, and freedom!" Arko shouted. "It's so easy to think that we young people invented everything radical, everything forward-thinking, but that's just self-serving nonsense! Our elders are radical, and visionary, and not expendable!"

I squeezed Arko's arm in warning. I knew he wanted to kill his youngest brother at this point. Heck, I wanted to kill his youngest brother at this point. But I also knew that Rontu was the key to us getting the money we needed to hire Bangoma and Bangomee. We didn't have to like Rontu's choices, but we did need him to open up the royal coffers for us.

"Rontu, I get that you're trying to cultivate a relationship with our rulers," I began, clearing my throat. "I'm sure it's a very clever, uh, plan on your part with only the benefit of your small kingdom in mind. I'm sure you're doing all this to benefit the people whom you effectively rule now that your own dear father is, well, out of commission."

"That's exactly right!" Rontu said, running his hand through his hair. I didn't want to tell him that all he'd done was get a bunch of sticky white rasagolla crumbs in his coiffure. He grinned at me in a besotted way. "I knew you would understand, Lady Pinki! Unlike other people in this room who shall remain nameless, you see me, you know me, you believe in me!"

Arko let out a barking laugh, that he very poorly tried to disguise as a cough. I stepped hard on his foot and smiled at the younger, sillier prince. "Yes, indeed! See you! Know you! Believe in you!" I repeated kind of blankly.

"Everything I did was acting out of a sense of duty to my position and my people!" Rontu was beaming at me now, his eyes all round and shining like a baby calf's. "Of course, I do enjoy a good game of pasha, and Sesha really is the most marvelous player."

"We don't need to hear about your gambling debauches with our serpent overlords!" Arko practically barked.

"No need to be so sensitive, Bor-da!" Rontu whined. "Just because you're not as good of a pasha player . . ."

With an incomprehensible expletive, Arko shot up from the sofa and stormed out of the room. "I need to get some air!" he growled as he left.

"He always was a very sensitive sort," Rontu sniveled, watching his older brother's departing back. "Worried about making inroads with other, lesser communities, like those filthy rakkhosh monsters . . ."

I seriously was going to deserve a medal for making it through this conversation without lighting this complete buffoon of a prince on fire. "So what do you say, Prince Rontu?" I tried to keep the disdain out of my voice, instead lacing it with a good deal of fake friendliness.

"That's Raja Rontu to you, my lady!" chirped Toto from his position on Rontu's shoulder.

"Yes, I suppose you're right, my young bird friend!" Rontu muttered with false humility. "I am the acting Raja of the Kingdom now. It's a heavy burden, but I take it on with full willingness to do my duty! Although"—and here, Rontu picked up my hand again in his own clammy fist—"that burden could be lightened if I had the right queen by my side."

I tried not to laugh. The thought of me marrying Rontu was the most ridiculous thing I'd ever heard. "Well, I think you're a bit young to be thinking of marriage just yet!" I said with tons of fake-jolly ha-ha in my voice. "But in the meantime, how about doing something really noble, really kingly, really romantic, like a hero out of one of those old folktales? Those guys who were always selflessly saving the day?"

Rontu did a little head tilt, cheesily smiling at me. I wondered that a little diamond-shaped light didn't reflect off his tooth, like *ching.* "I always did think of myself as exactly that sort of prince, you know?"

"Of course! I could tell the first time I met you!" I rushed on. "If you give us the money to hire the giant birds, I think you'd be in a win-win situation. I know you love your brothers, no matter if you disagree with their choices. Just give us the money and we'll hire those birds and try and bring the princes back. And I'm sure, as busy as they are with the resistance and fighting for justice and whatnot, they'd be perfectly happy to let you keep up with the business of ruling the Kingdom."

"It's an important business, this ruling of the Kingdom." Rontu frowned at me. "You know, my beautiful, strong lady,

I could never deny you anything, but if my new BFF, Sesha, found out . . ."

"There's no reason he would!" I protested enthusiastically. "That's the beauty of the plan! Your brother Arko and I take all the risk and you none! In fact, you get to keep yourself looking and smelling like a rose, as it were!"

Toto, who was proving to be a serious kiss-up, chirped, "You do smell good, my Raja."

Rontu puffed up at this. "I really do try to pay attention to my grooming, you know? There are so many princes these days who neglect thinking about the smell of their armpits, their breath, their feet."

"But not you!" I said with so much jocularity I thought my cheeks would burst from fake smiling.

Rontu grinned, his eyes becoming slits. "You've noticed my sweet, minty-smelling breath, have you, my lady?"

"Sure!" I agreed nervously, hoping he wasn't about to breathe on me to prove his point. Or, like, take off his nagra shoes and make me smell his feet. "So will you do it? Give us the money, I mean?"

"There was a time when we brothers were inseparable, when we Seven Brothers Champak did everything as one," said Rontu in a small voice. He looked so wistful and young all of sudden, I actually felt bad for him. Then the next thing he said erased that feeling entirely. "What would you give me if I could do you this favor?"

"Give you?" I coughed a plume of uncontrolled smoke. "Also, *this favor*? We're talking about saving your brothers, here. How is that a favor to me?"

Sensing the impending firestorm, Toto tweeted in alarm, flying around my head. He flapped his wings rapidly, effectively dissipating the smoke into the air. I rolled my eyes at the bird. I was pretty much at the end of my rope with this snake-loving prince, and if it wasn't for the fact that I felt seriously guilty for getting Arko's other brothers shot out into space, I would probably have lit Rontu's hair on fire by now.

"Sweet lady!" Toto chirped. "Cool-headed lady!"

Rontu noticed none of this exchange. Or if he did, he didn't understand it. Ignoring Toto, he edged closer to me. "You see, my dear, I know where Bangoma and Bangomee are. In fact, they are the ones who reversed the champak curse upon our household!"

"What are you telling me?" I was so surprised by this turn of events, I didn't even pull my hand away when Rontu took it in his clammy one. "That those magical, giant birds are, what . . . here in the palace?"

Rontu scratched at a spot of rasagolla syrup that had stickily congealed on his chin. "They're too big to house at the palace—it would be havoc to the interior design! They're staying in the stables!"

"But we'd still need money to pay them, right?" I narrowed my eyes, trying to understand exactly how deep Rontu was in with Sesha and the rest of the dirty snakes. Turns out, it was pretty darn deep.

Rontu smiled a secret and disturbing kind of smile. "No, actually. You won't need money to hire them. They'll do what I tell them."

"How?" It was Arko, who'd obviously not walked too far. Or had cooled down and returned in time to hear this last interchange between his brother and me.

Rontu spread his hands wide in a strange, magnanimous gesture. Like he was some kind of wannabe gangster. Or wannabe snake is more like it. "There are some secrets that I need to keep, even from my dearest brother."

Arko's dark brows drew together, and I could tell he was seriously reconsidering the whole ahimsa thing once again. So I jumped in before he could say—or do—anything he regretted.

"It doesn't matter how the birds came to be here, does it, Arko?" I looked, bright-eyed, at my friend. "All that matters is that they're here and under Rontu's control, right?"

"So then take us to them, brother!" Arko said. "What have you been waiting for?"

"Well, now that you mention it, there is something." He stood up from the divan and faced his older brother, Toto on his shoulder. "Something that could make the inevitable risk I face in defying Sesha a bit more worth my while."

"Worth your while!" rebuked Arko. "We're talking about rescuing our brothers here. Are you actually asking for a bribe?"

"Not a bribe! Not a bribe!" protested Rontu, rubbing his hands together in a strange snakelike gesture. "More like inducement for me to cross Sesha's will."

"What's your price?" Arko crossed his arms over his chest, looking absolutely disgusted.

Rontu licked his lips. "Word has come to me through some very, let's just say, reliable sources that you, Lady Pinki, are in some kind of royalty competition."

I carefully put down my teacup and stood up from the divan now too, so that the three of us were facing each other in a strange triangle of distrust. "Word has come to you about this through Sesha, you mean," I clarified.

The prince of snakes had told Rontu this, but he'd obviously not revealed my identity. What in the multiverse was

Sesha playing at? From his previous remarks, I didn't think Rontu would take kindly to finding out I was a rakkhoshi.

Rontu giggled in a weird, awkward way. "Perhaps, perhaps," he verified.

"So she's in a royalty competition, what of it?" Arko demanded, edging closer to me until our shoulders brushed. I could tell he too was nervous about Rontu realizing I wasn't human.

"And I've heard that it's customary for whoever wins this competition to choose a consort, or even two." Rontu shot me a sly look.

"What are you suggesting?" I could feel my three hearts beating hard and fierce, like trapped birds in my chest. *Please don't let him be suggesting what I think he is, please don't let him be suggesting what I think he is*, I thought desperately.

Rontu grinned at me than, his eyes twinkling in a very Sesha-like way. "I've heard you've already promised one particular person that you would have them be your consort if you were elected Queen, Lady Pinki," said Rontu smoothly. "All I'm asking is that for your second choice of consort, you consider someone more human, like yourself?"

"Whoever can you mean, brother?" Arko snapped.

Rontu had the grace to look embarrassed. "Why, that she should choose me, of course!" he said, beaming with pleasure. "So will you do it, Lady Pinki? Will you choose me as your consort if you win this competition?"

CHAPTER 24

That Was Way Too High a Price to Hire Some Magic Wormhole Birds

I coughed. Loudly. Hoping that it might drown out the horror of what I'd just heard. "I'm afraid I must have missed what you said there, Prince Rontu."

Arko was looking at me with a strange expression, and I shot him a look of desperation. I had declared I would take Arko as my second consort—but I hadn't promised it! And if Rontu made me promise to make *him* my second consort instead, there would be no going back on it.

"I want you to choose me as your second consort if you win this queen contest." Rontu raised his voice, practically shouting at me as he said this.

"But, Prince Rontu, you're so young! Also, we hardly know each other! Also, I snore! Not that the consort thing is a romantic partnership—it's more like a political one! But seriously, I do snore, like a dragon!" I was babbling now, and knew it, but couldn't help it. I desperately wanted to get out of this situation but had no idea how to do so.

Arko addressed his brother directly. "Do you mean to say that you won't let us try to rescue our own brothers unless Lady Pinki promises to make you her consort? That's blackmail."

"Blue mail! Red mail! Purple mail!" chirped Toto, jumping from one of Rontu's shoulders to the other.

"Blackmail's such an ugly word, brother." Rontu spread out his hands in a weird evil-genius sort of way. "Think of it more like making it worth my while to risk the wrath of my new BFF, Sesha."

"You disgust me," Arko spat out, looking again like he was ready to plant a punch on his brother's nose.

"Well, why don't I leave you to cool down and then discuss it with Lady Pinki for a moment, brother," Rontu suggested. "I'm going to get a quick change of clothes from last night's rather bedraggled ones, and then I'll meet you in the royal stables, where Bangoma and Bangomee are being kept." Rontu gave me a knowing look that honestly made me want to punch him in the nose too. "I'm assuming you'll have an answer for me by then, lady?"

With Toto still perched on his shoulder, Rontu made a low bow to me and then swept from the room.

Arko spun into action, grabbing my wrist. "Come on, let's get out of here."

I shook him off. "What do you mean, 'get out of here'? Rontu's going to be waiting for us at the stables. Where, by the way, Bangoma and Bangomee are!"

"There's got to be a better way," Arko said, a fierce look on his face. "I'm not going to let you do this."

"Let me?" I bristled, heaving sparks of fire. "You may be a prince, my friend, but have you forgotten I'm a fearsome rakkhoshi? This isn't a question of anyone letting me or not letting me. I do what I want."

"I didn't mean it like that." Arko let out a big, frustrated sigh. Then, unexpectedly, he kind of threw one of the divan pillows from one side of the room to the other. I wanted to say something snarky about nonviolence and decorative pillows but decided against it. Arko made another angry sound—this time more of a muted yell. "I just mean you don't have to go along with Rontu's ridiculous blackmail. We can figure out a different way."

"If I don't do what he asks, he's probably going to stop Bangoma and Bangomee from working with us. And if those giant birds don't make us a wormhole, how will you get your brothers back?" I asked, my voice already resigned.

Arko was pacing around now, absently pulling at his hair until it stuck up in all sorts of weird directions. "I don't know. I don't know. But we'll think of something. We have to think of something."

"What other option do we have?" I asked, feeling both heartbroken and, suddenly, very clear. "Even if we found the money somehow, Bangoma and Bangomee are probably not for sale to anyone that Sesha and your brother don't approve of."

"I can't believe that!" said Arko, sounding like he actually did believe it. "How could Sesha have predicted that we'd come here?"

And then it hit me. That little, secret smile Sesha had given me when we were leaving that mockery of a trial. He probably knew we'd try something like this. And that's probably why he planted the idea about being my consort in Rontu's head. Sesha had been two steps ahead of us this whole time. We'd been doomed to fail from the start.

I felt very, very tired all of a sudden. I turned to Arko, who was rubbing at his neck. "Let's go to the stables," I said simply.

We walked in silence, both lost in our own thoughts,

back over the wide expanse of lawn. Behind us rose the high marble turrets of the palace, now shining with morning sunlight. There were birds singing from the trees, and the peacocks we'd seen dancing before were now by the forest. We stopped for a moment and watched their dance, their beautiful plumage splashed as if a canvas for some other-worldly artist.

I turned my face up, soaking in the warmth of the sun even as I shaded my eyes from its glare. "I'm not sure I'm cut out to be Demon Queen anyway," I confessed.

"I know you don't think so, but you are," Arko answered simply. There was something in his voice that made my three hearts squeeze painfully in my chest.

I kicked a clump of grass a gardener had overlooked when cutting the beautiful lawn. "The truth is, I'm kind of relieved that Hidimbi's crown got stolen. So even if I win, I can't get found out as the imposter I am."

"You're not an imposter," Arko said, his voice gravelly and rough. "But you also don't need a crown to make you the queen you already are."

I felt like crying at his words. Why did he believe so much in me when I didn't even really believe that much in myself? Maybe that's what a true friend was.

"What if I do become Queen, but I'm corrupted by all

that power? I mean, look at your brother, look at Sesha!" I couldn't believe that I was saying the words out loud, from the most inner, secret sanctum of my own insecurities. "What if I gain the crown but wield its power for evil? What if I side with the snakes for shiny favors instead of seeking freedom for my people?"

"You will be a powerful and just queen." Arko took my hands in his own, shaking them a little until I met his eyes. "Do you hear me? I see the goodness in you!"

"Goodness?" I scoffed, involuntarily letting out a puff of smoke.

"Yes, goodness." Arko coughed a little at the smoke, but kept squeezing my hands fiercely. "Righteous, fierce, fiery goodness, like a torch burning for justice!"

"What if I choose the wrong path?" I whispered.

Arko laughed, his own eyes wet now. "Don't you remember, there is no right or wrong path, at least not made by someone else! You will make your right path as you walk it, as you've always done!"

We stood there for a moment, staring at each other, hand in hand. Like the coward I was, I was the first one to break off the eye contact.

My own voice shook as I said, "You know what it means

when a rakkhosh promises something—we can't break our word. Not easily, anyway."

There was a muscle working fiercely in Arko's cheek. "He certainly has a way of getting what he wants, that snake."

I nodded, not sure what to say to that. I looked out beyond the expanse of green toward the palace stables. There were etchings of flying pakkhiraj horses all along the beautiful walls of the building. I thought of flying through the sky with Arko on Raat's back. Until now, I hadn't admitted there was something about being with Arko that made even flying through the air actually tolerable. I thought of all the adventures that I'd assumed were laid out before us. Now all those expectations seemed like they were burning to dust.

"I had an idea of asking someone different to be my second consort, you know." My voice was hoarse, sounding a bit strangled in my throat.

Arko gave me a sideways glance, accompanied by a crooked sort of grin. "You hadn't always been planning on asking Rontu, you mean?"

I let out a bitter little laugh. "I'd never been planning on asking Rontu, and you know that perfectly well."

We walked on a few steps, still holding hands. I could hear the wind moving some distant chimes somewhere. Everything was so golden right in that moment—the light, the peacocks, the chimes; it all made me feel open and raw.

"I was going to ask someone else," I repeated, looking at Arko in the eye. "If he would have me."

"I know. You saved me at the tribunal by declaring it pretty loudly." Arko smiled in a sad way, a movement of his mouth that didn't really reach his eyes. "Pinki, I wish situations were different."

I gulped down a hot fireball of emotion. "Really?" I squeaked, spitting smoke.

Arko didn't say anything for a moment, staring down at his long fingers as he fidgeted with the sleeves of his kurta. "I have to rescue my brothers. You know that, right?" he finally said, squinting at me. "And after that, I have to continue leading the nonviolent revolution."

I nodded, coughing a little from the smoke. "I would never ask you to be someone you weren't," I said unnecessarily abruptly.

Arko looked down at his feet. "I know that, Pinki. In the same way I would never ask you to be who you're not."

I rolled my eyes, gesturing ruefully at my hornless,

fangless self. "Except when you ask me to disguise myself as a human when we visit your home."

Arko chuckled as we kept walking toward the stables. "Can you imagine Rontu's reaction if he really knew who you were?"

I was quiet, as I could imagine what that reaction would be. And it wouldn't be something good. But that didn't matter now. All that mattered was getting Rontu to let us have access to Bangoma and Bangomee.

"I'll do it." I stared at the dancing peacocks as if their beauty would make what I was saying less awful. "I'll promise your brother the consortship, if it'll get him to make us that wormhole."

Arko sighed. "I wish you didn't have to."

I nodded, feeling my stomach twisting painfully. "But I do. How else will you ever find your brothers?"

When Arko didn't answer, I knew he agreed. Something felt broken inside me, and I knew that as much as violence left a scar inside you, nonviolence could too. Neither of us spoke again until we entered the stable, where Rontu was waiting for us.

We entered the high-ceilinged space, smelling like hay and horses and the special honey nectar favored by pakkhiraj horses. As soon as he saw us, Toto flew off Rontu's shoulder in a flutter of excitement. "I've got the job! I've got the job!" the little bird burbled in utter glee.

"Job?" Arko caught Toto and brought him to our face height. "What job?"

The little bird puffed out his chest proudly. "I'm going to be the Raja Rontu's Minister of Humor!"

"Minister of what?" I asked, giving Rontu a quizzical glance. "To be a minister of humor, you'd have to actually be funny, right?"

Toto let out a few tail feathers in annoyance. "I'm funny!"

Rontu smiled and shrugged. "I need a minister of humor. I find my life is rather humorless these days."

"Oh, I think you calling yourself Raja Rontu is plenty funny," snapped Arko, giving his brother a less-than-pleasant stare.

"Well, *acting* Raja Rontu, of course—or rather, Raja Fatteshwar Orebaba, parentheses, Rontu," concluded Arko's brother hastily. He shot me a nervous look, grinning pathetically as he did so.

"Acting Raja, my throne!" Arko took a few big steps toward Rontu, practically growling. "You're going to have to reverse the spell that's over Father. Before we make any kind of deal with you about any kind of consort business."

We'd all walked to the back of the stables, past the pak-khiraj stalls and through to the largest stalls at the back, where the huge, human-faced birds Bangoma and Bangomee were sleeping on enormous piles of hay. They blinked their eyes open at our noisy approach.

"Your Raja father will continue to sleep," said Bangoma with a twirl of his moustaches. "While the snakes in this kingdom do creep."

"What? The fate of my father is connected to the freedom of the Kingdom?" Arko spluttered. "How can this be?"

"Magically his fate is bound," Bangomee intoned, her kohl-lined eyes ancient and inscrutable. All the jewelry she was wearing on her human head, ears, and neck jangled as she spoke. "To those who rule the Kingdom Beyond!"

"That doesn't really rhyme," Toto sniffed from Rontu's shoulder. But he said it in such a low voice, the giant birds didn't hear him.

I had to say, I was on Toto's side on this one. I'd never seen Bangoma and Bangomee this close up, and frankly, the magic human-faced birds were giving me the serious creeps.

"Are you soothsayers as well as wormhole makers?" I scoffed, my nervousness manifesting, as usual, in an extra dosing of aggression. "Why should we listen to the dramatic predictions of some giant and, quite frankly, disturbing-looking birdie freaks?"

I realized right away I'd probably spoken too hastily, because both Bangoma and Bangomee squawked and grew even bigger, ruffling their feathers so much they looked like they were about to explode out of the confines of their stall.

"Lady Pinki didn't mean that!" Rontu reassured the birds, his hands up in a calming gesture. "She's simply awed by your magical magnificence, your eminences!"

"It is not exactly within our rules," Bangoma squawked, his moustaches quivering with annoyance.

"To make a wormhole for any fool," Bangomee concluded. She settled herself rather ostentatiously back on her nest as she spoke.

"My dear friends," Rontu said, bowing to the giant birds. "Please excuse any unintended slights. But we were hoping that we might ask you to create a wormhole for us."

"To the same place your last wormhole went," Arko added quickly. "The one that took the five princes, our brothers."

"We are obviously up to the task," Bangomee said. "But on whose authority do you ask?"

"Well, at least that was better meter, better rhythmicity," muttered Toto.

"Shush! Those giant birds could eat you for breakfast and still be hungry!" I whispered to the yellow parakeet.

"We won't make wormholes for any flakes," Bangoma said, a mercenary gleam in his eye. "Right now we only work for the snakes!"

"They're on retainer from Sesha," explained Rontu self-importantly. "The only reason I'm housing them here in my stables is because I'm Sesha's *particular friend*."

"*Your* stables?" Arko looked angry enough to spit. "Our father isn't dead yet, brother. And if you haven't forgotten, you're not the eldest brother."

"Oh, I haven't forgotten." Rontu turned on his brother, a strange look on his face. I began to see exactly how much influence Sesha had exerted on him in a short period of time. "In fact, you and my other elder brothers never let me forget it. Not in my whole life. And so isn't it interesting that while you all are off playing rebel-rebel, I'm the one stuck here with all the power and responsibility?"

"Maybe if you hadn't allowed the curse you lifted to fall directly on our father, you wouldn't be in this position!" snapped Arko, his brows like thunderclouds.

"Now, boys, this isn't getting us anywhere," I said firmly, stepping in between them. "Let's keep our eyes on the prize?"

"Making the wormhole? Rescuing the princes?" Toto said, stating the obvious.

"I'm not sure my new best friend, Sesha, would be very pleased to hear that I ordered a wormhole made outside of official serpentine business." Rontu raised his eyebrow at me in a poor imitation of the serpent prince. "It's very risky for me."

"Oh, gee, I wonder what could make it worth it for you?" I asked sarcastically.

"Don't you remember?" chirped Toto. "If you were to make him your consort when you won De—"

Before Toto could finish saying the word *Demon*, I squeezed his little beak between my fingers. "Yes, I remember, thank you, Toto. If I win the contest I'm involved in, then you would want to be appointed my consort."

"Your second consort," amended Rontu.

"Right, because you realize you'll always be second to that new friend of yours," said Arko in a dangerous voice.

Rontu ignored his brother. "So will you do it, Lady Pinki?"

"Will I make you my consort if I win the contest I'm in and become Queen?" I repeated, hedging for time. I snuck a look at Arko, but he didn't seem to be able to meet my eye. Instead, the prince seemed very preoccupied with a particularly interesting pile of hay on the floor of the stables.

"Yes," I said, the word shooting out of my mouth like an uncontrolled flame. "I promise to make you my second consort, Rontu, if I get elected Queen."

Arko let out a strangled sound, and now it was me who wasn't able to meet his eye. I too studied that terribly interesting pile of hay.

"Rontu and Pinki, sitting in a tree," began Toto, before I grabbed him, harder than I probably needed to, and shook him a little.

"Enough, bird!" snapped Arko. His voice sounded heavy and rough and sad. Kind of like how I felt inside.

Rontu, on the other hand, looked as pleased as punch. He grinned at me, grabbing my hand before I could pull it away and planting a sloppy kiss on it. "I am so pleased, my lady! I will make you a wonderful consort. Of course, we must discuss what this 'first consort, second consort' business means at some point."

I wondered how Rontu would react if I told him that historically, rakkhosh sometimes killed one consort while picking the other. Not that he even knew I was a rakkhoshi. But now wasn't the time to worry about any of that. Now was the time for action.

"I fulfilled my end of the bargain," I said urgently. "Will you get the birds to make the wormhole?"

"Any risk is worth it for you!" Rontu said in a disgustingly gooby way. He turned to Bangoma and Bangomee. "Will you please make another wormhole to where my brothers went?"

I thought for a second the birds would protest and all my promising would be for nothing. But after a quick, low-voiced consultation with each other, they shrugged and then flew out of the open back doors of the royal stables and into the air. Flying around and around in a circle, they created a pulsing, humming hole between them. A space of possibility vibrating in a range of colors that danced and sang in harmony.

"Time to go, princie!" announced Toto from my shoulder.

"Bon voyage, brother!" Rontu waved with bizarre nonchalance.

"Be careful," I said, suddenly feeling full of far too many things to say to Arko. I grabbed his hand. "Come back quickly."

"I'll try," Arko said, his face sad and intense as it gazed into mine. "But, Pinki, if I don't return . . ."

"Don't say that!" I exclaimed, putting his hand up to my face. "You'll come back as soon as you find your brothers. Say it! Promise it!"

Even though I knew that human promises, unlike rakkhosh ones, were able to be broken, I needed to hear the words.

"I promise," said Arko softly. His brown eyes were alive with heat. Or was he just reflecting my own flames? "I promise, Pinki, I'll return soon."

I felt the fires of hope, fear, and possibility all burning inside me. "Promise!" I whispered again, feeling like the entire multiverse was crashing down on me to see him go. "Promise!"

"I do," he whispered, clutching my hand that one last time. "I will come back."

I had no idea then that Arko, non-rakkhosh human that he was, wouldn't be able to keep his promise.

CHAPTER 25

In Which I Underestimate Rontu's Growing Snakiness

As luck would have it, Chandni showed up at the palace just as Rontu, Toto, and I were walking away from the stables. She had arrived just minutes too late to have seen Arko. I know it wasn't noble or good of me, but it gave me a little spark of joy even in my sorrow that I'd been able to say goodbye to Arko alone and have that time with him to myself.

"Lady Chandni!" gushed an obviously guilty-feeling Rontu as he bowed low over her hand. "What a pleasure to see you again! And looking as shimmery as ever!"

"What do newlywed bees eat on the moon?" asked Toto with an excited chirp.

"I don't know, my friend, what?" said Chandni with a tired smile. I felt like growling inside. Why was the moon girl always so pleasant when I felt like smashing things? I knew I was being unfair. She didn't know what had just happened to Arko. She didn't know that everything felt like it was breaking.

"What do newlywed bees eat on the moon?" Toto flew around our heads laughing in his little birdie way. "Why, they eat moon honey on their honeymoon!"

Chandni gave a polite laugh. Rontu, who obviously had no sense of humor, guffawed loudly. I didn't crack a smile.

"Where is Arko?" Chandni asked, turning to me.

What I told her next wiped that gooby smile right off her face. In fact, true to her character, Chandni immediately started to cry.

"He left without saying goodbye?" she choked out, her face awash with glistening tears.

"There, there, my lady!" With a flowery gesture, Rontu handed her a lace embroidered handkerchief that he pulled, unbelievably, out of his sleeve. He, unsurprisingly, didn't seem upset at all by Arko's departure.

"Arko left to find his younger brothers," I reminded Chandni. "There was no time to lose, no time for goodbyes."

"He said goodbye to you," Chandni said. She didn't say it in an accusing way, but still, it somehow felt like an accusation.

"Come, my ladies! May I offer you a small luncheon? Six or seven courses only. Simple food, really!" Rontu bowed at both of us, obviously delighted to have both our company.

From Chandni's expression, she didn't feel particularly delighted. I didn't either.

"I'm sorry, we should get back." Chandni shook her head politely, her face tense. "I only came to bring Arko and Pinki the news. Something shocking has happened—there's been a coup!"

"A coup?" I repeated. Wasn't that when those in governmental power were overthrown? But the snakes were still in charge, weren't they?

Rontu's face spread in a pleased grin. "So he did it, did he? He actually did it!"

"Who did what?" I repeated. "What are both of you talking about?"

"Sesha." Chandni looked at me with wide eyes. "He's overthrown his father and put himself at the head of the Serpentine Government. He's crowned himself the Serpent King!"

"That's ridiculous!" My mind was whirling with the news. "The snaky army is loyal to the Governor-General, aren't they?"

Rontu's smile widened, and he rubbed his hands together

like some kind of cheesy storybook villain who has success-
fully finished a caper. "Not really. Sesha's been cultivating their
loyalty for years!"

I studied Rontu's face, the pieces of the puzzle forming
an image in my mind. Rontu had, after all, only recently
done something very similar. Just as he had gotten rid of his
own father, the Raja, in order to assume power, so too had
Sesha done the same thing.

"And that's not all," Chandni went on grimly. "As his first
act, Sesha has gotten the Intergalactic Sacrifice Program up
and running. And the first sacrifice through the wormhole
was none other than his own father!"

"What?" I took in a shocked breath. I mean, it's not
like I had any affection for that slimeball of a Serpentine
Governor-General, but for Sesha to send his own father
shooting out through the multiverse! I'd always thought
the kid was scared of his cruel dad! But to yeet him into the
universe like this? It was unbelievable!

"That's why I came!" Chandni explained. "Now the snakes
are already beginning to expel all the elders from the entire
kingdom through the transit corridor! Sesha's actually
making the case that since he sacrificed his own dad, everyone else should be willing to sacrifice their elders!"

I felt a shot of panic at the thought of elders being

separated from their homes, families, and communities—
the only country they'd ever known—sent out to fend for
themselves all alone, who knows where in the multiverse.
"Yesterday the snakes couldn't even get the wormhole
to work!"

"Well, apparently, they fixed it!" Chandni said heatedly,
the color rising in her light brown cheeks.

I whirled on Arko's brother. "And you obviously knew
about all this?"

"I am King Sesha's *particular friend.*" Rontu shrugged
in what I suppose was meant to be a nonchalant gesture but
just looked awkward and goofy. "And he and I agree on one
thing—no need to keep around old folks who are holding
us back! All that cultural respect and honor we're supposed
to pay to them—bah! Why? Old people are a drag!"

"How can you say that?" Chandni asked, her eyes wide
with shock. "So many of our elders lived through so much
more difficult times. Take Lady Pinki's parents; they were
legendary revolutionaries!"

Rontu waved his hand dismissively. "That was a long
time ago!"

"Not really!" Chandni argued sincerely, as if convinced
of the possibility of changing Rontu's mind. "Some of our
elders were, and continue to be, so much more radical than

we are—so much more visionary! It's just ignorance and ageism that makes us think otherwise!"

"That, and the fact that erasing such revolutionary histories serves the oppressor's narrative!" I grumbled. "The snakes will happily glorify their founding serpent fathers, the snaky kings who came before them, but it's really convenient to forget that there is a long history of resistance and strength among their subjects!"

"The snakes have saved this country, made it great again!" Rontu insisted huffily, his face getting sweaty with irritation. "Without them, our foreparents would have run this country into the ground!"

I narrowed my eyes, feeling like biting off a limb from the pompous prince. But I couldn't afford to lose his trust, because I still needed him to do something for me. I forced a pleasant expression on my face, cleared my throat, and tried to change the subject. "So you'll let us know when Arko and your other brothers return?" I asked. "Send a message to Chandni?"

Rontu started. "There's no guarantee my eldest brother finds our lost siblings, of course!" he said, as if to himself.

"What?" Chandni and I both turned on him in practically the same stance—hands on hips, accusing looks on our faces.

"W-well," Rontu stammered, backing up a little. "Wormhole making isn't an exact science, you know. And even if Bangoma and Bangomee were able to send him back to the same place, there's no guarantee he'll be able to find our brothers that easily. And even if he does, how will he get back?"

The heat of fury roared within me, like someone had switched on a flame. My hearts were hammering inside me like three angry drums. Still, I said my next words slowly and carefully. "Arko will get back because that wormhole that Bangoma and Bangomee created will still be there, right?"

"Oh, no." Rontu shook his head, making his ridiculously long hair flip-flop against his head. "Not necessarily. Created wormholes don't last very long."

"Wait a minute." I advanced on Rontu rapidly, threateningly, making the prince reverse directions until his back was against a tree. I pointed my finger into his chest. "The deal we made was to send Arko through that wormhole to find your brothers *and then bring them back!*"

"Well, actually, technically, Lady Pinki, if you remember . . ." Rontu licked his dry lips, looking seriously nervous. As well he should. "The deal was for me to get

Bangoma and Bangomee to *make* the wormhole. We didn't talk about them making a second one to get everyone back."

"Are you being serious right now with this?" I grabbed Rontu's collar. "You better forget about that whole consort business if this is the way that you're deciding to honor our agreement."

"Consort business?" Chandni blurted out, her voice screeching a little on the words.

"I'll explain later," I reminded her through gritted teeth.

Rontu, in the meanwhile, was looking seriously shaken. "Lady Pinki, I didn't mean it like that! Please, don't take offense! I will of course honor our agreement! I just need to, uh, speak with Bangoma and Bangomee to emphasize that they must create another wormhole when my brother is ready to return."

"But how will they know to do that?" Chandni demanded. Even Toto chirped as if echoing the question.

Rontu remained conspicuously silent as Chandni and I exchanged horrified looks.

"Prince Rontu?" Chandni's voice rose with emotion. "How will you know when to bring Arko back?"

That's when something really terrible occurred to me. "Rontu, did you do this on purpose? Are you trying to keep all your older brothers out in the multiverse so you can keep being in charge of the Kingdom?"

I hadn't guessed that Prince Rontu would be so self-serving, but I would put nothing past Sesha. And now that I'd learned what Sesha had done to his father, it didn't seem that unlikely he would convince Rontu to undermine his entire family to keep hold of power.

"No, no, of course not! I would never do something so underhanded—and to my own family!" Rontu protested. His cheeks were now blotchy with red spots of emotion. "Lady Pinki, you cannot think so ill of me! I mean, I do think someone who isn't involved in the rebellion should be running the day-to-day business of our kingdom, but still, I would never do that to my dear brothers!"

"You better not!" I said in my most vicious tone, the rakkhoshi coming out even though I was in human form. Rontu took a couple obvious steps back from the fire of my wrath. "Or else I'm coming after you! And you better forget the whole consort thing!"

"No, of course! I will do exactly as you say!" Rontu promised, his eyes wide and wild. "I will tell the birds right now to make sure they facilitate my brother Arko's return!"

"Toto, you'll tell us the moment Arko comes back to this dimension?" I turned to the bird and stroked his little yellow head. I was realizing it might not be such a bad thing to have a friend—a spy of sorts—employed in Rontu's kingdom.

The bird saluted me in a typically ridiculous way. "Yes, ma'am! Absolutely, ma'am! I will keep my eyes peeled for any sign of Prince Arko's return and let you know posthaste!"

"Let's go, then?" Chandni looked at me doubtfully. I could tell she was troubled, as I was. But what else could we do?

I nodded, suddenly feeling very exhausted. I remembered that I'd been up all night. But more importantly, the fact that I'd arrived here with Arko and now was leaving without him felt downright terrible.

"Let's go see what's going on with those sacrifices at the transit corridor," I said to Chandni as we headed toward her horse and my helicocroc.

It wasn't until we were flying that Chandni turned to me from Raat's back, her face full of horror. "You let Arko go without a plan to get him back? And for that, you promised Rontu he could be your consort too? How did *that* happen, for demon's sake?"

I stretched my fingers on the helicocroc reins and sighed. "Sesha must have planted the idea in Rontu's head. I mean, the kid doesn't even realize I'm a rakkhosh! He just thinks I'm competing in some human royalty contest during which I'll get to choose a consort."

"It's all very fishy," observed Chandni with a sigh. "And in the wake of Sesha getting rid of his father like that!"

"The guy was pretty awful—hitting Sesha all the time and whatever." I remembered how violent the Governor-General had been to his son.

"But to retaliate like this—not in self-defense but in such a cold, calculated way!" The wind lifted Chandni's long hair all around her. "I'm not saying he didn't have cause, but committing that kind of violence will leave a scar on his soul."

"What do you care about Sesha's soul?" I scoffed even as my helicocroc flew way faster than the air speed limit. If only these stupid things had brakes!

Chandni didn't answer right away. When she did look over at me, her eyes were moist with tears. "I've always cared about him. Even when he turned away from the resistance and joined his awful father's cause. Maybe even more then, to tell you the truth."

I felt the shock jolt through me. Had all of Sesha's and my ridiculous attempts at making Chandni jealous actually worked? But Chandni didn't operate on base emotions like jealousy, did she? "What, do you have some kind of a savior complex about Sesha? Think you can reform him or something corny like that?"

From Snowy's back, Chandni shot me a look of pure malice. Huh. Maybe her heart wasn't all full of fuzzy unicorn rainbows all the time. "You wouldn't understand my feelings for Sesha. You wouldn't understand what it means to want the best for someone, to protect someone."

I started in offense. "What do you mean by that?"

Chandni's face was cold and moonlike as she snapped, "Well, you let Arko get sent off into the multiverse without a plan to get him back, didn't you?"

Her words felt like a sock to the gut. But I couldn't argue with her. She was right. I had. And if the prince didn't get back safely, I'd never forgive myself.

CHAPTER 26

Yeeting Elders into Outer Space Is Not Great for a Country's Morale

By the time Chandni and I arrived at the market, I was exhausted. The stress of everything Chandni had accused me of—letting Arko go through the wormhole without a good plan for getting him back—was hitting me. Plus the not sleeping all night. Plus the flying all the way over from Rontu's palace in a tense silence. But it was nothing compared to how stressed I felt when I saw the scene at the bazaar.

As soon as we dismounted our horses, we could hear the sounds. The sounds were horrible, full of sorrow and anger, downright bone-chilling.

"What is that?" I asked Chandni. I thought of shak-chunni, petni, and all the other types of ghosts that usually haunted bamboo groves and muddy bogs. Had the market been taken over by bhoot?

But no, I was wrong. "It's the families," Chandni said, wincing a little as a particularly piercing sound rent the air, cutting through our ears like knives. "It's the families wailing for their grandparents."

I'd never heard a sound of such deep and utter human distress. It made me feel like running away, or screaming, or sticking my fingers in my ears, or burning something down. But instead, I stayed quiet, biting my lip as we continued to walk toward the sounds. If they were feeling such sorrow, the least I could do was witness it.

They were lined up well before we got to the transit corridor, snaking this way and that through the main path of the market. Resigned elders, waiting in line stoically, their years of love and wisdom about to be sacrificed into the ether. Their adult children and small grandchildren clutched at them, crying. Some of the elders were crying too, but most were too stunned to cry, their faces dry and shocked. What kind of a society sacrificed their grandparents without a second thought? They were all being guarded by menacing-looking serpent soldiers who were forcing people forward in line with a poke of their bayonets. There were so many stunned elders, so many weeping parents, so many frightened children, it was quite overwhelming.

"This is unbelievable!" I muttered, glad I'd been too tired to change out of my human disguise just yet. I spotted the sticky-uppy-haired merchant's child who had hugged me on my first visit to the transit officer. He was clutching his grandmother's leg like a barnacle on a rock, a look of terror on his grubby little face. His poor grandmother, white-sari clad but unbent by age, had tears streaming silently down her pained face.

"What are you doing here?" I asked the grandmother angrily, pulling at her thin arm. "Who else is there to care for this child if you are gone?"

The grandmother turned to me, her traumatized face barely registering any recognition. I was still in human form, but still, she looked so shell-shocked she was probably incapable of recognizing anyone. "What can I do? What do you want me to do? If I don't go willingly, the snakes will make him go with me." She pointed to a sign that was plastered on almost all the buildings around us.

Thank You for Participating in the
Intergalactic Sacrifice!
Jettison One Grandparent Into Space

**Today So We Don't Jettison All Your Elders
and Children Tomorrow!
Fill Out All Forms in Triplicate, With
Signatures and Seals Affixed
Tears Will Not Be Accepted as a
Form of Payment
Have a Good Day
#ComplianceOverDefiance**

"How is this happening?" I fumed, turning to Chandni. "Why is this happening so quickly? How were you all-knowing rebels not on top of this more?"

"I was in serpent prison, and then on trial, if you don't remember," Chandni snapped. Then, tiredly, she rubbed her hand over her eyes. "After the coup, this was the first thing that Sesha did, accelerate the Intergalactic Sacrifice Program."

"What in the demon butts is his rush?" I grated out. "Is he trying to erase every family's history just like he's effectively erased his own?"

"Probably." Chandni looked at me sadly, then echoed Arko's words: "Not to mention breaking down the will, the spirit of the people. You take away a people's children, you take away their future. You take away their elders, you take away their anchor, their history, their crown."

Chandni's choice of words, about elders being a family's crown, made me pause. Something was fluttering with fear in my hearts. Then all chaos broke loose.

"It's all you revolutionaries' fault!" screamed a father who was standing nearby us. He pointed accusingly at Chandni, who I guess was a recognizable rebel now, after the recent march, arrest, and trial. "You did this by opposing the snakes and building up our hopes about freedom!"

"Nothing good comes from dreaming about liberty!" shrieked another woman in the line, her face streaked with tears. In her arms was a sleeping toddler, and on her other side was an old man, his face twisted at the thought of leaving his daughter and grandchild. His terror-filled gaze kept shooting to the front of the line, clearly wondering what lay in store for him ahead. "This is the fault of the rebels!"

Others in the line caught on to her sentiment, and I heard them repeating, "The rebels' fault! The rebels' fault!"

I felt my hearts sink, and for a moment, I was glad Arko wasn't here to hear this. The serpents wielded cruelty like a weapon and knew exactly how to break the people down. With this Intergalactic Sacrifice Program, they'd effectively broken the spirit of the people of the Kingdom Beyond and turned them against the rebellion. Instead of seeking freedom, the people were blaming those who sought to break their chains.

I was just turning my face away from the distraught families when I saw her far at the front of the line. Too far to get to. But there was no mistaking her. No, it couldn't be! But it was—that height, that thin-haired bun, those sloping shoulders, those glowing green wrist cuffs.

"Ai-Ma!" I shrieked, and despite the distance, my mother heard and turned toward my voice, my need. As she always had my entire life.

"Pinkoo, no!" Ai-Ma yelled, tears erupted from her eyes. "Go! There's nothing you can do!"

I looked desperately around me. Chandni had spotted Ai-Ma too and had begun trying to jostle her way through the impenetrable crowd. "Ai-Ma!" she howled. "They're taking Ai-Ma!"

"You think?" I spat out, desperation and fear making me mean.

Chandni met my eyes with her own tear-filled ones, and I felt myself melt a little. As much as we'd been at odds lately, I knew Chandni loved Ai-Ma, and I knew she was as desperate to rescue her as I was.

"Stop!" I yelled, feeling the panic building up in me.

As much as I didn't like to admit it, Ai-Ma was the anchor keeping me from getting swept up by every storm—even those created by myself; she was what kept me from sinking in this life. Or more to the metaphor, what kept me from burning myself up from the inside out. And she was a hero, so much more kind and noble than I was—probably could ever be. She had sacrificed so much for the country, for me, and now *this* indignity was to be her fate? *This* was how it would end—lined up like livestock, waiting to be jettisoned into space like so much garbage?

"Stop!" I yelled again. I wasn't sure if I was begging Chandni, my mother, or the serpentine soldiers when I yelled, "Please, don't do this! Please, don't take my mother!"

"Get away from here, you filthy rebel scum!" shouted a snake, lifting the butt of his bayonet as if to pummel me with it. I still looked like a human, so I suppose he was confident in being able to bully me. The soldier was quite surprised, I think, to find his feet suddenly burning from an inexplicable trash fire that spontaneously lit up under him.

"Hey, how did you do that?" he yelped as some of his snaky friends helped him put out the angry inferno.

It gave Chandni and me a chance to run away from the soldiers and view the scene from behind the awning of an abandoned shop. I looked at my friend in desperation. We had to rescue Ai-Ma before she reached that transit corridor. And there was only one of us powerful enough to take on all these soldiers.

"Do your moon-magic trick! Where you summon your staff and fell everyone in sight!" I was practically shaking the girl now. "My fire power can't take on all these soldiers—not without risking harming these innocents in line too! Only you have the power to stop this!"

"But, Didi, you know I can't use violence." Chandni's voice choked a little as she said this.

"Are you kidding me?" I protested. "Enough with the ahimsa stuff! If there was ever a time for violence, it's now!"

Chandni looked like she was about to cry. She shot another worried look at Ai-Ma, way forward in the snaking line of elderly prisoners, all lined up for sacrifice. I looked too, the grim realization dawning on me that plenty of the elders in front of and behind Ai-Ma were also wearing the glowing green shackles. The snakes had obviously used those magic bracelets to transport all these legendary ex-resistance fighters here when they wanted.

"I think I have another plan," Chandni said, her voice shaking.

"Think? Or know?" I demanded.

"We have to speak to Sesha," she said firmly.

"How did I know you were going to say that?" I muttered bitterly.

Chandni whirled and demanded of one of the soldiers, "We need to see the prince . . . I mean, the King of Snakes!"

The soldiers began laughing rudely. "Oh yeah? And I need to dance the cha-cha with the Queen!"

I groaned. Chandni was such a dope. Did she really think that just asking to speak to Sesha would cause the guy to spontaneously appear from thin air?

But apparently, when it was the moon maiden asking, that was exactly what happened.

CHAPTER 27

Blargh! We Have to Negotiate with Sesha, Again.

Y ou wanted to see me?" asked a deep voice from above us.

The laughing soldiers shut up abruptly, bowing low when we all realized who was in the balcony of the building just behind us.

"Sesha!" Chandni began, but he gestured impatiently for us to join him up in the balcony.

Desperately, Chandni and I dashed up the stairs to the balcony on which Sesha was standing. There were no niceties, no polite chitchat. Sesha was leaning against the railing in another velvet outfit like some kind of overdressed troubadour. I was in no mood for his self-important posturing. I whirled back into my full rakkhoshi form, then charged at him, spitting fire.

"What do you want to make this horror stop?" I demanded, pointing down to the snaking line of frightened elders waiting to be sacrificed. My voice was shaking from emotion and exhaustion, but I didn't care.

Sesha blinked at me a few times, as if clearing dust from his eyes. Then he looked at Chandni for a long, hard moment before turning his gaze back to me. He dug a pomegranate out of his ridiculous velvet capes and cracked it open with just his palms, allowing the red juice to pour messily over his hands like blood.

"Sesha, are you okay?" Chandni demanded, her voice shrill and high. "What happened with you and your dad?"

Sesha raised that one wicked eyebrow of his as he messily scooped a bunch of seeds into his mouth, not caring that his face and hands were now covered in juice. Carefully, deliberately, he chewed and swallowed. "I'm more than okay, my dear. I'm the king of the entire Serpentine Empire! And no irritating Daddy Dearest to hamper me!"

"That's not what I'm asking!" Chandni insisted. She pointed at Sesha's chest, as if at the very location of his heart. "I'm asking about *you*. The boy I know is still somewhere inside there."

I rolled my eyes. I honestly didn't care that much about what happened with Sesha and his dad. I mean, wasn't it obvious? Sesha's dad was a violent jerk, so Sesha decided to become a bigger jerk and yeet his dad into the multiverse while taking over all his power. Seemed pretty simple to me. And no matter what Chandni liked to tell herself, there was no sweet-hearted boy inside Sesha's mean exterior. I mean, what was she even thinking?

"How do we get you to stop the intergalactic sacrifices, Sesha?" I demanded. "You can't throw the grandparents of this realm away from their families and out into who knows what galaxy like this! You're taking away their history, their strength! Also, my mom!"

"Also, her mom, who is awesome!" added Chandni, reaching out to touch my shoulder.

Sesha wiped his messy lips with the back of an even messier hand before looking at Chandni with an intensity I'd never really seen before. "You want me to rescue Pinki's Ai-Ma?"

Chandni smiled, seemingly sure of her hold over him. "Yes, with all my heart."

Sesha studied her face for a moment, then looked over at me, digging out another bunch of pomegranate seeds as he did so. He tossed them back, saying, around his full mouth, "Fine, Pinks, I'll save your mother. I'll even save all these other worthless elders." He made a vague gesture to all those lined up below, before fixing his gaze at me again. "For a price."

Chandni took in a shocked breath, like she couldn't believe this guy who she knew perfectly well was a villain was actually acting like . . . a villain. I narrowed my gaze, crossing my arms over my chest. "What do you want this time?"

Sesha noisily finished chewing and swallowing, then grinned, his mouth shiny and red with fruit. "Become Demon Queen now. Make me your consort now."

Chandni and I stared at Sesha, open-mouthed, both unable to process what he was telling us.

"You've got to be kidding—" Chandni said, but Sesha cut her off with an elegant wave of his hand.

"I never kid. Especially not on a matter like this." He raised a dark eyebrow in my direction before slurping up a few more pomegranate seeds.

"I know you're not serious!" Chandni protested again in her delicate voice. "Sesha—"

He cut her off again with a sharp gesture of his ringed hand. "You know nothing about me," he said harshly, slamming the fruit he was holding against the balcony railing and effectively decimating it. The soldiers below looked up in alarm, but he waved them off impatiently, wiping his hands on his cloak.

"Sesha!" Chandni tried again.

"What?" he snapped, finally whirling toward her. Unlike at our last meeting, when Sesha looked at Chandni with almost-unhidden puppy-dog love, now his lip kind of sneered in mockery. I felt her tense next to me, unused to this kind of treatment from him. But I could tell, even if the moon girl could not, that Sesha was still in love with her. He was just using anger to mask it. It was ironic that I could see the parts of Sesha's personality that Chandni was clueless about. Because the other thing he was using to mask his emotion was, well, me. I was like an emotional shield he was holding up in between his beloved moon girl and himself.

"Become Demon Queen. Make me your consort," repeated Sesha, looking at me with those intense eyes of his. "And if you do, then I'll call off the IGSP, the Intergalactic Sacrifice Program."

I stared down at the lines of elders below me, trying to find Ai-Ma's tall gray head in the masses. It felt like a punch to the gut when I found her, still there, still patiently waiting to be sacrificed. Then I stared over at Chandni's stricken face, feeling something bitter and vengeful coursing through me.

"Yes, fine, great," I said in a much louder voice than I had to.

"What?" Both Chandni and Sesha turned to me.

"I'll become Demon Queen as fast as possible. I'll be delighted to make you my consort, oh, you little sneaky serpent of sin!" I crooned, my voice over-drippy with fake emotion.

There was a moment or two of utter silence, as Chandni and Sesha continued to stare at me. Chandni's luminous face changed colors, and her mouth and brows tightened ominously.

Sesha, on the other hand, grinned slyly. "Well, that's fantastic to hear because it's certainly my heart's desire to become your consort, Queen Pinki, my darling demented demonic dear!"

"Why?" Chandni had her hands crossed over her chest and an adamant expression on her face. "Why do you want to be her consort so badly?"

Sesha raised that wicked eyebrow again. "Why do you think?"

Chandni flushed uncomfortably but still held her ground. "Why really?"

Sesha gave her a look so full of jealousy and insecurity and attraction I felt like flicking Chandni upside the head. Didn't she get it? This entire consort thing wasn't about me at all. It was about making her—Chandni—jealous. It always had been and still was. And at some level Chandni had to know that, which was what frustrated me even more. I felt the flames of irritation burning at me. It really didn't feel good to be a pawn in somebody else's game.

"Is it so hard for you to imagine he's transferred his affections to me? Or that maybe he respects me as a rebel more than he respects you?" I spun on Chandni, throwing words at her like weapons. "All this nonviolence crap. I mean, has it ever occurred to you, moon girl, that what he liked you for was your strength and bravery? And that maybe this wimpy version of you is disgusting to him?"

Chandni stared at me open-mouthed, her eyes filling with moisture. Then she cleared her throat. "Well, all that matters is that we shut down that evil transport of grandparents into outer space."

I had the grace to feel bad. I don't know why my words always came out harsher than I meant them, especially with Chandni. And the truth was, I didn't think nonviolence was as useless as I initially had—hadn't I used Arko's teachings as a way to get out of some scrapes of my own?

In the meantime, Sesha looked at us and raised an eyebrow, making me feel like I was talking to Rontu again. "As I've said, in order for me to shut down the IGSP, you have to make it worth my while."

Chandni grunted with disgust, which only made Sesha grin wider. Clearly, his plan to bother her by using me was working.

"You're a snake, you know that, right?" I volunteered, feeling just too beat down to fight any of it anymore.

"Clearly." Sesha made a showy hand gesture, indicating his whole body. "And you love it."

"Every second we wait, there's more elders getting sent out into the multiverse," Chandni ground out, her voice shrill and stressed. "Just stop it, now."

Sesha nonchalantly fixed his cuffs. Then ostentatiously cracked his neck. "You want something from me. I want something from you."

"You want me to make you my consort, but I have to win first," I blurted out.

"Then I guess you'll have to convince your little air- and water-rakkhosh friends to drop out, won't you?" Sesha gave me a seriously creepy smile. "I heard they both got pretty injured recently. So it might not be that hard to convince them."

"How did you know about Aakash and Kumi getting hurt?" I shivered as a cool breeze shot through the forest like a warning. "It was the middle of the night, in the middle of the sky."

"There are a lot of things I know about, my little demonic darling. If you hadn't noticed, I am the most powerful person in this land now; there's nothing beyond my noticing!" Sesha said with a sinister smile. "Whether in darkness or light, whether on land, in air, or in water."

"But not fire," I couldn't help retorting. I wasn't even sure what I meant by that, but I couldn't bear to let slimy Sesha get the last word.

"Well, that's why I want to be your consort so badly, don't ya know." Sesha reached out a lazy finger and twirled a strand of my curly hair in it. I slapped his hand away, making him smile even broader.

"Why *do* you want to be my consort so badly?" I couldn't help asking.

Sesha gave a long, hard look at Chandni, and I saw, in a passing moment of vulnerability, his past self. The Sesha who had been a revolutionary, working at cross-purposes to his father. The Sesha who had been Chandni's friend. I realized in a flash that his love for Chandni was as much about her as it was about Sesha's desire to go back in time and find that past version of himself, that past self he could better like and respect. He wanted to find and walk that path again, and thought I might illuminate his way, like a light in the darkness.

As if remembering my question, Sesha finally turned to me. "Why do *you* think I want to be your consort?" Sesha dropped his voice into a growl, like he was playacting the role of a dashing hero in a romantic movie. It felt gross, and fake, and if the situation wasn't so dire, I would have laughed. As it was, I really didn't feel like laughing at all.

"Isn't that why you got rid of your father and became the ruler of the Serpent Empire?" Chandni asked in a soft voice. She played with a strand of her hair as she did so. "So you could do things differently? So you could do things right?"

I raised my eyebrows in surprise. It seemed Sesha wasn't the only one good at playacting here.

The prince of snakes looked like he was going to take the bait. He pitched and swayed as if being pulled toward Chandni by some invisible, magical force in the air. But then he coughed and righted himself.

"When I'm consort to the duly elected Demon Queen, then and only then will I stop the transit corridor program," he said firmly. "Although, to show you my goodwill, I will happily halt the sacrifice of Pinki's demonic mother."

I couldn't help but feel my hearts lift as Sesha gestured to the guards below and, with a quick few commands, got them to pull Ai-Ma out of the line. She looked startled as they got to her, shielding her eyes and looking up at me on the building's balcony as I waved. But my pleasure was short-lived. Even as the snake guards pulled Ai-Ma out of the queue for sacrifices, there were so many other mothers, fathers, grandparents—others' loved ones—who remained.

I felt disgusted. "You better get ready to shut the whole thing down soon," I spat.

Sesha made a tsk-tsk noise with his tongue, faking a hurt expression. "Now, is that any way to thank your future consort for saving your demented demon mother, my darling?"

"We'll be in touch soon, Sesha." I tried to make it sound like both a promise and a threat.

"I'm sure you will." Sesha smiled thinly. "Just think of all those decrepit granddads and grandmas you'll be saving."

"You're disgusting, you know that?" I gave him a dirty look as I passed by toward the stairs.

"Oh, keep speaking those sweet nothings to me, demonic

darling mine!" Sesha cooed dramatically. "And you'll have me eating out of your hand!"

"Sesha, I didn't think you were capable of this!" Chandni snapped.

Again, a look of vulnerable hurt crossed Sesha's face. "You know what?" he said in a falsely light tone. "I didn't either."

And then he turned on his heel and walked away.

CHAPTER 28

Strawberries and Chocolate Are Nasty and You Will Never Convince Me Otherwise

By the time I got back to Ghatatkach, it was done.

"The Serpentine Empire has issued a decree." Surpanakha rolled out a parchment, reading from it in a loud voice. "We must, before sunset on this very day, declare the winner of the Demonic Royalty Contest."

"But Kumi and Aakash are hurt and in the infirmary." I wasn't sure why I was arguing, but the whole thing just felt like a trick being played on me within another trick. I'd come back to school prepared to ask my friends if they would consider dropping out of the competition, only to hear that the decision might be out of their—and my—hands anyway. "It's not fair to them if we end the competition today."

We were in the banyan grove classroom, where the

headmistress and I had been going around and around on this topic for a good half hour at this point. Chandni was up visiting our friends in the infirmary while I'd been stuck down here trying to figure out what exactly Sesha was up to.

Finally, it was the headmistress and not me who stopped pretending. She sighed roughly, staring at me like she wished she could just yeet me into outer space and be done with it. But instead of resorting to her usual insults, she simply asked, "What's actually going on here between you and that snake Sesha, fire demoness?"

"What do you mean?" I asked in what I hoped was an innocent-sounding voice.

"Oh, enough lies!" yelled Surpanakha. In a swift move, she removed a small stoppered bottle from her sari waist-line, then grabbed me, forcing me to drink a couple drops of the liquid inside. I could probably have matched strength with the older rakkhoshi, but her attack was so sudden, I was startled into submission.

As soon as I tasted the liquid she had forced me to drink, I knew what it was. Egads, it tasted monstrous—like strawberries and chocolate. Only a few weeks ago, Professor Ravan had used the same potion on Kumi and Aakash!

"Disgusting!" I spat out what I could from my mouth,

rubbing my raw tongue with the end of my sari. "You made me drink truth serum?"

"Unlike my brother, I hate using it on students!" snarled the headmistress. "But how else will I know what you are up to?" She stared at me, her eyes fierce. "So tell me, fire demoness, are you working with the snakes?"

"I . . . am, I guess, in a way," I admitted despite myself. With a shocked gasp, I clapped my hands to my mouth.

The headmistress growled, showing her sharp fangs. "What do you mean *in a way*?"

"I've promised Sesha he can be my consort if I win Demon Queen." Again, the words spilled from my mouth unbidden.

"Yes, yes, I know about that!" snapped Surpanakha. "But what else are you planning with the snakes?"

"Only that Sesha said he would stop the Intergalactic Sacrifice Program through the transit corridor if I would become Demon Queen right away and make him my consort immediately," I admitted.

"Why do you care so much about the IGSP?" demanded my headmistress. "Aren't you all about looking out for yourself and your power?"

"How can you still believe that after the raid on the

undersea training school?" I asked. Inside my mouth, my tongue buzzed and burned from the magic of the truth serum, making it impossible not to say exactly what I was thinking. "He was going to send my mother into that worm-hole! Not to mention all those other elders! And the people now blame the rebels for their troubles, instead of placing blame where it belongs—on the serpents!"

"I didn't realize you actually cared so much about the revolution, and not just controlling your fire!" the head-mistress snapped.

Her words set off an inferno of anger within me, an anger I'd once been afraid of but now was more than com-fortable tapping into. "I care about the revolution, unlike you!" I snapped. "You're the one willing to use your broth-er's soul-bee, not to mention Kumi's and Aakash's bees, to try and get me out of the competition. And what about using my little cousins in the combat competition? And you're probably the one who stole Hidimbi's crown in the first place!"

"Why would I do that? If we had Hidimbi's crown, I wouldn't have to go to so much trouble to get you out of the competition! We can all see you're not worthy to be Demon Queen, you selfish slug!" Surpanakha cracked her neck even as she roared with fury. "If we're to free our land from the snakes, we need a real leader, one who will do what needs to be done, not a show-off only wanting to blast her fire at everyone!"

"I am a real leader!" I shouted, realizing the words were coming from the depth of my soul. "And I have learned about other ways of leading except for brute force! Didn't you see how I got around your test with the bees? How I fought my cousins but didn't hurt them? How I've promised Sesha and Rontu consortships instead of just burning them with fire, which is honestly all I really wanted to do?"

To my surprise, Surpanakha seemed to deflate at this. The red tinge receded from her eyes, and her expression grew thoughtful. She nodded calmly. Like she believed me. I guess she had to, what with the truth serum still inside me. "You know, you remind me of myself in many ways, Pinki."

"Is that why you had it out for me so much?" I asked, before I could stop myself. I gulped, sure Surpanakha would lose her cool and destroy me now.

But instead of getting mad, the headmistress laughed, shaking her head. "I suppose so. Being reckless and impulsive, overconfident—it didn't always get me where I wanted." She gestured to her face. "But I'm not willing to let you cut off the nose of all of rakkhosh-kind, if you know what I mean."

"I know I'm not perfect," I began.

"That's a bit of an understatement!" Surpanakha guffawed.

I scowled, feeling the flames tickling my throat. "But I really do want to lead our kin, and all the peoples of the Kingdom Beyond, to freedom."

The headmistress stared at me for a moment, then nodded, and I knew she believed me. "So Sesha said he'd stop the IGSP if you made your friends quit," she murmured. "I guess he didn't trust you'd be able to get it to happen fast enough." She paused, as if considering something extremely confusing to her. "But why in the world is that little snaky father killer, or at least father banisher, so eager to become your consort anyway?"

"He isn't. Or I don't think he is, anyway," I admitted. "I think he just really wants to make the moon maiden Chandni jealous. They were once friends, when he was briefly in the resistance, and I don't know, he seems to want to find that past part of himself."

Surpanakha narrowed her eyes. "Well, then we can make that work toward our advantage, can't we?"

The effects of the serum were already wearing off, but still, I couldn't stop myself from asking the question that popped into my mind. "Are you still on the side of the resistance? You're not working with the snakes yourself?"

Surpanakha narrowed her eyes at me. "Just because someone does things differently than you, or doesn't think the way you do, doesn't make them an enemy. You know that, right?"

I nodded, feeling foolish.

The headmistress went on. "There are many paths to freedom, and as long as someone is heading to that same destination, they are on your side. No matter if they believe different things, or behave in different ways, or disagree with you."

I nodded again, thinking of Arko, and sighed. "So now what? I win? Yippee?"

Surpanakha nodded. "As long as your competitors—your friends, should I say, agree, then you win, yes. It's our best chance of getting Sesha where we want him." She bent down and whispered her plan in my ear.

It was a flimsy and risky plan at best. I had no idea if it would work. And more importantly, I had no idea if, when the time came, I'd be able to do what needed to be done.

CHAPTER 29

Sesha and I Put on a Show That Fools, Well, Only Fools

I don't know how the moon girl did it, but only a few hours later, that very evening, I found myself standing on the balcony outside my now-single set of rooms with Sesha. How Chandni had gotten the message to Sesha, and then convinced Sesha to come without a guard, I didn't know. In the meantime, Surpanakha had been hard at work too, making sure the coronation ceremony for Demon Queen could take place that very evening. And for both their efforts, here he was, Sesha the serpentine prince, on my balcony, holding my hand.

"Oh, my suave serpentine suitor!" I said, trying to lay it on thick like Surpanakha had directed me. "How patient you have been!"

I heard a rustling out in the gardens below the balcony and wondered if it was my classmates spying on us, as Surpanakha had arranged. But for Sesha's benefit, I whispered, "I think that's Chandni down there, listening to us!"

That seemed to inspire Sesha plenty. He grabbed my hand and began to gush, in a far louder voice than was strictly necessary. "Oh, my demonic darling! You are more than worth waiting for!"

There was a stifled gasp from below, and then the rustling from the gardens got louder, as if whoever was down there was trying to stay still but failing.

I went on, feeling utterly foolish. "Tonight is the night we have been waiting for, my darling! The night of the choosing ceremony! When I choose you as my consort and declare our love openly!" The light was behind me, shining brightly out of my room, and the garden was in darkness, but I was sure I could see some movement down there, by a large tree below us. Was this ridiculous plan going to work? I really hoped so. Otherwise, I was humiliating myself acting like a goober for no reason.

Sesha too seemed to have heard whoever was doing such a bad job at staying quiet down there, because he practically bellowed his next words in my ear. "Everyone will know and we won't care, my sadistic sugarplum!"

He really was laying it on thick, for what he thought was Chandni's benefit. But hey, two could play at that game. I cleared my throat, shouting, "I won the title of Demon Queen fair and square—after so many tests of intellect, bravery, and rodent disembowelment!" Woodenly, like I was a bad actress in a play, I placed my hand on Sesha's arm.

"That you did, my clever, bloodthirsty, disemboweling minx!" Sesha awkwardly tweaked my nose as he said this, which made me want to seriously burn his face off.

I barely controlled the furious impulse, instead digging my claws into Sesha's arms as I yelled, "And tonight's choosing ceremony will show everyone that I know how to chart the best course for our people's future!" Sesha tried to shake me off, but I only dug my fingers in harder as I continued with my shouty bad acting. "I'll show them that love is the answer to the riddles of the multiverse!"

Sesha stepped on my toes, hard, effectively getting me to let go of his arm. He kept the artificial lovelorn look on his face, though, continuing, "We will combine our powers and rule them all! Tonight, after you choose me at the ceremony and not that nincompoop Rontu, the human prince from the Kingdom Beyond!"

"You're overdoing it!" I muttered. "Everyone knows who Rontu is! And stop talking like that, like you're a C-list actor auditioning for a part you're not going to get."

"Stick to the plan, fire-breath!" said Sesha through clenched teeth. "I need Chandni to buy this!"

I stared at him, raising my eyebrow in an imitation of him. This was the first time Sesha had admitted his feelings for Chandni, at least out loud, and at least to me. It was a weird context for him to do it, but somehow, despite all the absolutely rotten things he'd done in the recent and not-so-recent past, it softened some small corner of my feelings toward him. Okay, maybe softened is overstating it. I still detested him, but maybe just a smidgen less.

"I can't believe my mother and Headmistress Surpanakha want me to marry that buffoon of a human prince!" I widened my eyes, batting them at Sesha with as much artificial flirtatiousness as I could muster. "They say it's important for the future of demon-kind and human-kind. I mean, blah, blah, blah! Who cares about that?"

Sesha's next words made me want to either burst out laughing or flame vomit all over him. "All that matters is our eternal love," he drawled.

"Gross!" I whispered, kicking him in the shin.

"Not as gross as you!" Sesha whispered back.

"Oh, Seshi!" I tittered loudly, kicking him for a second time. "You're such a dreamboat!"

Sesha ground his heel into my foot. "I adore you, my sly sweetheart, my fanged femme fatale!"

"Oh, yuck, that's just over the line!" I muttered. On an impulse, I dragged Sesha by the hair toward me, ready to slam his head into the wall.

He struggled free, grating out, "Our love may be forbidden now, but it won't be after you choose me as your consort!"

"They say you just want me for my power!" I screeched. Would whoever was in the garden notice if I body-slammed him into the wall? "I know you love me for myself!"

Sesha's nostrils flared, and he looked like he was trying not to throw up, or maybe laugh. "Oh, I do! I do!" He really was the worst actor. How could anyone overhearing this actually believe this drivel? "I adore you, my demented dumpling!"

"I'll see you at the ceremony!" I singsonged. "Don't be late, now. You're allowed to wander around Ghatatkach freely only for another few minutes. I had to work on the headmistress hard to get you special permission!"

Special permission, my demonic butt. This was, of course, all a part of Surpanakha's complicated plan. I only hoped it would actually work. I was starting to have some serious doubts based on both Sesha's and my iffy acting skills.

"I told you, as soon as you choose me and we are officially engaged, the centuries-long trouble between our people will be over!" Sesha said smoothly.

"'Trouble between our people'?" I muttered. "You mean like you snakes oppressing us, ruling our lands with an iron fists, and taking away all our rights, including the fundamental right of self-determination?"

"Shove it, rebel scum!" Sesha whispered back, his face still in a fixed mask of a romantic smile. Then, louder, he went on. "The Empire of Serpents has decided the rakkhosh will be given their own homeland, separate from the humans! The newly formed Demon Land and the Empire of Serpents will be allies now and forevermore! And we will reduce what's left of the Kingdom Beyond Seven Oceans and Thirteen Rivers to ashes!"

I practically gasped at his words. Keeping my expression as unchanging as I could make it, I hate-whispered, "Are you serious, you power-mad buffoon? You think we rakkhosh would ever allow you slimy snakes to do that? Yes, we want our own homeland, but not at the expense and pain of every other species!"

He kept grinning like a killer clown as he muttered back, "Just try and stop me!"

I wanted to burn him to cinders, gouge out his eyes, punch him in the nose, something. Instead, all I could say, loudly, was "Not long now, my love!" Even as I said this, though, I pinched his side, hard, grinning when I made him yelp and bat my hand away. "Among all the others at Ghatatkach Academy of Murder and Mayhem, I was chosen as Demon Queen. So it's my decision to choose my consort, and mine alone, no matter what Ai-Ma or the headmistress think about you."

That wasn't, of course, entirely true, but Sesha didn't need to know that.

"Oh, those old biddies are just jealous that you get to have me and they don't," said Sesha obnoxiously, spitting into my face a little just for spite.

I wiped my cheek, then stuck a talon back in his arm, purring, "Oh, I adore you, my slithering snaky suitor!"

He gave me a serious black-and-blue toe as he answered, "I worship you, my ravishing rakkhosh radish!"

I pushed him from me with a bit more force than an actual love interest might perhaps use. "Now go, silly snake boy. Let me get ready for the ceremony!"

I gave him a ridiculously over-the-top wave goodbye. Then, for good measure, blew him flying kiss after slobbery kiss.

He looked like he was about to leave when he stopped and turned around, saying, "And, by the way, I got you the most wonderful coronation gift!"

"What?" I gasped, catching the dastardly look on his face. Realization dawned on me, horrible and creeping like a fungus. Oh no. No, it couldn't be. "Hidimbi's crown?" I guessed. "You had it all along?"

Sesha smiled in a way that curled my stomach. "Maybe. Maybe not."

"Is this why you wanted me to get crowned immediately?" I breathed, feeling the smokes of fury erupting through my ears. "You think it's going to burn me up?"

"Why would I think that, my dearest dung blossom?" Sesha grinned evilly. "Unless *you're* worried that you're not Hidimbi's true successor?"

My hearts slamming in my chest now told me that was exactly what I was worried about. But I wasn't about to tell Sesha that. I gulped. Hard. "No, not at all."

"Wonderful, we're all set, then! I'll see you there, my demonic darling!" Sesha called loudly as he sauntered from the room.

I slammed the door behind him, muttering, "Not if I see you first!"

A few moments after Sesha left, however, there was a strange, repetitive sound on my balcony, like someone was throwing rocks up to get my attention. I whirled around, expecting to see Kumi, Aakash, or maybe even Chandni, but whoever was standing out there was a stranger to me.

I squinted against the darkness, leaning down over the railing and trying to see more clearly. "Who's there? Aakash, is that you, you air-clan loser?" I threw in a couple more insults in case it was a classmate unaware that Aakash had willingly given up the crown for the greater good. "Still upset I beat you for the crown? Still whining you didn't become Demon King?"

The voice that spoke to me was strange, and completely unfamiliar. "Listen to us—we're friends, my lady!" it wheezed. "Here to tell you Sesha's way shady!"

They were rhyming, which meant they couldn't be rakkhosh. Every rakkhosh in the Kingdom older than ten knew about the ban against using our rhyming dialect. Who the heck was down there in the garden?

"How do you know about Sesha? Who are you?" I demanded, leaning out even farther and squinting into the night. My mind was still whirling at the possibility that

Sesha had brought me Hidimbi's crown. I really didn't need to deal with strange spies on top of that stress.

Another voice spoke then, a voice equally unknown that yet sparked something familiar and warm inside me. "He wants you for your power," said the second voice. There was a pause, as if the speaker was searching for an appropriate rhyme at the last minute. Finally, the voice said, "Not because he thinks you're a flower!"

Since the imposter rakkhosh were rhyming, I figured I might as well too. Who were these strangers so new to our ways? Could these be serpent spies, brought into Ghatatkach by Sesha, even though he'd promised Chandni that he'd come alone? But the many guards, not to mention magical barriers of protection around the school, would stop that from happening. Then who the demon butt was in the garden?

"Show your faces, you rakkhosh rubes!" I shouted. "Or I'll mince you into little cubes!"

I hadn't rhymed in a while, but it felt good to do it again.

The first voice then called out, "Rontu's soft, him you can control." Adding, after a beat, "But Sesha will dump you in a dark hole!"

I listened carefully to the strangers' voices, feeling more confused than ever. They sounded human—but how could that be?

"Not true!" I called out, leaning over the parapet into the darkness. "Who are you?"

The second voice, the one that felt vaguely familiar, called out, "Isn't it better to be independent?" There was an even bigger gap this time, and I guessed this rakkhosh impersonator wasn't very good at rhyming. After quite a few moments of inaudible, furious whispering from the garden, they finally concluded, "Than to give birth to a bunch of snaky descendants?"

"How dare you, Sonny Jim!" I exploded, turning away from the balcony and getting ready to run into the garden to catch these losers. "I'm coming down there to rip you limb from limb!"

But when I dashed down to the garden, no one was there.

CHAPTER 30

A Ceremony of Some More Really Bad Acting

The banyan grove was decorated for a party, and the students were in a raucous mood. All the rakkhosh were dressed according to their house colors, and the trees were draped with clan banners—waves for water clan, flames for fire clan, wings for air clan, and a rocky mountain for land clan. The darkness was heavy with the smells of night-blooming flowers—the jasmine so thick in the air I felt downright dizzy. On top of the chatter and yells of all my classmates were the endless crickets and the relentless rushing of the nearby stream. The path from the main entrance of Ghatatkach down to the grove was lined with rows of glowing prodeep, each stake designed to look like beautifully disembodied rakkhosh arms. That touch was really very tasteful, and I made a mental note to compliment the headmistress at a later time on those glowing arm lights. I still didn't really like her, but she was, I had to admit, growing on me.

My stomach churned with acid and anticipation as I stood next to the central dais, waiting for everyone to file in and sit by their designated trees. There was an empty throne in the middle of the stage, waiting for me, and in front of the throne, two empty chairs for my potential consorts. I couldn't see any sign of Hidimbi's crown, but I was sure that's what Sesha had brought for me. My palms felt clammy, and I could feel serious trickles of nervous sweat making their way from my hairline down my back and neck. I licked my lips, willing myself to calm down. I'm not sure I succeeded. I remembered the feeling of the ancient queen's burning crown on my head and shuddered. How was I going to make it out of this coronation alive?

Next to the dais was the school's beloved blue champak tree, fluttering with blue butterfly-like flowers. I breathed in their scent, thinking of Arko and his brothers, who had once been cursed to become champak flowers. I wondered where in the multiverse my friends were and if I'd ever see them again. I stared for a moment up at the starry night, thinking of Arko and hoping he was safe. If he was here, he would have told me to believe in myself, that I had nothing to fear from the crown of flames. But I couldn't have the same amount of confidence in myself as he had in me.

Then it was time for the ceremony to begin. The headmistress came out, wearing her silk sari shot with all the Ghatatkach clan colors. She had draped around her shoulders a shawl mixed with all the same colors too—brown and green for land clan, red and orange for fire clan, shades of blue for water clan, and light blue and white for air clan. Surpanakha's hair was in that giant vertical bun she favored, and she stared out at the school through the horn-rimmed glasses she balanced on her noseless face.

"Headmistress!" I hissed through the side of my mouth. "Can I talk to you for a minute?" I wanted to ask her about the crown and find out if there was a way for me to get out of this mess before it was too late.

"You can't lose your nerve now!" Surpanakha hissed back. "The ceremony is about to begin!"

"But—" I tried again.

She cut me off. "Everything depends on you now, Pinki. Your people depend on you."

I gave a little squeak. "But I . . ."

Then she turned to face the audience, ignoring me. "Students of Ghatatkach Academy. As you know, today is the day of the great choosing ceremony. When our newly elected Rakkhoshi Rani—our new Demon Queen—will become settled into her powers and select her consort for life!" The headmistress raised her hands above her head in a dramatic gesture.

A shehnai wailed, and there was the ulu-ulu call that marks auspicious occasions. This meant it was my turn to stand up in front of everyone dressed in an elaborately stupid wedding sari. Surpanakha had insisted I wear it. It was actually Ai-Ma's own wedding wear she had worn to marry Babu—a red sari embroidered with golden thread. I was wearing Ai-Ma's jewelry too—golden rings attached by chains to the bangles on my arms. I was even wearing a nose ring attached by a gilded chain to the ornaments in my hair.

Although they were still recovering from their injuries, Kumi and Aakash had felt well enough to help me get ready. Like during the comportment contest, Kumi had helped me put on my sari and jewels, while Aakash had done my hair, arranging the white shola pith tiara in my updo. They had been weirdly unfazed when Surpanakha asked them to officially drop out of the contest—like they could see the greater good and the fact that this might just be the way to defeat the Serpent Empire forever. I was proud to be their friend, and even prouder to be my mother's daughter. Surpanakha had brought Ai-Ma over for the ceremony, and I realized that what I was doing today was continuing my parents' legacy—the revolutionary fight they had begun for freedom, but that my friends and I had continued.

Then, with another wail of the shehnai and a tabla drum roll, my two less-than-desirable consorts—Rontu and Sesha—were led onto the stage, decked out ridiculously in white wedding clothes. They were both dressed in sparkling kurta and dhoti and even the pointy topor caps that bride-grooms wore all through the Kingdom Beyond. I really felt like running away then, but I knew I couldn't. I could only hope that Sesha had been bluffing, letting me believe he had the crown when he didn't, just to freak me out. That did seem like something he would do. My palm and hairline sweat got worse, and I could feel the fiery acid churning in my intestines.

The moment the consorts sat down, there appeared around their chairs two giant, glowing cages. The entire audience burst out in hoots and curses.

Rontu, who of course didn't know what I was, couldn't be allowed to see that he was in a school for rakkhosh, so he had been magicked to see us all as very tall humans. But

I could tell the magic must not be working exactly right, because he gave a frightened look around and let out a small whimper from inside his cage.

Sesha, in the meantime, looked like he thought the cage was a joke. He grinned stupidly at me through the bars, blowing me all manner of gooby fake kisses and actually waving like he was a king and not an imprisoned consort. I could tell he was looking around for Chandni and not seeing her. I had to let him continue to believe she was still here, otherwise our plan wouldn't work. But when he winked at me like a complete cheeseball, I looked away from him with disgust. None of this was how I'd planned to become Demon Queen. But there was nothing I could do about it now.

"Pinki of the fire clan has been elected our new Demon Queen due to her skill in the classroom and the combat yard, and of course due to all your faith that she will fulfill the great cosmic duties of demon-kind." Surpanakha peered around the clearing with her clever eyes as she said this, mostly to prevent any snickerers or doubters who were surprised that the contest had ended so abruptly—and that I had been made Queen. On either side of her lounged her two jackals on golden leashes, their sharp eyes roaming over the student body too.

Surpanakha went on, as much for Sesha's and Rontu's

benefit as anyone else's. "Tonight, as has been our custom since the beginning of time, we have captured the princely sons from two neighboring kingdoms. One of these future—er, or current—rulers, Pinki will choose as her consort."

I made a choking sound in the back of my throat, and the headmistress threw me a quelling glance, then continued. "Before our new queen makes her choice, she must swear to keep the balance of the multiverse. For the seeds of the multiverse's origins reside in our queen, and on her shoulders falls the responsibility of rakkhosh-kind: to keep in balance the light and the dark, birth and death, story and silence. On her shoulders falls the responsibility to keep the diversity of the multiverse ever expanding."

I tried not to roll my eyes. I knew this was mostly an act on Surpanakha's part, but still, all this talk about universe, stories, light, dark, blah, blah, was making me seriously gassy. How about freedom from our oppressors? How about kicking the snakes out of our country once and for all? How about getting Arko and his brothers back home, as well as all those grannies and grandpops who'd been punted through the transit corridor and who knows where into the multiverse?

"To fulfill this great duty," Surpanakha went on, "our queen must gain the power of all four clans. She already has the power of her own fire clan . . ."

"Finally!" somebody yelled from the audience.

"Took her long enough," somebody else added.

"Just a few classrooms burned down," said a third voice, then broke into titters.

I whirled toward them but couldn't locate the annoying titterers. How I would love to show them just how well I could control my fire now!

But I wasn't the only one annoyed by the interruption. The jackals growled, and Surpanakha gave a general death glare in the direction of the hecklers. It felt good to have my headmistress on my side for once.

"As I was saying," Surpanakha continued, "our queen already has the power of her own fire clan, but tonight the other three clans will be sharing their power with her with offerings of symbolic gifts. I call first upon the air clan to make their offering."

The headmistress plucked one of the blue champak flowers from the tree. It fluttered in her hand as if it had wings. Then the wings turned into lips, and the magicked flower announced, "Gift giver for the air clan will be the flier Aakash!"

Aakash gasped as his name was called, putting his hands up to his face like he was so thrilled and surprised. "What? Little ole me?" he shrieked in the fakest accent.

I rolled my eyes. This was all, of course, planned out. But we had to make it look like it was a prophecy, or a happenstance, or whatever. Which was seriously pushing all of our acting abilities to the brink.

Even though his wing was still healing, Aakash looked as powerful and handsome as ever, muscles practically busting out from beneath his blue-and-white house shawl. He stood up from the air-clan banyan and took a bow. The leaves and branches of the tree above him waved in what appeared to be a gusty storm, making his elaborately styled hair look even more stylish and windblown. As usual, rakkhosh and rakkhoshi from all the clans ogled and sighed at the sight of my handsome friend.

Aakash approached me and bowed, but not before giving me a cheeky little wink. "For our awesome queen, the air clan offers, like, the power of flight."

My airhead friend made a little gesture, making a blue pulsating energy appear in his hand, like a little swirling storm. It was a tiny ball with even tinier wings.

I gave Aakash a critical look and asked, "Was it you calling me today from the garden?"

Aakash looked dumbfounded. He really didn't have to act at all for this part, as it came pretty naturally to him. "My . . . uh . . . Queen?"

"Never mind!" With what I hoped was a regal incline of my now-regal head, I took the winged storm from my friend's hand, hoping he knew how grateful I was for his support and friendship. If Hidimbi's crown was here, it would surely kill me, and then either he or Kumi would be the next ruler. And I knew that whoever it was would be great. I tried to communicate all of this with my eyes, but my friend just grinned at me.

Loudly, I said, "Thank you, air clan, for sharing with me your power of flight!" I let out a little burp of frustration, and the air-clan rakkhosh cheered.

The moment I accepted Aakash's gift, there appeared on my arms the same tattoo-like markings that swirled up the champak tree. I was being marked, body and soul, as Rakkhoshi Queen, and it was quite a heady experience. I remembered what Arko had said, about future generations telling our stories and being guided by them, and felt the weight of responsibility to that future seeping into my skin.

"Stories!" Surpanakha bellowed, holding my arm up to the crowd, like I was some kind of prize fighter. "All the stories of the air clan and the creatures of flight are now the responsibility of our queen. They are etched into her very skin!"

Almost as soon as the headmistress finished speaking, my mehendi disappeared, as if being sucked into my skin. I couldn't see them anymore, but I felt their power there, under the surface, humming beneath my skin. Aakash, still bowing, backed away from the throne. Then Surpanakha picked the next magical champak flower, which called out, predictably, that the gift giver for the water clan would be my friend and ex-roommate, Kumi.

Kumi approached the throne with a deep bow. Maybe no one but me could tell, but she was holding her arm tightly against herself, and I wondered how much pain she was in still, but not showing. My friend knelt before me, sticking out her tongue in my direction when she was out of everyone else's sight. Then she waved her hands and produced what looked like a giant teardrop. "From the water clan, we offer our new queen power over water in all her many forms."

I was sorely tempted to just burst out and tell my friend to take my place, that I couldn't do it. I wanted to scream that I didn't deserve to be crowned, that I didn't dare to be. But everyone was looking at me, so I just took Kumi's gift as graciously as I could. "I thank you, water clan, for your gift."

As before, as soon as I said the words, my skin was covered by the mehendi designs—this time in the flowing shapes of waves and teardrops, rain and rivers. I felt the weight of these stories too, and my responsibility to them.

"All the stories of the water clan and the creatures of the water are now etched into your skin," said Surpanakha.

"Don't screw it up, Your Royalness!" Kumi whispered as she backed away. It was all I could do not to bust out crying that I wasn't just worried about screwing up a little bit, but screwing up so royally that I might die.

Which was why I wasn't really paying attention when Surpanakha picked the next blue champak flower. When it called out the unfamiliar name, however, I felt shocked into full attention.

CHAPTER 31

The Jewels of the Crown

I'd thought the land-clan gift giver would be the oldest and strongest of that clan, the annoying muscle-head rakkhosh called Gorgor. Or maybe Harimati, the land-clan rakkhoshi who had been a reporter during the comportment contest. But instead the flower announced a name I'd never heard before. Yet, like the voice in the garden, the name resonated inside me, calling forth a memory I didn't even have yet.

"Our gift giver representing the land clan will be . . . Kiranmala!" shouted the small flower.

The headmistress looked as confused as I, muttering about how we didn't have a student of that name at the school. There was a murmuring from out among the students too, but then a bunch of land-clan students hoisted a perky little rakkhoshi with a long braid and a backpack up on their shoulders, carrying her toward the stage.

Behind her ran a young rakkhosh boy who felt so familiar to me I almost cried out. But I also knew I didn't know him. Yet I felt, deep in my bones, that we were somehow connected. With a jolt, I remembered the boy and girl from my dream. They hadn't been a rakkhosh and rakkhoshi then, but they still looked the same. And I remembered the boy's name, the one that Hidimbi had told me—Neel. His name had been Neel, the color of the sky that holds the sun.

But someone couldn't travel out of a dream and into your real life, could they? I shot Surpanakha a worried look. What was going on?

Ai-Ma, who had been quiet up until now, leaned forward and stared at the land rakkhoshi named Kiranmala, like she too had dreamed about her. "I feel like I know you from somewhere, little demon-ling," she murmured.

The little rakkhoshi looked up at me. How did I know her? "Oh, Queen. The air clan has offered you flight, and the water clan control over water itself. What can the land clan offer you to compare?"

The non-land clans hooted while I heard some serious grumbling from the land clans. The little rakkhoshi pulled out pulsing white and yellow jewels from her backpack and held them out to me. "We offer you these jewels, fallen to land from the heavens themselves. Powerful enough to give their owner wealth beyond compare, or even control over death!"

Everyone in the grove gasped. I felt my legs threaten to give way from underneath me. Here they were, magically reappeared, the Chintamoni and Poroshmoni, the missing jewels from Hidimbi's crown! But how could that be? Didn't the legend say that the jewels would reappear only for the rightful heir to the crown? And if that was true, well, then did that mean the rightful Demon Queen was . . . me?

Everyone seemed frozen in place. Surpanakha and Ai-Ma were looking at me with such expressions of pride on their faces, I knew they were thinking the same thing I was. But before any of us had the time to speak, Sesha yelled out from his cage.

"What a wonderful gift!" he shouted. "Perhaps I should keep them for you, oh Queen, for safekeeping!"

The entire grove burst into laughter, pointing at Sesha. Yeah, no, that was not about to happen.

"You are in no position to make such an offer, Prince of Serpents!" snapped Surpanakha. "The gifts of the clans are for the Queen alone, not her consort. Besides, what makes you so sure she will choose you and not the prince Rontu?"

"Oh, she will choose me," protested Sesha, and now I could really hear the desperation in his voice. He leered at me with a disgusting expression. "And she wants to give those jewels to me, don't you, my dear darling Pinki?"

That was it. I couldn't keep up the farce anymore. "Don't tell me what I want or don't want. I am no weakling to be controlled by a consort," I growled. I grabbed the jewels the little land rakkhoshi was offering me and stood up. As soon as I held them, my skin was again covered by the elaborate mehendi stories. They glowed bright red before fading into my skin as the others had done before. The weight of these stories was heavier than the others had been, as if I were carrying the burden of tales from not just this multiverse but all the others as well.

I cleared my throat ferociously. "In fact, let me declare it now, loud and proud. As my headmistress and mother have chosen, my consort will be none other than Prince and acting Raja Fatteshwar Orebaba, aka Rontu!"

With these words, the cage around Rontu disappeared. With a triumphant look at Sesha, I handed Rontu both the magic jewels. As I did so, my fellow rakkhosh students cheered. Ai-Ma and Surpanakha looked pleased. And Sesha, for the first time, looked seriously frightened.

It was all, of course, part of the plan. This was how we were going to get rid of Sesha for good—by invoking our ancient rakkhosh traditions and killing him. We knew that Sesha's ego would never let him believe that I could choose Rontu over him, and that's how we had caught him—with his own vanity. Only now that it was time to carry out the plan, I felt something inside me hesitating. Could I kill Sesha like this—while he was within a cage, without a weapon? As much as I detested the snake boy, there was a part of me that also, I don't know—somehow understood him. We'd been through a lot together, Sesha and I, and while I could imagine using violence if he attacked me or mine, the thought of killing someone like this, even a snake, in cold blood, made my reflux seriously act up. It was like I could hear Arko's voice whispering across the multiverse, telling me that using violence in this way would only scar me—a horrible story that would seep into my skin, my bones, my very soul. It would change me. It would be a stain I could never be rid of. I thought of what Arko had said, about wielding a shield and not a sword. Had I, without my knowledge, been so altered by Arko's beliefs that they now felt like they were my own? Had his philosophy seeped into me, changing me forever?

In the meantime, Rontu, unfortunately, seemed to have been slipping out of his magic spell. He looked around himself, stunned. "But . . . you're a rakkhoshi! I don't want to be your consort!"

Ai-Ma waved her hands before Rontu's eyes. "True love will you see when you see Pinki's face. No demon anymore, but with human replaced." And with these words, she snapped her fingers, and Rontu's expression changed entirely.

"Oh, I adore you, my Queen, my love!" he burbled, grasping me simperingly by the hand.

I felt revulsion well up in me at the sight of his familiar and yet not-familiar face. How I wished it were not Rontu holding my hand, but his brother Arko.

"It's time, fire demoness!" Surpanakha muttered to me through clenched teeth. "Do the deed! Kill the snake!"

Even though he couldn't hear the headmistress's words, Sesha howled and snarled, rattling his cage with all his might.

"How dare you, you stupid demoness?" he yelled. "How dare you not choose me?"

"You want my power!" I yelled back. "You thought I wasn't the rightful heir to Hidimbi, that I would die if I put her mukut on, and then you could just take over and rule Demon Land in my stead. But that's not what's happening, is it? Since I'm the one who was presented the Chintamoni and Poroshmoni Stones, the missing jewels in Hidimbi's crown!"

"You'll regret this for the rest of your life!" shrieked Sesha. He turned, snarling, to my classmates, almost unhinged in his fury. "All of demon-kind will regret this. I will destroy your kind if it's the last thing I do! No one will remember who you are! I will erase your stories from the multiverse!"

As Sesha raged inside his cage, making the school guards hop onstage and surround him, I felt my fury burning within me. I was sick of having to pretend I felt anything but utter loathing and contempt toward the serpent prince.

"Do you know what our traditions dictate?" I spat out at him, sending a wave of hot fumes into his cage. "That once the Rakkhoshi Queen picks one out of two consorts, she gets to kill the other one! So when I kill you, by your very own laws, there's nothing the serpent government can do to stop me. I'm completely within my rights to follow my ancient cultural practice."

"You'll never get away with this!" Sesha snarled, but I could tell he was scared. He lost that confident expression he usually wore, and his left eye started twitching.

"Really? Why not?" I scoffed in a low voice. "Your own father wrote the rulebook on respecting the traditions of his subjects in order to better rule over them."

Surpanakha smiled again. She looked so confident in me, in my ability to kill Sesha in cold blood. I was really not looking forward to disappointing her. Even though I detested him, I didn't think I could follow through with straight-up murder. But how was I going to break all that to my headmistress? The conundrum made my acid reflux go wild. Before I had to do or say anything, someone completely unexpected stepped in.

"My Queen!" that familiar voice sang out from the land-clan tree, the boy Neel. "You can't kill the snake prince!"

I studied the rakkhosh boy's familiar, handsome face, his dark hair, his joyous eyes. I had thought he reminded me of Arko, but now, I wondered with shock if the person the boy reminded me of was me. The past and future flickered together before my eyes, like elders and children linked by bonds of family and tradition, history, and connection.

I felt myself soften toward the boy, even as I said, "Tell me, then. Why can't I kill Sesha?"

"Because . . . because . . . you're better than that?" Neel suggested with a hopeful shrug.

Students all around the banyan grove began to laugh, and I saw Gorgor slap the boy on the back. "That's a good one, kid!"

"Better than that!" I scoffed. Despite my words, I was torn. Arko would agree with him, I knew it. But at the same time, I felt the mounting pressure of all rakkhosh-kind upon me, the hopes of my classmates and teachers, expecting me to do what was necessary. I felt that pressure mounting inside too. After all, I loathed Sesha. Besides, look where believing in all that nonviolence stuff got Arko—punted into outer space! Which left me alone here to deal with all this mess and lead the revolution practically alone. And I wasn't a namby-pamby pacifist like Chandni; I was the most powerful rakkhoshi of the land—the Demon Queen!

With a growl, I shouted, "I'm not better than that. Why should I be better than that? What a thought!"

Sesha was babbling about how he was sure I was in love with him, or how he was in love with me, or some similar blather, all of which was a complete joke. Then Rontu tried to get in on it, shouting about some other nonsense about love and marriage. I let them both ramble on for a while, before I zapped Rontu into a quick sleep. Man, that guy could talk a lot. It was a relief not to hear his buzzing voice in my ear, like an annoying bee.

I turned to Sesha, narrowing my eyes at him. "You know, you can drop the 'I'm in love with you' act. Because Chandni isn't here. She's back at the rebel headquarters, working on a way to get Arko and his brothers back."

"You told me she was here!" Sesha breathed. "How could you let me believe she was here? Forget about Hidimbi's crown, I'm going to kill you myself, you beast!"

"I lied." I shrugged. "And guess what, you don't get to kill me, because I'm going to kill you first!"

I jumped forward, reaching through the bars of the cage and putting my hands around his throat. Sesha gasped, and the crowd cheered. The snake prince was strong, but his power was blunted inside his magical cage. So he could do nothing. He was helpless. I saw Arko's face floating in front of me, talking about the ways that violence seeps under your skin and changes you. I heard his voice talking about forging our own path, not letting our oppressors force us into false choices. I heard my own hearts asking me if I could find a third way, a better path to walk. I loosened my grip. No matter how much I hated Sesha, how evil and cruel he was, I couldn't kill him like this. I couldn't let this violence stain me and scar me. I couldn't. I wouldn't. But how could I refuse the heady call of violence? Everyone would be disappointed in me, and Surpanakha would undoubtedly kick me out of school. I'd probably lose my title of Demon Queen. No one wanted a Demon Queen who was a pacifist! I mean, the thought was enough to make me both laugh and cry.

The next thing that happened, though, saved me from having to make any public declaration about being able to use or not use violence. My hands were still around Sesha's throat when I saw that Neel was speaking to Ai-Ma, as well as his little friend Kiranmala. And then, completely unexpectedly, Ai-Ma stood up, holding the little rakkhoshi's fist in the air with her own. "Halt, my daughter, Pinki! This young rasagolla of a demon-ling invokes the right of challenge kill!"

"What?" I sputtered sharp blades of fire. Taking

advantage of my confusion, Sesha somehow pushed my hands off his neck and took in some big shuddering breaths. "You invoke challenge kill? Based on what right?"

"Based on the right of . . . relation," Ai-Ma said, a bit shiftily.

I peered at Kiranmala, this little rakkhoshi who had saved me from having to embarrass myself and publicly refuse to kill Sesha. Was I imagining things, or was there something luminous and moonlike about this girl— something that reminded me of Chandni?

Ai-Ma went on. "This young rakkhoshi has had, um, loved ones harmed by Sesha's malice."

"What?" snarled Sesha. "I've never seen that hideous rakkhoshi wench before in my life!"

"Well, I've seen you before!" snapped the surprisingly brave little rakkhoshi. "But I guess you've forgotten me!"

Some students around us erupted in shrieks of mocking laughter. And then I heard some young, rhyming rakkhosh shout out, "Water, air, land, and flame, the snake's gone and forgot his name!" I looked over and realized it was Kawla, Mawla, and Deembo, all dressed up in finery for the ceremony. I felt a lurch of protectiveness as Sesha completely lost his cool at all this.

Sesha's reddened eyes widened as he caught sight of my little cousins. Then he pointed at me with a shaking finger. "My name will never be forgotten! But yours will be—I will erase all of rakkhosh-kind from the multiverse's memory." He was totally losing it, even frothing a little at the mouth. "Just you wait! No one will remember you; no one will tell your stories. You will become beasts from a long-ago and forgotten culture!"

"No, Sesha!" said Kiranmala, pulling out a bow and arrow and aiming right at Sesha's head. "It's your name that will be forgotten!"

"Wait a minute, wait a minute!" I protested, both relieved and miffed that I wouldn't have to go through with Surpanakha's plan. "I haven't granted you the right of challenge kill. What makes you think you have more right to kill Sesha than me?"

Surpanakha stepped in between Kiranmala and me. "Challenge kill is an ancient right among our kind, and if this rakkhoshi has the right of injury on her side, it cannot be denied. You say this serpent prince has harmed your loved ones, land demoness. If that is so, you must bind yourself to him and let fate decide if you have the right of vengeance upon him."

Swift as a storm, the headmistress magically extracted a fountain of poison from one of Sesha's teeth. She caught it in a little vial and handed it to the rakkhoshi, instructing her to drink. We all stared, fully aware that if Kiranmala had the right of challenge kill over Sesha, the poison would not harm her.

The little rakkhoshi was brave, I'll give her that. With a little bottoms-up-type gesture, she lifted the vial and downed it. She swayed a little but didn't fall, staring straight ahead at Sesha the whole time.

"Who are you?" Sesha hissed, maybe recognizing the similarity the young rakkhoshi had to Chandni too.

And then, through who knows what magic, Kiranmala somehow summoned the flowers on the champak tree to turn into a swarm of living, breathing butterflies. As if under her control, they swooped down among the crowd, then swarmed upon and into Sesha's cage. They covered him so thickly, I couldn't even see him anymore.

"What is this? Get off! Get off!" Sesha sputtered. But the butterflies were relentless, flapping in his eyes, his hair, his ears, his nose, his mouth.

"Make them take him away from here!" I told the girl. "Make them send him off through the transit corridor, like all those precious elders he's sacrificed!"

With that same mysterious magic, the little rakkhoshi waved her hands, opening the cage that held Sesha. As easily as if he were a child, the butterflies carried him up and out of the cage, along the length of the banyan tree clearing, and finally out into the now-starry night. His yells and curses filled the night, but he was out of our grasp, and soon, out of our sight.

"No!" howled Surpanakha, turning on me. "You lost your chance to kill him! You lost your chance to free our land from the snakes forever!"

"Do you think my killing Sesha would have freed us?" I said, not with anger but with tired, quiet patience. I saw things so clearly all of a sudden. "Killing Sesha would only have brought the wrath of the Serpent Empire even more mercilessly on our heads. Their oppressive power would continue, even without Sesha. Their power isn't about one individual but an entire unfair system. And it's not rakkhosh-kind who would have suffered the most, but the most defenseless among us. Those human kids, those grandparents, our most vulnerable neighbors."

"You're right, Mother," said the boy Neel. And at that word, I whirled around.

"What did you call me?" I shrieked, my hearts thudding with wild recognition.

And then I felt it: how this boy and this girl were my descendants, and I their elder. How they were the past, present, and future all rolled up in one. And then I saw it, time itself, not a straight line but a circle coiling around and around in a never-ending cycle like a serpent biting its own tail. And then I knew it, something I needed to know, now that I was not just Demon Queen but keeper of all the clan stories. The secret was simple: that all those who came before us, and all those who came after us, could coexist, and had always done so. Like the flimsy veils separating one dimension from the next, time too was something to dance through and between, and stories were the vehicles that took us to those places we thought were long forgotten, those magical destinations not even yet here. Through stories, our ancestors and our children and our own selves could exist together, weaving in and out of each other's imaginations, hearts, and lives.

I cannot explain any of what happened next. Neel's and Kiranmala's rakkhosh disguises fell away, revealing them to be humans. And next to them stood Hidimbi the ancient queen, her crown gleaming tall on her powerful head. She shimmered, as if she was both here and not here, living outside of time.

"I believe this is yours," she said in an echoing voice, lifting her crown from her head and placing it upon mine.

But unlike the times before, I wasn't afraid. I didn't flinch, or cry, or refuse it. I simply bent my head and accepted my destiny. The crown was heavy upon my head, but it did not burn me. Instead, I felt on fire with its power.

"I believe this is yours," I said to Kiranmala and Neel, handing them a silver-covered copy of *Thakurmar Jhuli* they had left on the clan benches. The book looked like the one I'd been reading from, if just a little older. And as they opened the pages and began reading aloud, they disappeared, returning, I knew, to their own time in the future. At the same time, so too disappeared Hidimbi, back to the past. And upon my head, her crown glowed and hummed as if speaking to me, calling back the Chintamoni and Poroshmoni jewels to their regal home.

"It's over!" whispered Surpanakha, her plan having been destroyed before her eyes.

"No, Headmistress, it's just beginning," I said with a firm assuredness born from my new role.

My country still wasn't free. But I could imagine now what freedom might look like because of Arko. Freedom was not choosing between two paths that another set out before you. Freedom was making your own path, setting your own rules, and refusing to believe that unfair choices were all the possibilities there were.

Unlike the headmistress, I was not upset that I had lost my chance to kill Sesha. But I was devastated that I had lost my friend Arko. Yet the boy and girl from the future had shown me hope. I did not need to limit myself to this time and place. I was connected by spirit and stories to the past of my elders' glory, to the present we chose to inhabit, and to the future of all of our wildest imaginings. I would find Arko, and I would free my country on my own terms, not on those set forth by our oppressors.

I flexed my arms, feeling the now-invisible stories of all the clans coursing beneath my skin, weaving themselves into all that I was, connecting me to not just this time and this place, but all of time coursing before and behind me, all the dimensions beyond and beyond.

I was Demon Queen now, and with that title, with this ancient crown, came a power that lit my head and hearts on fire. A fire that wasn't destructive or frightening, but purifying and strong.

Like Arko's song, I knew that I must now fashion myself as a beacon in the darkness. I must be reborn as the spark of light that would illuminate our oppression's bleak night.

Destiny was calling my name, reminding me that I was its flame.

Author's Note

Crown of Flames is the second Fire Queen novel, taking up where *Force of Fire* leaves off. Both stories, like the three Kiranmala and the Kingdom Beyond books (*The Serpent's Secret*, *Game of Stars*, and *The Chaos Curse*), draw from many traditional Bengali folktales and children's stories. These are stories beloved in West Bengal (India), Bangladesh, and throughout the Bengali–speaking diaspora.

Thakurmar Jhuli and Rakkhosh Stories

Folktales involving rakkhosh are very popular throughout South Asia. The word is sometimes spelled "rakshasa" in other parts of the region, but in this book, it is spelled like the word sounds in Bengali. Folktales are an oral tradition, passed on from one generation to the next, with each teller adding nuance to their own version. In 1907, Dakshinaranjan Mitra Majumdar published some classic Bengali folktales in a book called *Thakurmar Jhuli* ("Grandmother's Satchel"). This collection is full of tales about princes and princesses from the Kingdom Beyond Seven Oceans and Thirteen Rivers, as well as stories about evil serpent kings, soul-stealing bhoot, and rhyming, carnivorous rakkhosh—who are the monsters everyone loves to hate.

Crown of Flames, like *Force of Fire*, is an imagined origin story for the same demon queen who appears in the original Neelkamal and Lalkamal tale, as well as my own Kiranmala trilogy. Her mother, Ai-Ma, also appears in the original Neelkamal and Lalkamal story as well as my previous books. Prince Sesha, who eventually becomes the serpent king, is a character of my own making in the Kingdom Beyond novels, but he is based on all the evil serpent kings of the original *Thakurmar Jhuli* tales. Chandni, the moon girl, is the younger version of Kiranmala's own moon mother (the word *Chandni* means "moonlight" just as *Kiranmala* means "garland of moonbeams"). The Seven Brothers Champak come from the *Thakurmar Jhuli* story of shat bhai chompa—seven princes who were turned into champak flowers by their evil stepmothers.

The rakkhosh figures Ravan, Surpanakha, Hidimbi, and Ghatatkach in *Force of Fire* are not from *Thakurmar Jhuli*, but from Hindu epics. Surpanakha is the sister of Ravan, the main antagonist of the Ramayana. She's attracted to the hero Ram, but when she approaches him, he rejects her. When she then tries the same tactics with his younger brother Laxshman she is again rejected. Humiliated by the two brothers, the demoness goes to attack Ram's wife, Sita, but has her nose cut off by Laxshman instead. She tells her brother Ravan about this shameful event and sets off the events of the epic, including Ravan's kidnapping of Sita. I always thought that *The Ramayana* treated Surpanakha pretty unfairly, so I made her the headmistress of the rakkhosh academy in the Fire Queen books and *The Chaos Curse*. Ghatatkach (after whom the made-up demon Academy of Murder and Mayhem is named) is a rakkhosh from another epic, the Mahabharata. The son of the second heroic Pandav brother Bhim and the rakkhoshi Hidimbi, enormously strong Ghatatkach fought alongside his father and Pandav uncles in the great war upon which the epic is based. Even though he was raised by his rakkhoshi mother, he was enormously loyal to his father and family and was an almost undefeatable warrior, so it made sense to me that he would have a rakkhosh school named after him! Hidimbi, Ghatatkach's mother, should have been the queen of the Pandavs, but as a rakkhoshi she was denied that honor in *The Mahabharata*. So I thought it only fitting to make her the last ancient Demon Queen whose crown is in the novel's title!

Thakurmar Jhuli stories are still very popular in West Bengal and Bangladesh, and have inspired translations, films, television cartoons, comic books, and more. Rakkhosh are very popular as well—the demons everyone loves to hate—and appear not just in folk stories but also Hindu mythology. Images of bloodthirsty, long-fanged rakkhosh can be seen everywhere—even on the back of colorful Indian trucks and auto rikshaws, as a warning to other drivers not to tailgate or drive too fast!

The Indian Revolution

The other backdrop to both *Crown of Flames* and *Force of Fire* is the Indian freedom struggle against the British. Although Britain ruled mercilessly over South Asia for over two hundred years, Indian revolutionary fighters of multiple generations fought valiantly against imperialist rule. Freedom for the region was finally achieved in 1947, due to the activities of both nonviolent revolutionaries like Mahatma Gandhi, and revolutionaries who believed in meeting force with force like Bengali revolutionary leader Netaji Subash Chandra Bose. In this novel, Pinki struggles with the idea of nonviolence but ends up understanding how it is a new way to undertake her work as a revolutionary. In trying to convince her, Arko and Chandni both refer to "2-D philosopher" Audre Lorde, who said, "The master's tools will never dismantle the master's house," and the Reverend Dr. Martin Luther King Jr., who famously said, "Darkness cannot drive out darkness, only light can do that. Hate cannot drive out hate, only love can do that." They also refer to ideas that Mahatma Gandhi upheld, including that of ahimsa (refraining from harming another) and satyagraha (the force of truth). Pinki argues back, however, pointing out that it's often the least powerful in society who are expected to use nonviolence while being oppressed violently.

Like Pinki's parents, many members of my own family were imprisoned for their revolutionary activities against the British. My entire life, I heard stories about and from these heroic family members, wondering at how much they had sacrificed for an idea called freedom. Like Pinki, I had to figure out my own place in this revolutionary family history. My father's aunt Banalata DasGupta was imprisoned by the British in her early twenties, when she was still a college student. Far too young, she died in captivity from a lack of treatment for her (curable) thyroid goiter. My maternal grandfather, Sunil Kumar Das, was only fifteen when he was jailed by the British for his involvement in the Chittagong Armory Raid (a raid which I loosely refer to in *Force of Fire*, when Chandni comments that Pinki's parents were involved in a raid against the snakes). My grandfather survived years of imprisonment but suffered many ailments his entire life due to the poor treatment he received at the hands of the British. When he died in his nineties, he was one of the oldest recognized Indian freedom fighters. I wish now that I had recorded more of his wonderful stories, that I had him on video telling me about all that he had done. I can only hope that this story, combining the folktales I heard from my grandmother with the real-life revolutionary tales I heard from my grandfather, is some sort of small tribute to all I have inherited from them.

The Sacrificing of Elders

The systematic sacrificing of elders that the snakes are planning in *Crown of Flames* is inspired by a much more recent experience in this country. Throughout the COVID-19 pandemic, the health and well-being of not only elders, but individuals with chronic illnesses, disabilities, and other conditions have been pushed to the side in order for the rest of society to "get back to normal." Elders in prison, like Ai-Ma, are particularly vulnerable to COVID-19, and many real-life activists have been trying to get such individuals released—in the same way that Arko and Chandni work to get Ai-Ma released. Both in and outside of prison, so many elders have been lost, and continue to be lost, in the pandemic. With these deaths, our society has lost much wisdom, stories, and guidance—after all, grandparents and other elders are our families' crowns. Although many segments of society have stepped forward to protect the health and well-being of those more vulnerable to COVID-19, there is much more we can do to recognize that the health of our society depends on the health of the most vulnerable, not the most powerful.

Rabindranath Tagore and Other Bengali Songs

As are many Bengalis, growing up in South Asia or throughout the diaspora, I was raised on the poetry, prose, and songs of Nobel Laureate Rabindranath Tagore. Many of his poems and songs were in fact written about Indian independence. The song that appears several times in *Force of Fire*, "Ekla Chalo Re," was written in 1905 by Tagore and is a revolutionary song that Mahatma Gandhi often referred to as one of his favorites. One line in the song becomes the heart of Pinki's story and is loosely translated by me as: *If there is no light, if the path before you rages with dark, then light your own heart on fire. Be the beacon. Be the spark.* In *Crown of Flames*, both "Ekla Cholo Re" and the Tagore song "Agun Jalo" are sung by the revolutionaries.

The names of Kanchkawla, Kaanmawla, and Deembo are all borrowed from a well-known absurd Bengali song called "Shing Nei Tobu Nam Tar Shingho" that was sung by Kishore Kumar in the 1958 Bengali film *Lukochuri*. The original lyrics were by Gauriprasanna Mazumder and the music by Hemanta Mukherjee. While *Kanchkawla* are underripe bananas, *Kaanmawla* means "boxing someone's ears." While *deem* are eggs, *Deembo* implies a nothing sandwich—a whole lotta nothing.

Toto/Tuntuni

Toto is a character of my own making, but I imagine that he is the father of the wisecracking bird Tuntuni who appears in the Kiranmala books. Tuntuni is a favorite, and recurrent, character of Bengali children's folktales. Upendrakishore Ray Chowdhury (also known as Upendrakishore Ray) collected a number of these stories starring the clever tailor bird Tuntuni in a 1910 book called *Tuntunir Boi* (*The Tailor Bird's Book*).

Chintamoni and Poroshmoni Stones

These stones, which first appeared in *Game of Stars*, are also sometimes spelled Chintamani and Parasmani. Here, it's important to note that *moni/mani* means "jewel," and these stones appear in both ancient Hindu and Buddhist texts and are often considered equivalents to the European philosopher's stone. It is unclear if they granted wishes, changed other metals into gold, granted immortality, or all three. Sometimes the stone is pictured in Hindu texts as in the possession of Naga, the Snake King (not the same character as in this book!).

Riddles and Other Recurring Things

Some of the same jokes and riddles that appear in the Kiranmala books also appear in *Crown of Flames*. In fact, an entire few scenes from near the end of *The Chaos Curse* is re-narrated in *Crown of Flames* from Pinki's point of view. This is where, through the magic of intergalactic time travel, the Kiranmala series intersects with the Fire Queen series, and Kiranmala and Neel are able to meet their parents as young people!

Astronomy

Like *The Serpent's Secret*, *Game of Stars*, and *The Chaos Curse*, which have quite a few references to astronomy, *Crown of Flames* deals with the multiverse. It also introduces the transit officer and transit corridor from *The Serpent's Secret*, a wormhole-like passage between the Kingdom Beyond and the rest of the multiverse. These ideas stem from string or multiverse theory, the notion that there may exist many universes in parallel to one another, which are simply not aware of the other universes' existences. String/multiverse theory appears in all the Kingdom Beyond books because it feels in keeping with the immigrant experience—the idea that immigrant communities are space explorers and universe straddlers.

Like in the Kiranmala books, rakkhosh in *Crown of Flames* are the manifestation of black holes. Even though this pairing of folktales and cosmology may seem strange, I did so to tear down the stereotype that cultural stories are somehow unconnected to science. In fact, like in every culture, traditional Bengali stories are often infused with stories about the stars and planets. That said, please don't take anything in this book as scientific fact, but rather use the story to inspire some more research about astronomy, black holes, and string theory!

Acknowledgments

The world has felt a bit like it's lit on fire in the past few years. But I'm so lucky to have a team helping me take that fire and use it to create stories. So many have helped light this path of my writing career. Thank you to my agent team of Brent Taylor and Uwe Stender at TriadaUS for believing in me and walking this path with me. So many thank-yous for the love and light given by the generous (and hilarious) editorial collaboration of Abigail McAden and Talia Seidenfeld. All of you make me hopeful about this world that we're creating, one story at a time.

Thank you to Vivienne To and Elizabeth Parisi for the beauty of this cover and the book's illustrations. Gratitude to my production editor, Melissa Schirmer, my copyeditor, Jessica White, and to the rest of my Scholastic family, including Ellie Berger, David Levithan, Rachel Feld, Lizette Serrano, Emily Heddleson, Danielle Yadao, Lauren Donovan, and Elisabeth Ferrari! Thank you to the team from Scholastic Book Clubs, and the team from Scholastic Book Fairs, for getting this series into the hands of so many readers.

Thank you to all those author friends I've made on this wonderful journey, including my We Need Diverse Books, Kidlit Writers of Color, and Desi Writers families. Thank you to my narrative medicine/health humanities colleagues and students at Columbia and around the country. Thank you to my extended family, as well as my wonderful Bengali immigrant community of aunties, uncles, and friends.

To my beloved parents, Sujan and Shamita, my husband, Boris, and my darlings, Kirin, Sunaya, and Khushi—love, love, and more love.